MAN AGAINST WOLF!

The handle of his knife was wet with perspiration. He dried his palm hastily on the sand, and then refreshed his grip. At least, he determined, thrusting out his jaw, he would die fighting—he would account for one among their number. Strange that he, a man, should feel such a savage satisfaction in the thought of striking down a beast and paying a death for a death. But would he be able actually to kill one of them? The thick, loose hide was admirably adapted to make the tooth of an enemy slide from the chosen mark, and it was tough enough to turn all but the keenest edge. Beneath that wire hair and the loose, rolling hide, there were stone-hard muscles and strong bones. Only by luck, no matter how strong his arm and how sure his thrust, would he be able to cut through to life in a single stroke. And more than a single stroke, he well knew, he could not have. Before he could strike twice, those deadly teeth would be in his throat.

MAX BRAND

SLUMBER MOUNTAIN

LEISURE BOOKS NEW YORK CITY

A LEISURE BOOK®

October 1998

Published by special arrangement with Golden West Literary Agency.

Dorchester Publishing Co., Inc.
276 Fifth Avenue
New York, NY 10001

ISBN 0-8439-4442-0

TABLE OF CONTENTS

SLUMBER MOUNTAIN

A Western Trio

The Outlaw Crew

Frederick Faust completed the short novel that follows in September, 1931, and titled it, "The Manners of Little Minnie." It was first published in Street & Smith's *Western Story Magazine* in the issue dated February 20, 1932 under the title "Outlaw Crew" by Max Brand. In the same issue the first installment of Faust's six-part serial, "Rancher's Legacy," appeared under the byline Peter Henry Morland. For the appearance of this short novel in book form the text as Faust wrote it has been fully restored.

Chapter One

"A Hard Problem"

Trent and Wayland, when they developed their mine a little, knew perfectly well that there was a fortune for them if they could find many hands to work in it. There was plenty of the ore, but the grade was not high; the pair of them, grinding away at this coffee mill the rest of their lives, would just about make good day wages, and little more. They had now made the experiment thoroughly, and they had been thoroughly beaten.

Twenty miles from them, as the bird flies, thirty as the mustang runs, forty as wheels must go, was the town of Sunnydale. In spite of its name, it was not sunny. It was the center of a mining rush. For six months it had been growing wilder and more crowded, more lawless, and more confident that Sunnydale need not pay the slightest attention to the rest of the world.

11

There were thousands of men in Sunnydale. The majority of them were the sharpsters, gamblers, crooks of all sorts, who come to exploit the honest prosperity of others. But there were laborers also—a limitless supply of them. The trouble was that they were only willing to work for bonanza prices. And bonanza prices were exactly what Wayland and Trent could not afford to pay. They could offer two dollars a day and found, but that was all. And how could those excited men in the gorge of Sunnydale be tempted away from a spot where every one of them hoped to find his individual fortune sooner or later? The laborers in that valley were willing to work in the rich, easy placer diggings for from six to ten dollars a day. But how could they be induced to come up the forty-mile trail and there, in the midst of the naked cliffs, break the hard face of granite at two dollars a day?

It seemed an insuperable problem. And as Trent and Wayland sat in front of their lean-to, which was built conveniently near the dump of the mine, they were deciding, on this evening, that it was better to give up the game for the present. Trent, as usual, made the downright decision. He was a big, fierce man of fifty with an unshaven gray beard, straggling like a stormy mist over his face. It was he who had prospected and found the claim. It was Wayland who had grubstaked the expedition out of his savings as a country doctor. His slender hands and narrower shoulders were not of much use in handling a drill. His spectacled eyes could not look so sharply into this kind of a future, either.

Wayland had risked much in leaving his home

and coming up here with his daughter. A younger man had moved in and was taking his practice. It was toward his daughter that he was continually glancing with troubled eyes on this evening. The scheme was that Harriet Wayland should do the cooking for the required gang of miners until the proceeds from the mine began to stack up and a regular cook and cook's assistant could be hired. They had attempted to work the mine on a shoe-string, and she was a necessary part of the string. Now she worked quietly, scrubbing up the pans after supper and making all orderly, never speaking, pretending that she did not hear the gloomy words of her father and his partner.

All that day it had been blistering hot, for the mountain shoulder on which they had opened the shaft faced south and west and the mountain itself was a series of naked, rocky steps that reflected the brilliance of the clear sun. There were no trees for shade, but only a scattering of tough shrubbery good enough for firewood, but little use for anything else. They had constructed a winding footpath that led down a quarter of a mile to a point where the mountain shelved out toward the valley. That was the highest point possible for freighting in by wheels, and there the buckboard was standing, covered with tarpaulin. There, also, the two mules were hobbled for grazing.

There was only one blessing of a practical sort in this situation, and that was the meager trickle of water that broke from the rock above and ran down onto the shoulder where the mine was opened. There it gathered in a shallow pool and then ran

13

on toward the valley. There was another blessing in the way of beauty, for the eye leaped from this high place across gigantic distances to other ranges, green and brown and blue, and some darkened by a growth of pines, and others offering the clear sheen of naked rocks, and some, about the summits, offering to the eye cool bits of snow-like little, white clouds, blowing in the sky.

However, neither of the men had any interest in the scenery just now. Trent, as he tamped the coal of his hot pipe with a horny forefinger and dusted off the finger against his sweat-marked overalls, was saying: "You take it this way . . . the pair of us, we work like the deuce, and we break enough ground and work enough of it to clear up about five dollars a day apiece. There's not much to be said for that. But suppose that we had twenty men working here. They would get out enough for us to pay them two dollars a day and three or four dollars more for our profit. Even more than that, maybe. We could make a lot of savings in extras. There'd be one gent traveling all the time to town and back with supplies. There'd be a cook. There'd be a hunter and general roustabout. There'd be you and me to keep the gang working.

"The gang would have nothing to do but break ground for us. Maybe that way we'd begin to clear seven or eight dollars a head for every dog-gone one of them. That way we could have something like a hundred or two hundred dollars a day coming in. And it would come in steady. It would come in regular as a clock. That vein is gonna go right on down to China. It ain't high grade, but it's steady.

"After a while we could get some machinery out here and an engineer to handle it, and then we'd rip into things and make a fortune fast. But the way it is now, you and me just about make enough to break even. We gotta quit and leave the thing to stand for a while. After a time . . . when the Sunnydale rush settles down . . . in six months . . . or a year . . . or maybe two years, we can get men out here, willing and glad to work for the right kind of wages. That's the only way to tackle the game."

He spoke grimly, almost brutally, for he knew how much pain this decision was giving to the doctor. The latter's business in his home town was now practically destroyed. If he returned to his house, he would be going back as a failure. And failures are rarely trusted by clients. However, Wayland met the future with a set jaw and a determined eye.

"If it has to be this way," he said, "it has to be. I'll take my medicine, and we'll wait. Only,"—here he lowered his voice—"Harriet, yonder, is. . . ." He paused.

"I know," muttered Trent. "It's hard on her. She's come out here and slaved. All she's got out of it has been sunburn . . . and the knowing that she's done her duty by you, Wayland."

"Her duty by me. Her duty by me," murmured the doctor sadly. "She's always done that. It looks as though she will keep on doing it. And in the meantime she pays no attention to men of her age. Boys, I mean to say. She won't go to dances because she won't spend the money on clothes. She won't go to boy-and-girl parties because she's been busy with housework. *She's* the one, Trent, who did most of the work for the last two years to save the money we needed for this experiment. And now the money's thrown away. I don't mind. I'm not thinking of myself . . . for once in my life. But I'm thinking of her wasted time. The young years are the time for a girl to be gay. She's not gay, Trent. Sad labor and very few hopes have been her share."

Trent said nothing. He felt the truth of these things, but he also felt the impossibility of offering comfort through words, and words were all he had to offer.

The girl herself had just finished the work she had been doing, and now she walked out to the edge of the little plateau to look over the sunset light that filled the great valley with russet dust. There was no comfort to the men in that beauty, but for her it made life bearable. The weariness of the day fell away from her, and out of the blue twilight always there was an assurance that no matter what success or failure had marked the day, the end of it was all that was profoundly worthwhile

From the darkening mountains she looked down at last to the darker valley. There was still dull gold on the heights and what seemed like old gilt along the faces of the cliffs, but the valley beneath was blue as water, and through this mist of thin color she saw a man coming, not on a horse, but walking swiftly. It seemed a very extraordinary thing, indeed, that he was on foot—no one traveled in this country without a mule, or at the least a burro. He came straight on, and, while he was still in the distance, she could see that he was a very big man, and as wiry as he was large, for he carried his poundage swiftly up the slope, then turned, and came striding with unabated strength up the winding trail toward the mine.

"There's someone coming," she said over her shoulder.

"Who?"

"Man on foot . . . a great big fellow, alone on foot."

"Who'd be coming on foot through this kind of a country?" demanded Trent, standing up.

The girl did not answer that reflection. She was too intent on the pedestrian. The exhaustless strength of him lifted her own heart. She began to smile long before she clearly made out his face.

Trent joined her on the edge of the plateau. "I've seen that fellow before," he said. "I've seen him somewhere . . . it's somebody that I ain't got any kindness for, I guess. Them shoulders, and that head . . . by thunder, it's little Minnie Trent! It's my own nephew! It's that same worthless scatterhead and vagabond. Works harder than any man in the world *to get out of* work."

Harriet Wayland moved back toward the lean-to as the big fellow gained the level of the plateau. Her pleasure in him disappeared, partly because of what his uncle had said, and more because of his ugliness. She never had seen such a face before; she hoped that she would never have to see one again. For he was a black man, with black hair, black eyes, a swarthy skin, and over it the growth of four or five days of beard that was as solidly black as a

17

painted mask. It was a face not modeled by the hand, but hewed with a blunt edge. The lines of brow and nose and jaw had been knocked out rudely, and never finished. It was a drawing, blocked out, but never completed. And she felt, as she looked at him, an uneasy sense of alarm.

Chapter Two

"Little Minnie"

"This is Minder Paul Trent," the uncle said to the Waylands, "but you don't have to call him that. Nobody does. You talk of Minder Trent and there ain't a soul, hardly, that'll know who you mean. But talk of Little Minnie, and you'll see a whole lot of gents reaching for their guns or anything in the line of a club that's handy. Minnie, this is Miss Harriet Wayland. This is Doctor Wayland, her father and my partner. Now what the deuce are you here for?"

"I was at Crow Creek yesterday," said Little Minnie after he had acknowledged the introductions, "and over there I heard about you and your mine, so I came over to take a look at it."

His uncle snorted. "Yesterday? Crow Creek is seventy-five miles away. You mean that you walked it, eh?"

"I'm hungry," said the big man. "Got any hardtack and coffee around here? Yes, I walked over from Crow Creek. It's not so very far."

"You were broke, eh, and you came over here for a hand-out? That's the truth, ain't it?" demanded the uncle harshly.

"I'm not broke," said the nephew.

"No, you got a whole quarter left, maybe?"

"*And* a dollar," said the nephew.

"We don't feed tramps in this camp," said Trent savagely. "We need working men, and we pay 'em good, too. Two dollars a day. You lazy hound, how long is it since you done any work?"

"I'm working all the time, Uncle Jim," said the nephew. "Touring the world and completing my education. Have you got any fresh meat in the camp? I could eat a few steaks, between you and me."

"We have some bacon," said the girl. "I'll have something ready for you in a minute or two."

"Thanks," said Little Minnie, and sat down upon a rock.

"Look at you!" exclaimed Jim Trent. "Setting down to let a lady that's already tired go and wait on you, eh?"

"Why don't you have fresh meat?" asked the giant, pointing. "There's a couple of hundred pounds of it waiting to be snagged."

Through the blue and golden dimness of the evening, a hundred yards or so above them, a mountain goat appeared among the rocks, standing on the edge of a cliff and reaching for a tuft of grass.

"You can't shoot that goat," said Jim Trent. "I've used up twenty bullets on it. The dog-gone thing, it comes up and wags its beard in your face, but the minute that it sees a rifle, it jumps for cover, and it always gets there. I've hankered after that meat for days and days. And. . . ."

"I'm going to eat goat meat, roasted, tonight," said Little Minnie, and from beneath his coat he plucked forth a revolver that was bigger than any Harriet Wayland had ever seen before. The barrel of that Colt was built three inches longer than the ordinary pattern, and it seemed of a heavier frame throughout.

The mountain goat had seen the flash of the steel. It turned with the uncanny agility of its race and leaped for cover as the gun spoke.

It leaped, struck a root, and then fell limply back, making a long, blurred streak of white as it slid down the smooth face of the rock and landed on the plateau with a thump not a dozen strides away.

Little Minnie went to it, leaned above it, then he raised it from the ground.

"I was wrong by a hundred pounds," said the giant. "Three hundred pounds of bone and eating in this thing. Now, Uncle Jim, are you glad that Little Minnie came for supper?"

"If you could shoot your way to money," said Jim Trent, "you'd do pretty good. But you ain't even got the nerve to be a bandit. You're too bad to be good, and too damned lazy to be bad enough to count."

"A good, fat young goat," said the nephew. "Shall I dress him here?"

"That's all right," said the uncle. "How long since you ate?"

"Haven't had a thing but a couple of rabbits all day long," said the nephew.

"Yeah, you must be starved, then," agreed Jim Trent.

His nephew already had tied the heels of the dead goat together, and now he hung the bulk by the legs from a projecting point of a great boulder. He produced a great, wicked-looking knife with a scimitar-like curve in it, and with long, dexterous, powerful strokes he dressed the kill. In a few moments the thing was done, and by the time the fire was right for cookery, the meat was at hand.

Little Minnie went to wash. He began to sing as he splashed.

"This is a pretty good place, Uncle Jim," he said. "I might stay a while. Don't let that fire get too hot, Harry," he advised. "You have to cook grown-up goat with care. Otherwise it's like chewing rubber."

"Her name's Harriet, not Harry," corrected Jim Trent. "Don't be making a fresh mug of yourself, Minnie."

"Spoil the manners and save the meat is my motto," answered the giant. "Harriet's a long name to say, even if it means a lot. But I know a buckaroo by the name of Harry that was a good skate and fine company. I'm complimenting the lady, I'd have her know."

The girl flushed a little. The speech was not exactly insulting, but she tingled and grew misty-eyed with anger. Her father, sitting stiffly apart from the rest, just on the verge of the circle of the firelight, looked coldly upon the big stranger.

Jim Trent went back to the speech before the last

one. "If you stay here, you stay alone," he said. "We're moving along."

"Why?" asked Little Minnie.

"Because we haven't got enough hands here to break this ground," answered the prospector.

"There's Sunnydale just over the hill," said Little Minnie. "Lots of men down there."

"Yeah. Six-dollar, ten-dollar a day men. This is a two-dollar job, and a hard one, at that."

"Where there's a will, there's a way," said Little Minnie. "I'd have some of those boys up here if I were you."

"If I got 'em up here, they wouldn't stay. I've tried it," said his uncle.

"If I got 'em up here, I'd *make* 'em stay," declared Little Minnie.

"How would you make 'em?"

"Where's a will, there's a way," said Little Minnie with annoying complacence.

"Shut up, will you?" said his uncle. "You got a smart way of talking about you. To hear you, anybody might think that you amounted to something."

"I've got an appetite that amounts to something," said Little Minnie.

He sat down close to the fire, regardless of the heat of the flames, and the light shone over the surface of his growth of black beard. He began to toast goblets of meat at the fire, turning them with a careful attention. And when they were cooked to his satisfaction, he offered the wooden spits to the others, after sprinkling a little salt on the roast. Both the other men refused the tidbits. The girl, forced on by a sort of angry curiosity, made the attempt to eat a morsel, but shuddered at the taste and the rubbery toughness.

"How can you eat such stuff?" she asked.

"With a pair of real jaws," said Little Minnie. "The trouble with you, Harry, is that you've used your jaw muscles chiefly on cake and candy, and small talk, and singing hymns. But you take me . . . I've used my teeth the way God intended me to. A little gristle here and there in my friend, the goat, but gristle gives a substance to meat. Gives you something that stays with you a while. I need something like that, because I can see that I've got to round up some of those crooks in Sunnydale and bring them up here to the mine. How much do you pay me a head for 'em, Uncle Jim?"

"You're gonna go down and persuade 'em up here . . . for two dollars a day?" demanded his uncle.

"That's the idea. For a crop of ten, twenty, thirty of 'em, how much do you pay a head?"

"I pay," said Jim Trent, "a dollar a day for every working day that you make 'em put in up here."

"I'm going to be rich," said Little Minnie. "What do you say, Harry? A month or two of savings like that . . . ? How many men can you use?"

"Fifty!" said Jim Trent. "As many as you can get for me."

"Fifty dollars a day," said Little Minnie, "is fifteen hundred dollars a month of anybody's money. I'll be on the way to being rich. Is there that much gold in your diggings, Uncle Jim?"

"There's enough pay dirt here," said Jim Trent

firmly, "to keep a hundred men busy, working every day for a thousand years."

"The first fifty years is all that I care about," answered Little Minnie. "How about you, Harry? That would do for us, wouldn't it?"

She said nothing.

Jim Trent broke in: "Are you gonna try to make a fool of Miss Wayland? All that you can do is to make a fool of yourself, Minnie."

The girl filled the giant's emptied coffee cup in a disdainful silence.

"Thanks, Harry," he said. "You don't mind me thinking out loud, do you? I never had enough money to think of marrying before. But now that I see I'm going to be a rich man before long, why, I naturally look at the first girl, and there you are, Harry. Look me over."

As he spoke, he did not glance at her, but continued to eat busily, saying around his mouthfuls: "You'll see that I've been around the world long enough, and rubbed up against things hard enough to thicken my skin. I'm old enough to shave, and I'm young enough to eat goat meat. What more do you want in a husband? Easy man to have around the house, too. You'd have lots of my company. Never would be dashing off to an office. Handy man around a garden, too, if it's not too big, and handy at patching things around the house. Keep burglars away better than a bulldog, and never criticize the cook as long as there are plenty of beans in the pot."

"Now you've driven her away into the house,"

said Jim Trent furiously. "You're an insulting young hound, Minnie!"

"Every girl to her own fancy," said the giant. "If she's gone inside, just reach me that coffee pot, Uncle Jim, will you?"

Chapter Three

"Sunnydale"

Little Minnie went to Sunnydale the next day. When he came over the rim of the hills to the north of it, striding long and fast as usual, he paused just long enough to make out the long and sinuous windings of the narrow valley. And just at that moment, it being about the end of the day for most of the mines, the shots began to go off, up and down the length of the ravine. Down the trails that led from the holes to the town, he could see men walking, or riding, or driving. Far away over the hills, toward the southern side of the valley, he looked at the white windings of the road and saw no fewer than three freighters, coming in with three white clouds of dust about them, while another long outfit climbed the slope to leave Sunnydale. Day and night these outfits must be coming and going. Still, as the big man stepped forward once more, he heard the explosions from the mines, sometimes distant, and sometimes seeming to shake the very earth about his feet.

"The salute," he said, grinning. "They know the king's coming to town."

He had shaved from his face the black shadow of his gleaming beard, so that, without it, one was able to see his face and his smile more clearly. He looked much younger, so viewed, but also, in a sense, he looked more grim. One could see his mouth that was smiling, for instance, more clearly than when the shining black shadow had covered it. It was a mouth too large even on that face, and the wrinkles on the sides of the smile extended far into cheeks that appeared hollow, perhaps because of the size of the cheekbones and the bulge of the jaw muscles. It was a crooked smile and a crooked mouth, and one could hardly tell whether the expression of it were sneering or openly amused. This was a man who would draw the eye, but the judgment about him might remain distinctly divided.

When he got to the town, it was what he expected—only a little more so. There was the same single main length of the ravine. Down the creek there was the same gathering of shacks, big and small, made of board, of canvas, even pieced out with tin cans straightened out in thin sheets. A blast of heat reflected from the town, though the strength of the sun was now diminishing. It was hotter indoors than out. People had poured out to take the air. And what people!

He knew them of old—the thugs, the yeggs, the confidence men who smiled upon the world, the sedate gamblers, the active businessmen, the honest laborers of the mines. He had seen them all before, and the mixture pleased him. The air, for him, became loaded with excitement. He saw other signs of excitement, signs that were obvious to his eye. He passed half a dozen blackened sites where the destruction caused by fire was hardly allowed to cool before the new buildings began to rise on the ground.

He passed under a saloon sign on which was painted: NED KIMBAL, HONEST WHISKEY. The NED KIMBAL part of the sign was obviously new. In darker paint, beneath that name, appeared another, with a single brush stroke through it. DENNY ROURKE was the name of the former proprietor. It had a meaning to Mr. Minder Trent. He turned in through the swinging doors beneath that sign.

Inside, he expected to see few people since there were so many on the streets, but he saw that he was wrong. At least fifty people were in the long and narrow room.

He stopped a man who was leaving the place. "You know Denny Rourke?" he asked.

"No, but I've seen him," said the stranger.

"Lately?"

"He's using his last ten bucks on faro," said the other.

"This Rourke, what sort of a looking fellow is he?"

"He looks about your size," replied the other.

Big Minder Trent went on into the back room and saw Rourke readily. He was a red man—red of skin, red of hair, and fierce blue of eye. He was, in fact, as big as Little Minnie. Now he stood coatless in a blue flannel shirt before the faro table, biting on a cigar and snarling to himself as he played. Little Minnie waited until he had lost and then won. He waited until the winning was greater than the loss. Then he stepped through the choking wreaths of pipe and cigar and cigarette smoke and tapped the bulging, hard shoulder of the Irishman.

Rourke turned his big head and glared. The glare turned into a smile so vast that the cigar was suddenly no larger than a toothpick in the vast stretch of his mouth. "Little Minnie," he said, "blast my eyes, but it's you!" He turned all about and shook hands.

"How are you?" asked Little Minnie.

"Worse than I was when you last raised a lump on the side of my jaw," said the frank Irishman. "How's yourself?"

"Broke," said Little Minnie.

"That's nothing . . . for you," said the other. "But I got about a hundred left . . . here's fifty, if you want it."

"I don't want it," said Little Minnie. "I want five minutes of talk. Tell me about this town."

"It's a good town for a crook. It's no good for you and me," said the red man. "I tried to buck the game here, and I made thousands. Then they got to me. The yeggs cracked my safe. The gunmen shot up my place. I was pretty rich, one day. The next day I was on my uppers. I had to sell. I cleared five hundred. I've got a hundred left, and faro has the rest. That's Sunnydale. It's sunny, all right. You don't mind this kind of sun if you got an asbestos overcoat."

"I thought it looked that way," Little Minnie said. "Looks as though Sunnydale needs some law and order."

"It don't need anything else but law and order," said the red man. "What's your game here?"

"Law and order is my game," said Little Minnie. "Where would that kind of a game stand?"

"Clean off the boards," said the other. "They shoot a deputy sheriff every three or four days, and they got the sheriff himself laid up in bed. They got a judge here, but everybody that he sends to jail breaks out the next night. The boys don't mind the jail here. It just gives them a rest."

"The strong-arm boys friends of yours?" asked Little Minnie.

"Friends of mine?" snarled Denny Rourke. "I could eat their hearts. Some time I'm gonna do it, too. I know the skunks that sank their teeth in me. I was framed. They frame everybody that don't play their side of the game."

"Maybe I'll be calling on you again," said Little Minnie. "So long."

He left the saloon and inquired his way to the house of the sheriff. It was a little shack on the rim of the town, near the creek. It was distinguished by having, in its front yard, the only tree that had not yet been cut down for building purposes. When he knocked at the front door, a growling voice told him to enter. He stepped in and found himself looking at the double mouth of a riot gun. Behind the gun was a man in bed with a cigarette pressed

31

flat between hard lips—a middle-aged man with black circles of suffering beneath his eyes.

"Who are you, brother?" asked the man in the bed. "And what's your gag?"

"Just stepped in to call," answered Little Minnie. "Will this chair stand my weight? I don't know yet what I am to you."

"Take the stool over there under the window," said the sheriff, "and don't try to maneuver around behind me. From this time on I start shooting first and do my thinking afterward."

Little Minnie drew out the stool and sat down.

"This is nice and cozy," he said. "What's the matter with this town?"

"Why, nothing much," said the sheriff. "Just a big Western play town is what it is. Just a lot of fine, upstanding fellows here in Sunnydale, as long as you ask. You wouldn't want to see anything better. Now and then they crack a safe, or dynamite a shack or two, or shoot a few of the gents through the back, but they got a whole lot of style, you can take it from me. They're quick. Just a little quick-tempered, if you could call that a fault."

"Me? No, no, no," said Little Minnie hastily. "I wouldn't ever accuse anybody of being quick-tempered. What's your name, brother? Mine is Little Minnie."

"I've heard that moniker before," said the sheriff. "I'm Anton Breen. What's your game here, Little Minnie?"

"I don't know exactly," said Little Minnie. "But it looks to me as though I've got to stand for once on the side of law and order."

"You can't stand on that side," said the sheriff. "There's nothing to stand on. There was me, but now there's nothing left."

"I thought you had a judge and a jail and all that?" suggested the big black man.

"We got a jail that's just like a sieve," said the sheriff. "And we got the best judge you ever saw. He's real worked up, too. He'd put a sparrow in jail for flying between his window and the sun. He'd give you fifty days for coughing in church. But what good is that when there's nobody to arrest any crooks, and when the jail won't hold 'em when they're arrested?"

"Well, look at me," said Little Minnie.

"There's a lot of you to see," said the sheriff, "if all that ain't beef is brains."

"You think you're talking to a hobo, partner," protested Mr. Minder Trent. "But you're not. You're talking to a statesman."

"All the statesmen I ever seen" commented the sheriff, "were hobos, outside of the newspapers. So that's all right. I don't see your graft yet, though."

"I'm leading you to it, step by step," answered Little Minnie. "I'm going to clean up Sunnydale."

"You're going to which?"

"I'll say it another way," said Little Minnie. "I'm going to do so much that you'll buy a pair of crutches and come out to watch. You're going to cry with joy when you see what I'll do to this town."

The sheriff looked at him. "I dunno why it is," he said then. "I've heard gents talk like you do before this. But it's always kind of soothing to me."

33

"Open your heart, brother," said Little Minnie. "I've come to you with a message."

"Go right ahead," answered the sheriff. "I like you, the way you talk. You've got style."

"I'll have more style when I've dressed up with a steel shield. I'd feel safer behind it, too," declared Little Minnie.

"Maybe you're crying to be a deputy sheriff?" asked Anton Breen.

"You guessed that right away the tenth time," said Little Minnie. "You're wonderful. You're a statesman yourself, perhaps."

The sheriff pointed to a table. "Open that drawer," he said, "and you'll find a lot of shields. There's been so many of them shot all to pieces lately that I had to send in a wholesale order. Take a couple of handfuls . . . you'll find that they wear pretty thin fast in this air."

"Thanks," said Little Minnie, and stepping to the table, he helped himself.

"You got plenty of guns?" asked the sheriff. "Gimme that Bible, will you, and I'll swear you in. Got plenty of guns?"

"I've got a club and a gun together, a sort of a private combination. I always have thought that a steel nightstick with a bullet inside it would do pretty well in this sort of town. But I'm not through yet. I want to ask you some questions. I want to find out about the honest men. I've seen one already . . . Rourke."

"What's the way you define an honest man?" asked the sheriff.

"Anybody," said Little Minnie, "who stands behind you and me is honest. Anybody who stands on the other side is a crook."

"That's simple," said the sheriff. "That's good enough for me. What are you going to do about it?"

"I'm going to put all of the crooks in jail," declared Little Minnie.

"The jail won't hold 'em. The jail leaks," said the sheriff.

"The pouring of it full," said Little Minnie, "will be a lot more fun for me than for those who are dropped into the cooler."

"Brother," said the sheriff, "it seems to me that I ought to have met you long ago. Maybe you're my long lost brother."

"I thought so from the first," said Little Minnie, "but by nature I'm modest. It's only education that gave me my brass."

"I don't know exactly what you're after," said the sheriff. "But you can catch all the rabbits in this town that you're fast enough to grab. I only hope that you're made of tool-proof steel, is all I hope."

"That stuff was named after me," declared Little Minnie. "Where do I find the judge?"

"In the courthouse," said the sheriff. "That was one of the first things that they built in this town. The early comers, they come in with a whole flock of illusions, and all the tough birds west of the Mississippi have been laughing ever since."

Chapter Four

"An Understanding"

Little Minnie went to the courthouse. The hour was wearing late, but he found a one-legged janitor, pretending to sweep the main hall.

"Where's the judge?" he asked.

"Who are you?" demanded the cripple without enthusiasm.

"You're minus a leg, but you've got two eyes," said Little Minnie. "Can't you recognize a deputy sheriff when you see one?"

"Sure I can. I just wasn't thinking," said the janitor. "I've seen just your style and fashion before, only you're cut a little bigger and fuller in the sleeves. That's the judge's office, down there, but it's after hours. He don't see anybody this time of the day."

"I have an appointment to meet him," answered the big man, and went down the hall.

He knocked on the door.

"Keep out!" roared a hoarse voice within.

Little Minnie opened the door and stepped in. The light inside was rather dusky. A white-headed man sat by a window, reading a book. His face was as red as his hair was white; it turned redder still when he saw Little Minnie.

"I have a mind to give you fifty days!" he said. "What do you mean by breaking in here on me?"

"You're Judge Herbert Loring," declared Little Minnie.

"I'm Herbert Loring," said the other, "and I'd be a judge if anybody ever were brought into my court. I'd like to have you there, and I've got an idea that I may, before long. Get out and stay out."

"You can't give me the run," said Little Minnie. "I'm here on duty."

"You're here on . . . get out and stay out!" shouted the judge.

"If you can't get on with your own deputy sheriffs," said Little Minnie, "you can't get on with anybody."

"Are you half-wit enough to take that job?" said the judge. "The bigger they are, the harder they fall in Sunnydale."

"I always get up again," said Little Minnie. "I wear shoulder springs."

"I think I've seen you before," said Judge Loring. "Sit down, my boy. Where did I see you before, and how many months did I give you?"

"It must have been a cousin of mine," said Little Minnie.

"Maybe it was," said the judge. "How much time have you done?"

"I'm not that kind of a crook," answered Little Minnie. "I'm not on the bench yet, but I'm on my way to it."

"I ought to give you ninety days for that," said the judge. "But I won't. After all, this is a democracy, and a deputy sheriff today may be a dead man tomorrow. Promotion like that comes quickly in Sunnydale. What do you want?"

"A free hand," said Little Minnie.

"Your hands are not tied," said the other. "What do you want to do with them?"

"Plug up the holes in the jail and then fill it to the brim."

"I see," said the judge, "that if age is a disease of the body, youth is a disease of the brain. That jail is a sieve."

"I'll plaster up the holes."

"There's no money to pay for the repairs," said the judge.

"Why not? Aren't there any taxes in this town?"

"There are," said the judge, "and the tax money always goes to the first man who shoots the tax collectors. In Sunnydale, they never close the season on tax collectors . . . and deputy sheriffs. I hope I'm not discouraging you."

"Not a bit," replied Little Minnie. "My system pays its own way. It lives on the prisoners it arrests."

"Suppose you manage to hold some prisoners for a while," said the judge, "there's no money to pay for their food."

"I've got a cistern all arranged," said Little Minnie, "that would hold the overflow from the Sunnydale jail. It will pay for the chance to hold them."

"Go on," said the judge. "Here, have a cigar."

"I've smelled the one that you're smoking," said Little Minnie. "That'll do me, thank you."

"All right," said the judge. "Keep on talking. What can I do for you?"

"Everybody that I bring into your court is guilty," said Little Minnie.

"That's not law," said Judge Loring. "Before I condemn and pass sentence, I've got to have proof of guilt."

"What sort of proof?"

"Proof that you made the arrest in Sunnydale," said the judge with a glint like that of polished steel in his eyes.

"I see," said Little Minnie, "that there's only one mind between us."

"I see that you're a flatterer," said the ironic judge. "What will you do to keep your prisoners in jail?"

"I'll use men to wall them in."

"What sort of men?"

"I have a list ready," said Little Minnie, "of fellows who'll do the work for the love of it."

"I'm sorry that Anton Breen is confined to his bed," said the judge. "He'd like to be up and about in these stirring times. But how will you support your prisoners?"

"They fast on bread and water for a day or two," said Little Minnie. "That's a health measure."

"And when the jail's full?"

"I forgot to tell you what you sentence them to," said Little Minnie.

"Yes, you forgot to tell me that," answered the judge soberly. "But it's not too late. Tell me now."

"You sentence them to hard labor, and no sentence under a month."

"Labor on what?" asked the judge.

"An uncle of mine has a hole in the rocks twenty miles from here as the crow flies and forty miles by foot."

"Friend," said the judge, "I begin to see that I am talking to a distinguished man."

"You're slow, but you're sure," said Little Minnie. "My uncle pays two dollars a day and found for every head of convict labor. The two dollars goes to the town of Sunnydale, of course. It'll help to repair the jail, and it'll pay the back salaries of the judge and the sheriff. Is there a mayor?"

"He was shot last week," replied Judge Loring. "What sort of a salary does this deputy sheriff get?"

"Nothing but affectionate praise," said Little Minnie. "Not a blamed cent from the treasury of Sunnydale."

"Not only a great man, but a good man. I hope you last for a day or two . . . and I promise to attend your funeral."

"Thanks," said Little Minnie. "And I want to know that the law is behind me till I rob a bank."

"There are no banks left to rob," said the judge. "So, go as far as you like."

Chapter Five

"Minnie Goes Calling"

Little Minnie went calling. He hunted up several gentlemen named by the sheriff, and found three of them. The first was a gambler. A tall, lean, sallow-faced man with a look of pain about the eyes and a look of mirth about the mouth. He was sitting on the verandah of the hotel, and Little Minnie asked him to the sidewalk.

"I'm a friend of the sheriff," he said.

"Then you're no friend of mine," said Lew Eastern.

"You're wrong," Little Minnie said. "I'm practically a cousin of yours. Don't you remember my face?"

"No, I'm damned if I do."

"I'm the new deputy sheriff," said Little Minnie.

"I'll do this much for you," said Lew Eastern. "I'll put some flowers on your grave tomorrow."

41

"Thanks," said Little Minnie. "I knew that blood would tell in the end. I wanted to ask you if you know the boys that burned down your joint last week."

"What good does it do to know them?"

"So I can put them in jail."

"You couldn't put them in jail," said Eastern, "and if you did, you'd see 'em walk out again."

"They won't walk past the new jailer," said Little Minnie.

"Wouldn't they?"

"No, they wouldn't."

"Who's the new jailer?" asked the gambler.

"You are."

"Is this a joke, or who are you?" demanded Eastern.

"I'm the uncle of the sheriff and the favorite grandfather of Judge Loring," replied Little Minnie.

"I begin to think that I saw you somewhere before," said Eastern.

"Any good memory is worth refreshing," replied Little Minnie. "Do you take the job?"

"What's all this guff about?"

"This guff is worth thirty dollars a week to you," said the deputy.

"Paid in advance?"

"No, you work for your cash and your bonus."

"Ain't you a little rash?" asked Lew Eastern.

"No, I'm only far-sighted," replied Little Minnie. "Do you want the job?"

"If I can slam those hounds," said Lew Eastern,

"I'll take all the lead that can be salted away in my hide the very next day."

"Can you lead me to them?"

"Sure I can. They always hang out in one dump."

"Got any proof on 'em?"

"I haven't got any proof. But there's plenty of proof on them just the same. Let me fan one of those boys, and I'll turn up some of my own on 'em."

"This way, brother," said Little Minnie. "Right down the street with me. We have a couple of calls to make first."

And Lew Eastern, stepping long and soft, followed Little Minnie.

They found a short, wide-shouldered man in the room of the Oasis Bar. Little Minnie tapped that solid shoulder and motioned him back to the wall. He came as though he intended to walk straight on through the giant.

"You," he said, "whatcha want?"

"Both your hands and both your guns, Jack," said Little Minnie.

"You can have all four if you got the nerve to collect 'em," said the other.

"Don't be rough," answered Little Minnie. "I was raised with tender care, and my feelings are easily hurt. You'd be surprised to know how easily they're hurt."

"You may know yourself, but you don't know me," said the short man, looking more and more like a bulldog.

"I know that you're Jumping Jack Story," said the

Max Brand

deputy sheriff, "and I know some of the safes that you've cracked. Is that enough?"

"That's enough to get you a sock on the chin," declared Jack Story. "All I see of you is a yard of gab. Your chatter ain't funny to me."

"That's because you don't know me," said Little Minnie cheerfully.

"I'm not gonna know you," said Jumping Jack. "I don't like the looks of you, you big stuff!"

"Do you like the looks of this?" asked Little Minnie.

The Jumping Jack saw the flashing move, and his own hand was almost as fast—almost, but a vital degree too slow. Now the length of the largest revolver that Jack Story had ever seen was leveled at the third button of his coat.

Except for tall Lew Eastern, they were unnoticed by any other man in the room, for they were standing in a dim corner. Jack Story drew his hand from beneath his coat. There was no revolver in it. "I think I've seen you before," he said.

The long gun disappeared from the hand of Little Minnie. "I knew that you'd remember me pretty soon," he said pleasantly. "The next thing you'll be remembering will be the names of your pals who rolled you, after you and they split up a big melon here in town."

"I know their names," admitted Jack Story. "And I'm gonna get 'em, one by one, all for myself. I'm gonna taste the marrow in 'em after I've cracked 'em up."

"You'll never get 'em," suggested Little Minnie, "because they all work together. You've waited, and

44

they still keep in a herd. Isn't that true?"

"You read the mind all right," admitted Jack Story. "What's your game?"

"I'm the new deputy sheriff."

"You oughta be seeing the undertaker, not me," said Jumping Jack.

"That's funny, too," answered the big man, "but not as bright as I've seen you before. Before they bury me, I'll be worn so small that a shovelful will be enough to cover my bones. Jack, you're going to lead me to the hang-out where your friends are playing pinochle."

"And then what?"

"Then you can join the party, or just watch me and Lew Eastern, here, collect the fun."

"Are you on this band wagon, Lew?" asked Jack with interest.

"I'm on the driver's seat," answered Lew Eastern.

"Well," said Jumping Jack, "I'll get aboard and help make noise, I guess. Where did you get that rod, brother?" he demanded of Little Minnie.

"It was tailor-made to fit my chest," said Little Minnie. "Come on, boys. We've still got a couple of calls to make."

They found a small shack farther down the street, and, when the door was opened to their knock, a man in overalls and a coat of the same material appeared. He was of middle age, a little gray about the temples, and his clothes bulged significantly here and there. He had a wide face, as sour as cider vinegar.

"Hello, brother," said Little Minnie.

The other slammed the door and turned the lock.

The large boot of Little Minnie arose, and smashed the lock, and cast the door wide.

The householder waited in the gloom of the hall, with a gun in each hand.

"Put up your guns," said Little Minnie, "or I'll eat 'em and spit 'em back in your face in hunks."

"I know you," said the other. "You and your yegg friends, what in blazes d'you want here? I'm gonna slam you, is what I'm gonna do!"

"You don't know me, but I know you," said Little Minnie. "You're Buck Penrose, and you had a mine up the valley once upon a time."

The other cursed. "You know my name, but you don't know me. You're gonna pay for that busted lock with a busted head," said Buck Penrose.

"I'm Minder Trent," said the big man. "Better known as Little Minnie. I've come to give Sunnydale law and order, and I thought you might know where the first dose ought to be given. You know the boys that jumped your claim for you. They're still around the town."

"I'll find 'em, one by one," said Buck Penrose.

"Let me take them for you, brother," said Little Minnie. "I'm the deputy sheriff now."

"It's a good thing your ma don't know it," said Buck Penrose. "Just what sort of a deal is this, anyway?"

"The sheriff is holding the cards," said Little Minnie, "and Judge Loring is handling the bank."

Buck Penrose stepped out through the doorway.

"I kind of take some stock in you, kid," he said. "What's the deal?"

"Lead us to where your old chums are hanging

out. We'll do the rest, unless you want to warm your hands on 'em, too."

"I'll warm a knife and a couple of slugs of lead in 'em," said Buck Penrose. "You boys follow me."

"We've got one last call to make," answered Little Minnie. "Buck, this is Lew Eastern, and this is Jumping Jack Story. We've all seen the dogs eating grass, and so we know that there's a change of weather ahead for Sunnydale. This way, boys. Come along!"

At the saloon of Ned Kimbal, Little Minnie paused and then went through the swinging doors. It was not hard to find Denny Rourke. He had lost every penny at faro and was consoling himself with liquor that his friends were buying him.

"You know me, Denny?" asked Little Minnie.

"I don't know you," answered Denny, "and what's more, I don't wanta know you. Get out."

"Not till I hear a real man tell me to budge," said Little Minnie.

"You want a man? I'll be the man for you!" yelled the Irishman.

He turned and struck in, wheeling. Little Minnie brushed the blow aside with an arm of iron, and with a hand of iron, not too heavily, he tapped the wide jaw of the other. Then he picked up the sagging body of Denny Rourke in his arms and carried him to the outer air.

"What happened?" groaned Denny, opening his eyes and glaring about him as the other settled him carefully on his feet.

"A thug slugged you on the back of the head with a slung shot," said Little Minnie.

"Is that all?" gasped the Irishman. "I thought that a sledge hammer had socked me in the jaw. Hello, Little Minnie, where'd you drop from?"

"Out of the sky," said Little Minnie. "Are you with us, Denny?"

"Who else would I be with?" asked Denny Rourke. "I'm with anybody, but I gotta have action, Minnie. I simply gotta have action. My doctor, he went and put me on an action diet, and I gotta have action every day. Where's there some action in this little old town?"

"There's no action except where we're going," answered the giant. "So that's the right street for you, Denny, I guess."

"Good old Minnie," said Denny Rourke, rubbing his jaw. "It's sort of like the old days to see you ag'in. I gotta lay my hands on something. If you don't show me where to put 'em, I'm gonna put 'em on you, you big lump."

"I'll show you some places to work yourself out," said the other. "Have you got a gun?"

"No."

"Buck, give him a gun, will you? You've got plenty. Listen to me, Denny. Are you sober?"

"Sober?" exclaimed Denny Rourke. "I'm so dry that you could set me on fire with one touch of a match. But go on, man. Are we going to stand here all day and get our minds rusty?"

Chapter Six

"The Chief Crook"

They did not stand there all day. They proceeded down the street, while Little Minnie said to long-striding Lew Eastern beside him: "What's the lid on this town, brother? What's the head of the government, and the chief of the crooks?"

"You mean Fatty Orcutt, I guess," said Lew Eastern.

"It sounds as though I mean Fatty," said the deputy sheriff. "Who is he?"

"He runs the biggest saloon and gambling house and dance hall in the town. He's young, but he's so bright that he shines, I tell you."

"He sounds better and better," said Little Minnie. "Has he got a big gang around him?"

"He's got everybody," said Lew Eastern. "You can't fool with him. No thug dares to stay in town unless Fatty Orcutt has okayed him."

"He's the man I want. *I'll* do something to Fatty that'll take some of the fat off him. Is he a fighting man?"

"Nobody knows. He might be, and then again he might not. You never can tell about Fatty. He's a whole box of tricks."

"So am I," answered Little Minnie. "Which is his hang-out?"

"Why, right down there, with the big lanterns on top of the sign and underneath it. That's Orcutt's place. Can't you spell his name clear off here?"

"It's always easy to see what you know is there," answered Little Minnie. "Stop a minute, boys. We're going to drop in on Fatty Orcutt. This is the idea . . . guns ready, but no shooting until I give the signal, and the only signal I'll give will be to send a bullet smash into Fatty Orcutt's fat face."

"Lemme have that job," said Buck Penrose in an almost trembling tone of entreaty. "I been dreaming about Fatty for weeks. I been dreaming of spoiling his face for him."

"I like the way you talk, Buck," said Little Minnie. "I can see that you're a man to be depended on. But plenty will happen to Fatty later on. Understand? You'll be on hand to overlook some of the things that are going to happen to him. Now follow me."

When they got to the brightly lighted entrance, two gatekeepers, flanked by two bouncers, demanded admission fees.

"Boys," Little Minnie addressed them, "you think that we've come here for fun. You're wrong. We're here on business. We're here because Fatty Orcutt needs us. Take us straight in to him."

The two bouncers looked at one another.

"It's all right," said one of them. "These birds look like the pure quill. Come on, pals, and I'll show you the way. What's the racket now?"

He conducted them down a narrow corridor made of canvas tent material only, until they came to a door at the end of the alley. On this the bouncer knocked, and it was presently opened a trifle.

"Five-six fellows out here that wanta see Fatty pretty bad," said the bouncer.

"Wait a minute," came the answer as the door closed.

"It'll be all right, I guess," said the bouncer cheerfully as he turned on the others. "He's got a big conference or something on, but he always manages to see the boys. What's the game, anyway?"

"It's the biggest game in town that we're after," Little Minnie said confidently.

"Is it?" asked the other earnestly. "I wouldn't mind a cut in a deal like that. Look here . . . ain't I seen you before, brother?"

"Sure you have," replied Little Minnie, "and you're going to see a lot more of me, too, I think."

The door of Mr. Orcutt's room opened, and out came a man with great shoulders and a face on which seemed to be imprinted all the sins darkly.

"Fatty's all tied up, boys," he said. "He can't see you. But I'll take any message that you've got. I'm Tolliver. You know me, I guess?"

"Why, I've seen you before, Tolliver, haven't I?" said Little Minnie.

The other looked him over suddenly, but with rather a side glance. Then his ugly face brightened.

"Sure, and I've seen you, but I disrecollect where," he said.

"Let's go on in," said Little Minnie, "and I'll refresh your mind for you."

"Hey, don't be a fool!" exclaimed Mr. Tolliver. "I told you that the chief's all tied up in there."

"That's the way I want to find him," said Little Minnie, and laid the muzzle of the revolver on the place where Mr. Tolliver's stomach projected like a little shelf.

"What's this gag?" whispered Mr. Tolliver from the side of his mouth.

"This is poison, brother," said Little Minnie. "Just stick up your hands for a minute, will you? You boys take any weights you can find off of our bouncer friend, will you?" he asked without turning his head. In the meantime, he was taking a single, very beautifully decorated revolver from the person of Tolliver. Then he heard the muttering voice of Buck Penrose enumerating: "Three guns, a knife, a set of knuckles, and a slung shot. That's all this gent needed to keep himself warm. Look how chilly he is right away. He's all trembling with the cold."

"You lead the way in," said Little Minnie, "and step smiling, Mister Tolliver. If you remember me at all, you won't try any of your little tricks now."

"Nobody'll ever believe it," said Tolliver. "Nobody'll ever believe that anybody ever tried a gag like this right under the nose of the chief."

But he led the way as commanded, the prodding muzzle of the revolver helping him to make up his mind with greater speed. And so they stepped through the doorway into a little room which was so occupied by a fat desk that it seemed a miracle that there should be room for the five people who were seated here and there around the wall—a precious collection of rascals by their looks, and above all Mr. Fatty Orcutt shone. He was young, big, soft, smooth, and smiling. He looked like some rich old woman's favorite son. And yet again, as has been said, he shone. There were other men in that room who might have been considered far more formidable, but none had in their eyes the light that adorned the eyes of Fatty Orcutt. It was not remarkable that he ruled in Sunnydale. It was only wonderful that he had not chosen a much larger field.

He began: "Tolliver, you know better than to bring in. . . ."

Then, before he saw the guns, he saw something in the face of his lieutenant that made him reach for the lamp. He would have caught it, too, and washed that room into solid blackness in another moment had it not been for the length of Little Minnie's arm and the extra inches on the barrel of his gun. As it was, he was just able to flick the gambler across the forearm with the rim of the muzzle of that great Colt. The arm of Fatty Orcutt jumped away and was caressed by the other hand.

The four friends, or business associates, of Orcutt's were out of their chairs, but the game was too hard for them, hardy fellows though they were. Faces like Lew Eastern's and Buck Penrose's, looking down gun barrels, were too disheartening. Two of them half drew their weapons, but they all thought better of it.

Fatty Orcutt asked: "What sort of a gag is this, brothers? And who are you?" he went on, looking at Little Minnie. "Haven't I seen you before?"

"Most people have seen me before . . . nearly everybody that's ever had a good nightmare has seen me before," said Little Minnie, his broadest smile on his crooked mouth. "Jumping Jack, will you fan these gentlemen for me? And if any one of 'em tries a funny move, don't waste time talking or warning. Just bash in his skull with a butt end, or else ram a couple of bullets through his spine.

"You don't have to be delicate in handling this cargo," he went on. "Anyway, it won't be shipped in a refrigerator car, and some of it is bound to spoil before the shipment arrives. That's all right. There's plenty more of these melons, growing in the same fields. That's right . . . take the wallets, too, Jack. You've got a set of useful fingers on those hands of yours. I wouldn't be without them and you. Now a few bits of this twine wrapped around their wrists and put their hands behind their backs. Thanks very much, boys, but I'll do the tying myself. I know the job, and I like it."

Chapter Seven

"The First Installment"

There were three heavily armed men still at the entrance to Orcutt's place, but they gave no trouble. The sight of their chief's bulky form—their chief with his hands tied behind him—seemed to paralyze their bodies and their brains. They allowed themselves to be stuck up, fanned, and taken in tow. Rapidly the procession moved by back alleys to the jail, but not so rapidly that they failed to hear a murmur and then a humming that began to pass through the trembling air that overhung the town of Sunnydale.

Mr. Orcutt was calm and coldly indignant. He said to Little Minnie: "This is a good bluff. You boys can't do anything with me. I'm too big. There's too much of me. Know that? You can't throw me away, brother. This is only going to be trouble for you."

"I'm only doing this for your own good, Fatty," said Little Minnie.

"Are you?" murmured the other.

"Yeah. Only for your own good. The way that you've been putting on weight is pitiful, Fatty. Think of the days when you used to be so slim and so slender that you could dance all night long. Gone are those days, Fatty, but they'll return again. And remember when your skin was a fine, healthful brown? Now see how pale and pink it is. Not a manly color, old fellow. But we'll change that. In about sixty days we'll bring you back a perfect picture of all that a young man ought to be. You won't have to pay a tailor so much when that time comes, old son."

"Sixty days?" said Orcutt. "What in blazes are you talking about, partner?"

"I'm talking about a little summer resort that I know of. An uncle of mine is one of the proprietors. And it's a funny sort of a resort, at that. Mighty funny. You see, they actually pay the guests, instead of the guests having to pay the resort. It's a simple life, but it will do great things for you, Fatty. Any good doctor in the world would advise the course for you. And the delightful part of it is that you will be surrounded by your best friends. You see, we've thought of everything. We're simply doing you good by force."

So they arrived at the jail, where Little Minnie climbed the steps and knocked on the door.

A voice inside drawled: "Open that door, boy. Dog-gone me if it don't sound like somebody wanted to get inside."

A key grated in the lock. The door opened, and a grinning Negro stood before them. At a little distance, lolling in a comfortable chair with legs extended before him, was the sallow-faced jailer, yawning prodigiously.

"You can step right outside, fella," said Little Minnie, walking inside. "You won't be needed any more here."

The Negro took one look at the bared guns of that strange posse and then leaped into the outer darkness with a gurgling cry. Inside, the jailer looked up with amazement at the giant who advanced upon him.

"Hey, what's this gang want?" he demanded.

"More room," said Little Minnie. "We want all the space you're occupying in this jail, brother. You've been the hole in the cask that a lot of good liquor has run out through. You'll be the easy exit no more, friend. This way, please. This way!" With his left hand he took the other literally by the ear, while he rammed the portentous length of his Colt against the ribs of the unlucky jailer. A twist of his iron fingers made the jailer howl and prance. In this manner they came to the door of the building, and from that point Little Minnie started the other into the world with the longest first step he had ever made. For he was buoyed up and assisted from behind with such a mighty impact that, as he shot upward and outward into darkness, his yell went like a sword of fire before him.

Little Minnie turned back into the building. Already the cell room had been opened by Buck Penrose, and the prisoners were being herded inside.

Little Minnie made a brief inspection. Then he said: "Gentlemen, I've already explained to Mister Orcutt that our chief idea in arranging this little surprise party is to give you a healthful time of exercise and rest, on good, simple food, and plenty of the freshest air in the world. Only one thing we insist upon. This is discipline. We believe, in fact, that discipline is a thing which we can teach better than you have ever been taught it before. We are going to do our best, humbly and patiently, to keep you in strictly good order. Where humility and patience have no effect, we will use the whip. Where the whip is not sufficient, we'll use the riot gun.

"Lew, you'll be in charge of this first installment. We won't leave you alone with them very long. Others will be joining them, I'm sure, to fill out our little mission. But while you're here alone, I call your attention to the row of riot guns hanging along that wall. See if they're loaded, Buck."

"Every damned one is loaded," said Buck Penrose. "Double charges of number one buckshot, Minnie."

"The very thing. The very thing to encourage discipline. I'm delighted," said Little Minnie.

"Listen, Mister . . . ," began Fatty Orcutt in a hoarse voice.

"Always pleased to hear a man of your intelligence speak," said Little Minnie. "Mind the whip, Lew. That quirt ought to do pretty well."

Lew Eastern picked up the quirt with an avid hand.

Fatty Orcutt snarled: "You think, damn you, that you've pulled a pretty good trick here, don't you?

But lemme tell you that I'm going to break this jail to bits, and when I get through with the jail, I'm going to start in on you. You write that down in red, you. . . ."

Mr. Minder Trent raised one finger, and Lew Eastern struck through the bars of steel and slashed the quirt across the shoulders of Fatty Orcutt. A gasping oath was the answer, and then silence. Fatty Orcutt showed his teeth, but he dared not speak again. He merely writhed and rubbed the weals the lashes had raised upon his tender flesh.

His adherents and advisers stood dumbly, glowering behind their bars. They stared not at one another, but at this strange giant who had stepped so suddenly and so violently out of nowhere into their lives.

"This is a good little jail, a snug little jail, a tight little jail," said Little Minnie to Eastern. "Now, while we're gone, I want you to sit here with a riot gun across your knees, and two more, one on each side of your chair. That gives you six charges to pay off any trouble that starts inside of this place.

"No matter what happens, don't let that front door be opened until you hear my voice outside of it. If there's any trouble inside, I don't want you to hesitate. Just turn loose the buckshot and let it talk for you. If I come back and find seven dead men in the cells, I'll be hurt, but not surprised. Is all that clear?"

"Brother," said Lew Eastern, fondling one of the double-barreled, sawed-off shotguns, "nothing ever pleased me more than this here job. I never was so tickled in my life as I am to be right in here with these boys. I'm seeing some faces that mean a whole lot to me, Minnie.

"Look at that yegg with the one eye and the patch over the other. That's Dan Binney. Curse his black heart, he's cut more throats than any two hounds in this town. He's a butcher, is what he is. And there's Mister 'Green-Goods' Walters. I'm glad to see him, too. And they're glad to see me, too . . . they are *not!* They'd rather be throwed into a pit filled with snakes than be left here alone with me. Why, Minnie, there won't be a sound out of them. There won't even be a whisper while you're away. They're just going to sit around like so many little mice and wait for the cat to come back and eat 'em up."

As he spoke, he chuckled, and the sound of his laughter was very like the low growling of a bull-dog.

Little Minnie turned to his other adherents.

"Boys," he said, "the next part of our program is really pretty simple, though it seems complicated. Follow me and do as I do. First, you take your coats off."

It was done.

"Then you rip out the lining. You make the lining into a hood that comes over your head and shoulders, with holes for the eyes . . . look, Lew, how these boys seem to know exactly how to make masks . . . every one of them. I wonder where they all learned the trick. Oh, I have a talented posse with me."

In fact, hardly five minutes were needed before there stood before the leader three masked men. It seemed to Little Minnie that he could see the smiles of that trio behind the black cloth of the masks.

"Which way this time?" asked Jumping Jack Story.

"This time back to the same place," said Minder Trent.

"Back to the same place?" exclaimed Story.

"Look here, chief," protested Denny Rourke. "You may get past the wasps once, but not when they're all buzzing in the air and ready for trouble."

"It's throwin' ourselves away," said Buck Penrose. "A long pull and a strong pull and a pull altogether may turn a big trick, but not a trick as big as that."

"I have an idea, partners," Little Minnie answered. "Ideas are better than numbers, and there won't be a gun fired . . . except if one of you gets too nervous."

He could see their heads, nodding in agreement. They had seen something done, and they were willing to follow him quite blindly this time. So it was that they marched out of the jail behind him, down the steps, and into the darkness across the field, and so, by a back alley, they came again to the gambler's stronghold.

Even then Little Minnie did not try to get in by a back entrance, but around the side of the big, sprawling shack, now seething with the noise of excited voices. They came to the front of the building again and found at the entrance half a dozen angry men, armed, and apparently waiting for them.

Chapter Eight

"The Trick"

When Little Minnie started to enter, before any other question, a rifle barrel flashed, and the muzzle of the gun was pressed against his broad chest. "What are *you*?" asked the angry guard.

"I'm this," answered Little Minnie, and from under his arm he produced a double-barreled, sawed-off shotgun.

"That may be your first name, but it ain't your last name," said the guard. "Lookit here. What are you doing with masks on?"

"What fool wants to go to the jail wearing his right face?" asked Little Minnie. "The rest of you are yelling your heads off about Fatty Orcutt, but I'm going to *do* something about him. You just back up, brother, and don't waste your time bothering me. I'll just tell you this. Fatty knows that I'm here right now. You pass the word around. Say that

I want to see some armed men, wearing masks, in the big game room, will you?"

"You'll see me one of 'em, as soon as I can get a hood over my head," said the guard. "Damn it, but I think you mean business."

He stood back, and Little Minnie, with his three solemn followers, marched into the game room of the Orcutt establishment. There was room enough in that place for a hundred men to lose their money all at the same time, and now it was swirling with a tumult of excited men, not one of whom was seated at the tables. Guns were everywhere. It was a mob that simply wanted leading. All heads turned toward that grim procession which now entered in single file, four solemn forms. Three of them, obeying muttered instructions, moved to the right and the left of the entrance. Little Minnie went on until he stood upon that raised dais where the roulette wheel was mounted, a sort of eminence that Fatty Orcutt's most crooked device deserved.

By the time the giant had reached that post he had the attention of every man in the room. Then he raised a great arm, at the end of which the heavy riot gun looked no more than a mere clumsy revolver. He spoke: "You boys are talking about Fatty Orcutt in the jail. You're *talking*. But you're doing nothing about it. I intend to take you there . . . as many of you as are sorry to see Fatty in trouble. I don't want a man that wouldn't go through thick and thin for Fatty. I don't want a man who doesn't think that Fatty Orcutt is the best fellow in this town. Fatty and six of his partners are in the jail, tied and helpless. I'm going to lead some of you who have enough courage and grit to go to that jail. I want to see you, but I don't want to see your faces. You may have to do some things that you won't be talking about tomorrow. There may be some blood shed tonight. Or it may just amount to a few necks being squeezed by sliding nooses. Now, lemme see how many of you put on masks to follow me into the Sunnydale jail!"

The talking ended. On the spot there was a sudden bustling. Some men followed the obvious device of Little Minnie himself and ripped the linings out of their coats to make hoods for their heads. Others declared that they would have to get cloth elsewhere for that purpose. Still others said that they had not with them the right sort of weapons, and all of those who left the building under these pretexts never returned. Of the original crowd, hardly twenty remained. But others sifted in through the doorway, all armed to the teeth, and all masked.

The noise throughout Sunnydale began to die down. It was plain that the rumor that something important was about to happen had quelled the lesser spirits and sent scampering home all of those men who were more willing to talk than to act. And now, when no more newcomers entered the place, and when there were present a full fifty masked men, someone jumped on a table and called out: "Let's get together, boys. We wanta find out the best plan. We wanta. . . ."

The thunderous roll of Little Minnie's voice broke in upon this harangue and stopped it. "What we want to do is to get into the jail. Am I wrong?"

Story, Rourke, and Buck Penrose shouted heartily: "Aye! That's it! We want to get into the jail!"

"That's it!" called other voices.

The man who had climbed to the top of the table stood unnoticed.

Little Minnie continued: "I'll get you all in there in a jiffy. Look this way, all of you, and listen to me. D'you hear? Listen to me and try to understand that I mean what I say."

Every head turned toward him. Crowds of men are like crowds of sheep. Not the best, but the first leader is usually followed. So these men attended patiently on Little Minnie. He went on: "Buck, Jack, and Denny, cover this gang . . . and the first hand that tries to lift a gun, open up with those riot guns and blow them to blazes."

As he spoke, the gasp of the crowd seemed a single voice exclaiming, sharp and high, as the trick began to be apparent. Hardly a man there refrained from reaching for a weapon. Every man reached for one, but none was drawn, for now in the massive fists of Little Minnie appeared two sawed-off shotguns that he handled with absurd ease. The great muzzles swung slowly in a semicircle, covering the assembly. It seemed to every man that he was picked out for the particular attention of that masked giant on the dais of the roulette-wheel table. For there was hardly a man there who was not deserving of particular attention.

It was a hand-picked group, containing all of the most hardy spirits in the town. They were such men as would readily have taken their chances against revolvers, but chances against sawed-off shotguns do not exist. In the hands of Little Minnie and his three assistants there was enough of a hailstorm of lead to sweep the cheap pine boards of that floor with blood and death. And those grim figures very well knew it.

"Move over against the wall!" commanded Little Minnie. "The whole lot of you, crowd over there against the wall. Start in. Move, blast you, or we'll wash you out."

Suddenly he loosed the barrel of his left-hand gun. He fired down toward the floor, and when the sudden roar of the barking explosion was ended, those who were curious could see how the floor had been mangled by the sweeping effects of the heavy leaden shot. There was no hanging back.

One man groaned: "We're sold, boys, and that's all there is to it."

"We've been taken in. It's a low trick," protested another.

The hardiest of men or wildcats may be caught in a trap, and these fellows knew that they were trapped. They moved, they sidled and backed until they stood in what averaged a closely ordered double rank against the wall. When they reached that position, it was plain that their case was infinitely worse than before.

Straight before them stood the giant, with a gun in each hand. At the one end of their line was a masked man, kneeling, his riot gun pressed close to his shoulder, studying that line with the steady muzzles of his weapon. At the other end two more, in the same position, regarded them.

Little Minnie said: "Denny, you wade through

those boys and collect their hardware. Jack and Buck, if trouble starts, just turn loose. It doesn't matter if you have to shoot Denny along with the rest of 'em. He'll be glad to go out in that sort of company. Step along, Denny."

And Denny Rourke stepped along.

He was cursed by voices that quivered with rage. But no man attempted to harm him. The watch was too close. The chances against them were too great. Who would try to dodge at close range from the spray of a garden hose? And here were three steel hoses, and the drops they were ready to spray were of lead.

Denny Rourke was not nice. He plucked weapons right and left. He dropped rifles and revolvers to the floor and slid them out into the center of it. One of them exploded and knocked a little hole in the wall. That was all that happened. Even the cursing began to die out. Every one of these fellows had gambled heavily and lost before this evening. It was not exactly strange to them to lose again.

Presently a great heap of weapons appeared in the center of the floor. There were rifles, shotguns, revolvers predominantly, slung shots, knives of all sorts and sizes. And finally Denny Rourke stepped back with a nod and a grunt.

"They're a lot cleaner now than they were, chief," he said. "I ain't gleaned 'em to the skin. But I've got all the cream."

"Go back and take a gun," said the leader. "Watch those boys steady and sure. Now, Jack and Buck, take those lengths of twine and tie their hands. Tie 'em hard and fast. Take plenty of time. Nobody in

Sunnydale will come to help 'em, because there's nobody left in Sunnydale. We've got the whole town here, and we're going to take it along with us."

Heavy groans arose from the unlucky ones. But what could they do save submit? There were well-witnessed tales of how one desperado with a single revolver had stuck up a room filled with twenty armed men. And here were four against fifty, and the four carried riot guns. Step by step that hardy gang had been backed against the wall. Every step had made its position worse. Now there remained nothing except blank submission.

Their hands were tied. Then long ropes were passed from arm to arm, secured by half hitches. And so the procession was started through the doors of the gaming house, with Little Minnie, standing at the door, snatching off the hoods that masked them, one by one. Three abreast, they entered the principal street of Sunnydale, and three abreast, closely huddled, they marched down its length, while nearly every man, woman, and child of the rest of the population lined the street and looked on with murmurs.

It was plain that a change had come to the town. Upon the spot, certain of the gay spirits who had escaped that rope gang determined to leave for other places, for any place that was far away from this sort of trouble.

Chapter Nine

"Minnie's Justice"

When they reached the jail, Little Minnie mounted
the steps of the building and made a speech. It was
not a long speech, but the words of it sank deep.
He had taken off his mask by this time, but his face
and his smile were not pleasant to those who
looked up to him from the lower darkness.

"Boys," he said, "you all wanted to do something
about Fatty Orcutt. He was your friend. You knew
that he was in the jail, and you wanted to break the
jail open. You won't have to do that. You can see
that the doors of the jail are open for you. You all
like Fatty a lot, and I don't blame you. Fatty's a
pleasant fellow. He's taken some crooked money
now and then and here and there, but never out of
your pockets. A few people have been tapped over
the head in his place, and some of them never

opened their eyes again. But he never rolled any of you.

"He's spent a lot of money on thugs and gunmen, and a good many of you have that money in your pockets. No wonder you care about Fatty. Now you're going to be able to do something for him. You'll be able to keep him company where he's going. And he's going to a summer resort where he won't have to pay for board and lodging. Partly for his sake, and partly for your own, you're all going to have the same opportunity. Jack, start them up the steps. We'll bed them down in here for tonight."

It was a tight fit, but it was managed. Into the little jail the mob was brought and turned into the cells by threes. There were only a dozen cells, and therefore some of the men had to sleep in the corridors, their hands manacled to the bars.

They were amazingly quiet. Lew Eastern, striding up and down all night with a lantern, kept guard over them, and Jumping Jack Story, who had found his particular enemies in the throng, and who had to go and see them now and then, burst into loud and long laughter. As for the others—Little Minnie, Rourke, and Buck Penrose—they slept rolled in blankets in the jailer's room. And soundly they slept, and long, until the dawn turned from gray to red, and then the sun came up.

When Little Minnie arose, he said in his loud voice to the prisoners: "I'm going to get the court ready for you boys. This is a just country, and we want you to have nothing but justice. That summer resort wouldn't take any of you without a recommendation from a judge."

Then he left the jail and went to find Judge Herbert Loring. He found that gentleman taking a breakfast of ham and eggs in the little shack that served him as a home. The judge made him sit down at the same table. He paused long enough to pump a wash basin full of water. When he had soaped and washed his hands and face, he sat down opposite the judge. A one-legged veteran came stumping in with a new supply of food and coffee.

"You don't look as though you've been up all night, Mister Trent, alias Little Minnie," said the judge.

"I haven't," said Little Minnie. "I've had a good long sleep."

The judge nodded. "When you got through, I hear that there was no one left in Sunnydale to keep people awake. It's the quietest night the town has ever had since the gold rush started. But what are we to do with that collection of beauties that you've gathered in the jail?"

"Where did you hear about 'em?" asked Little Minnie.

"You can't keep people from talking," answered the judge. "They'll talk whenever they get a fair excuse. And you gave them more than a fair excuse, I take it. I hear that Jud Biddle is in that gang?"

"Who's Jud Biddle?" asked Little Minnie.

"Why," said the judge, "he's a fellow who's wanted for murder in Arizona and for arson in Nevada and for pushing the queer in California. There are enough charges against him to hang him three times and put him in prison for seven lifetimes.

71

Then I understand that you picked up the gentleman called Dagger Jim."

"That sounds interesting," said Little Minnie, "but I don't know Dagger Jim, either."

"Dagger Jim is a great artist," said the judge. "Murder is his special talent, and he uses it overtime. It's hard to keep an artist from using his hands, you know. And Dagger Jim uses his. He draws his pictures with a knife, and some of them have been very interesting. They've attracted world-wide attention. He's wanted for only one crime. But he's wanted in seven states, and always for murder. A lot of sheriffs in this country would almost cry for joy when it's known that Dagger Jim has been caught."

"Any more that have been spotted?" asked the captor, frowning.

"A lot more," said the judge. "Enough to keep me busy for six months, giving sentences. But there'll be a great deal of extradition. Lawyers are going to rub their hands when they hear about all of this."

"Judge Loring, I'm sorry."

"Why?" asked the judge.

"Because," said the giant, "I don't like lawyers."

"No?"

"Except in their own place."

"And what is their own place?"

"In a jail, or near it."

The judge grinned, his eyes sparkling with a sudden brightness. "Go on," he said.

"About these murderers and such . . . ," began Little Minnie.

"Yes, I've just been talking about them."

"We're going to have a new kind of justice in Sunnydale," said Little Minnie.

"I believe that," answered the judge. "We already have a new kind of justice. You got most of the foremost crooks in one sweep, and the others, the smaller fry, suddenly find the air of Sunnydale is bad for what ails them. All night long there have been buckboards and horses and mules starting out of town, all bound for parts unknown, all carrying a freight of thugs of one sort or another. I haven't closed my eyes since the first reports came in."

"Good," said Little Minnie. "And it's too bad, too. Pretty soon it won't be possible to raise enough crooks to make a poker game, not with a sheriff's posse to help collect 'em."

"Would that be hard on you, Trent?" asked the judge.

"I wouldn't stay in that kind of a town."

"*This* town would like to have a mayor again . . . it would like to have you, man," said the judge. "A handful of the leading citizens . . . citizens, I mean to say, who will lead now that Fatty Orcutt is out of the way . . . left my house just at dawn this morning. They all decided that you were the man for the job."

"I'm sorry," said Little Minnie. "But I've got to help my uncle run his summer resort for fifty days. And after that I'll be outward bound."

"Fifty days?"

"Fifty days," said the other, "is what I hear all those thugs are going to get from you by way of a sentence."

73

Max Brand

Herbert Loring bowed his head a little and looked up at the big man from under darkened brows.

"Those murderers, safe-crackers, counterfeiters, cut-throats . . . you think that they all will receive fifty days?" he demanded.

"Yes," said the other.

"Who told you that?"

"A still, small voice," answered the big man, grinning.

The judge did not smile in return. "You've done a great thing, a wonderful thing, Trent," he said. "You've broken up a hotbed of corruption. You've washed the poison out of Sunnydale's gold. But you can't interfere with justice."

The other shrugged his shoulders.

"What's your answer?" said the judge. "Some of these men are blackened by every crime in the calendar, and yet you want to let them off with sentences of fifty days apiece?"

"I'm blackened by a good many crimes myself," answered the giant slowly. "The only reason I was able to make this roundup is because I know a lot of roughs, and know how to handle 'em. This was partly business for me, but it was chiefly a game. I'm not going to turn it into more than fifty days of business. After that, they go free. There may be murderers and such in that gang. But I went after laborers, not thugs."

The judge struck the table with his fist, but he struck it lightly. "Things have gone so far that you can't interfere," he said.

"Suppose," said the giant more slowly than ever,

74

"that I go over to that jail and turn loose the whole hive of wasps on Sunnydale?"

"You can't do it!" exclaimed Judge Loring.

The big, crag-like jaw of the giant thrust forward. "I'll take some stopping," he said.

"Confound it, man," said Loring, "are you going to turn your invaluable contribution into a joke?"

"I'm going to turn my joke into fifty days of sweat for 'em," said Little Minnie. "I won't have their blood. I don't want their blood. I'd rather cut off my right hand than have it on my head."

"Are you afraid of 'em?" asked the judge suddenly.

"Afraid of them?" repeated Little Minnie, amazed. "Why, before they've finished raising blisters and headaches in my uncle's mine, every one of those thugs will be ready to starve for ten years to have one shot at me. If I get them hanged, I can't get them to hate me any more than they will."

"Then, under heaven," exclaimed Loring, "I don't understand why you want to let them off with paltry sentences."

The other thought for a moment. "It's an instinct with me, not a reason," he said. "But I suppose that I'd rather have the hatred of men and stand in their danger than have them dead and be haunted by the thought of them." Then he added: "I've broken enough laws myself. Who am I to bring other people to justice?"

Judge Herbert Loring actually rose from his chair, and then he made a swift turn up and down the room. At last he said: "Partner Trent, you confound me."

"I'm sorry," said Trent.

"But," continued the man of the law, "whatever it may be, justice or foolishness, I'm going to let you have your way. But let's get it over with quickly. Bring those rascals into my court at once, and I'll be there waiting. It's not law. It may mean that I'll be thrown off the bench, but I'll do what you want."

"Judge Loring," said the other, "I've an idea that after this morning anyone who tries to throw you off the bench will have to face every gun that Sunnydale can pull to keep you seated."

"From what I've heard," said Loring, grinning suddenly, "there are no guns left in the town."

Chapter Ten

"The Trial"

Since the French Revolution there was never such a trial. On the prisoner's bench, or rather grouped closely in front of it, stood fifty-seven men, their hands bound, long ropes holding them together. Nearby stood the formidable forms of Jumping Jack Story, crook, Lew Eastern, crooked gambler, Denny Rourke, saloonkeeper and general man of all trouble, and Buck Penrose, whose single love was a hard fight. The judge sat behind his desk on the raised platform. The clerk sat at the table below it. The old sergeant-at-arms was by the door, his eyes as big and round as apples. The only other man in the room was the giant, Little Minnie. The newspapers were not represented. The people of Sunnydale were not represented. The district attorney was not there. No lawyer attached to the court was on hand. The sheriff was not appearing.

77

But in the street was a crowd of three or four thousand, humming as ten million bees might hum.

The judge said: "Mister Deputy Sheriff, what is all this about?"

Mr. Minder Trent, deputy sheriff extraordinary, answered: "Your Honor, here are fifty-seven fellows whose names don't matter, all charged with breaking the peace."

"Are you standing in the witness stand, Mister Deputy Sheriff?" asked the judge, rubbing his knuckles across his chin.

"I'm standing in my boots," said the giant, grinning.

"How did they break the peace?" asked the judge.

"Most of them wore masks," said the giant. "And those who didn't wear a mask wore concealed weapons, all the way from knives of illegal length to Colt revolvers."

"This is a serious charge," said the judge, still faintly smiling. "What have you to substantiate it?"

"I have here," said the deputy sheriff, "one half gross of revolvers and eighteen rifles and twelve shotguns and three dozen of the knives that I talk about. There are also certain other illegal weapons, such as brass knuckles, slung shots, lead-pipe sections in hose, and other devices. There are burglar sets and several packages of counterfeit money. But the worst charge against the prisoners is the faces they wear. Look at those beauties!"

The judge looked, and he did not smile. Few people, other than Minder Trent, could have smiled at the glowering hatred and malice that darkened fifty-seven faces.

"A serious charge," said the judge. "I feel that I must proceed to sentence."

A loud, gasping voice, the voice of Fatty Orcutt, exclaimed: "Your Honor, what does this mean? I appeal to law and justice. I want my due rights as a citizen of the United States. I demand a chance to consult a lawyer. I protest against this mock trial of fifty men on one charge. I protest against evidence that. . . ."

"There's other evidence, Mister Orcutt," said the judge very dryly. "There are scores of men in the street who are aching to give evidence almost as much as they are aching to tie a rope around your fat neck. And if you are held for a week, there will be sheriffs and their deputies from half the states in the country to lay charges against you. Perhaps this is not a trial. Perhaps it *is* a mockery. But the mockery is of the law and the rights of the law, not of you and most of the other reptiles who are gathered around you.

"You, Orcutt, have serious charges of fraud pending against you. Five separate times officers of the law, to my certain knowledge, have come to Sunnydale to arrest you, with legal warrants. One of those men was found dead in the street. Another disappeared mysteriously. Another now lies recovering from wounds. Two more were able to leave the town alive, but not unhurt. Orcutt, do you seriously challenge full justice for yourself, or do you prefer to have me hand you over to Mister Trent for fifty days?"

"Damn him, and you, too," muttered the fat man, but his voice was barely audible.

"I would have held you for the full operation of the law," said the judge. "Legally or illegally, I would have held you all. But in this uncertain time, the power of Mister Trent is greater than mine, and he has refused to permit a single major charge to be offered against a single one of you. Such generosity is, in my opinion, more extraordinary than sensible. But some of you, in my belief, can thank him for your lives, and others that the rest of your days are not spent in prison. But I proceed to sentence, unless . . ."—he lifted his head and grimly glared along the rows of faces—"unless there are other voices raised to demand particular justice in each case?"

Not a voice answered, though the judge purposely maintained that grim silence for the whole of a long minute.

He said, at last: "Since everyone is satisfied, I now deliver you into the hands of Mister Minder Trent, deputy sheriff of this county. Each and every one of you is sentenced to fifty days of penal servitude . . . hard labor. Mister Deputy Sheriff, remove the prisoners. Mister clerk of the court, write nothing in your book. Sergeant-at-arms, attend the prisoners to the street and keep the mob from lynching them if you can."

That was the end of the most singular trial ever held west of the Mississippi. Perhaps there were trials for witchcraft in certain dark old days that might have matched it for freakishness. But though the trial had ended, the troubles of the prisoners, in a sense, and certainly their danger, had just begun. For when they were ushered down the steps to the street, a murmur, a groan, a shouting, and then one long, wild howl arose from the thousands gathered there.

A singular process went on in the mob at the same time. Women and children, as though by magic, were sifted to the rear of it. There remained in front only men. And rough men they were, and angry. They had seen murder done almost whole-sale in their town. They had been robbed, tricked, cheated in a thousand ways. They had seen rascal-ity walk bare-faced through the streets, and still there had seemed no way of organizing to put down crime. Now they saw crime itself gathered in ranks before them, helpless, hands tied. And the temptation was too great.

Single voices began to break through that gen-eral hymn of hatred.

"There's Fatty Orcutt! There he goes. Where's the rope to hang him?"

"Here's the rope for Orcutt. Here's another for Bill Levine, the gunman. He killed Pete Thomas. I saw him kill Pete Thomas."

"There's Gonzales, that murdered Steve Hamp-shire on a bet. Get him!"

And now, as the crowd began to rush, the thun-dering voice of Mr. Minder Trent arose and boomed down that street and put every man back on his heels.

"Gentlemen, keep back! If you start to make trou-ble, I'll turn the prisoners loose, and then handle 'em if you can. Keep back, or we'll turn loose on you with the riot guns. March on, there in front. Jack and Buck, clear the street. Use your gun butts if you have to. If that won't do, shoot, and I'll take the responsibility. Gentlemen of Sunnydale, we're giving you a safe town for the first time since it was built. But I won't see helpless men murdered, no matter what they've done before. March ahead! Fall back, you!"

He was everywhere. Those enormous strides carried him to the front and to the back. Wherever angry townsmen began to draw close and prepare to gather, the looming bulk of the deputy sheriff discouraged them before they could act.

So, down the main street to the first break in the houses moved that troop, the prisoners holding closely packed together. More than one lost both coat and shirt sleeves, as fingers hard with rage plucked at them. Such was the temper of the crowd that, once a man had been detached from the general mass, there would have been no question asked. Death on the spot would have been the order of the day. Now, down a side lane, they were marched into the open country behind the town, and, as though the clean, open spaces banished murder from their minds, the townsmen fell back and let the procession go forward.

There was talk of pursuit. There was even arming and the saddling of horses, but no sufficiently large group could draw to a head. The mighty form of Little Minnie remained, looming too formidably in the memories of these men.

In the meantime, the guards of the prisoners had mounted on mustangs. Six dozen confiscated revolvers and eighteen rifles and various sundry other weapons had been exchanged for the horses

and for the solid and heavy packs of provisions that
helped to weigh down the saddles. So Little Minnie
and his four men herded the captives quickly
across the plain, up the slope, and over the ridge.

By that time, the sun was beating with great
force upon them, and more than one was without
a hat. Moreover, though some of these men were
as tough as bands of iron and leather, yet many
others were, like Falstaff, larding the lean earth
they walked upon. Fatty Orcutt began to groan and
roll his eyes. Plenty of food and little exercise had
been very bad for the condition of Fatty. He was
cut loose. He was allowed to march at the rear of
the procession, and, when he lagged, a quirt,
snapped near his ears, taught him to hurry forward
once more. Presently every man in the lot was permitted to have free hands, and the controlling
ropes that grouped them all together were dis-
pensed with. For they were not needed. Beaten,
staggering, groaning, cursing, that mob of desper-
adoes of many kinds climbed the long slopes toward the mine.

It was forty miles that they had to cover, very
nearly. And the pace they were able to maintain
was not more than two and half miles an hour,
even at the first. It grew less and less as the day
progressed. Thrice in the day they came to water.
But there was no food.

"An empty belly makes a bright dog," said Mr.
Minder Trent.

The day ended as they started on the last long
pull. The darkness closed with the guards riding
busily here and there to make sure that no one of

the herd dared to try to slip behind a bush or a rock and so escape. Then the moon rose, and just above them it gilded the rocky face of the mountain where stood the mine of Tom Wayland and Jim Trent.

Chapter Eleven

"End of the Journey"

After supper, Jim Trent usually smoked one pipe, rolled in his blankets, and went to sleep. On this night he had smoked the pipe, rolled himself in his blankets, but sleep he could not. Between him and repose slid a thought of trouble that kept his eyes wide open. They began to ache and burn as he stared up into the darkness. Finally he got up and went striding out across the little plateau that extended before the mine.

He and Wayland, he knew, had reached the end of their tether. They really had reached it a long time before. The ground they were breaking was just as hard as ever; there was nothing softening of the strain in which they labored, nor did the vein become richer as they explored it further. They would have to give it up. Just as he had said, it seemed to extend clear down to China, but two men simply could not exploit it. They could make day's wages—hardly that, considering the overhead and the labor that the girl was forced to do. They would have to give up now.

He must press the issue upon Wayland at once. For himself he hardly minded. He had prospected for twenty years; he had labored in a thousand holes of his own discovery; he could return to the maddening and fascinating business once more. But it was a tragedy for Wayland. He would have to return to find his clients gone to other physicians. He would return so poor that his daughter would have to make her own living however she might manage it—as a camp cook, perhaps, or a slavey in a crossroads boarding house.

These thoughts darkened the mind of Jim Trent as he stood and stared at the moonlight that stepped across the mountaintops and dropped vainly into the blue deeps of the gorges. He was not a lover of beautiful pictures, but he was a lover of spaces, and some harmony in this gigantic composition entered his soul, unknown to him. Then it seemed to him that he heard upon the wind, from the valley beneath, a murmuring like the humming of bees when they are swarming not very far away. He had never heard such a sound as this in such a setting. So he shaded his eyes with a frown and peered into the depths beneath him.

Gradually he could make out something that moved close up under the rock. It seemed one unshaped monster, flowing slowly over the ground, reaching the cliff, entering upon the windings of the upper trail. But then, his eyes clearing with a start, he made out riders, five of them, and a multitude of men. The murmur was the scraping of their feet upon the ground and the groaning breaths they drew and the oaths they gasped out. They walked like drunkards, staggering. Sometimes a man went down. He was kicked to his feet by his companions and forced on. For who dared to drop by the wayside in this march and thereby prolong the agony of the entire group?

The riders had dismounted. One of them held the horses of the others and started to unsaddle them. Three more made a rear guard, with the faint sheen of guns in their hands. But the fifth man strode straight through the compact throng.

He seemed to step over the men, as well as among them. He came swiftly to the front, and then the bulky outlines of him were suddenly familiar to the eye of Trent. He shouted: "Little Minnie, is that you, you rascal?"

"Here I am!" thundered Little Minnie.

"What are you up to? What have you got there?" called Trent.

"Men to work the Wayland-Trent Mine!" shouted Little Minnie.

A swirling of dizzy hope mounted into the brain of Jim Trent. He would not believe what his eyes beheld—the steady, upward flooding of these men, come, as his nephew said, to work in the mine. Why, with as many hands as that they would simply be able to crack the mountain open like a nut and get at the rich kernel, if kernel there were.

The call of Trent brought out Wayland and the girl from the shack. The great voice of Little Minnie began to give orders before he had scaled the last of the steep trail.

"Get the coffee pot boiling. Slice some bacon. Stir up some bread. Here are fifty men that have to eat before they sleep, and sleep before they work. Uncle Jim, get the guns together and out of the way, where no hands but your own can work them. There may be gun work to do on this gang before they're ready to turn into honest miners."

Now the form of the giant loomed above the edge of the rimrock, looking more huge than ever with the moon behind his head and his great shadow streaming before him.

"Uncle Jim," he said, "and you, Wayland . . . I've brought a little present for Harry Wayland. Harry, where are your pretty manners and your thank yous? Here are fifty-seven thugs that I gathered here and there in Sunnydale. Sunnydale didn't want them. It was glad to get rid of them. And the judge sentenced them to fifty days of hard labor in this summer resort. You keep them busy and feed them, and you pay me a dollar a day for bringing them here and keeping them at work. I have four sheep dogs along with me that'll help to herd the sheep. Here they come, Harry. Look these fellows over. Some of them aren't pretty, and some of them never handled a double-jack before, but we'll teach them the rudiments of how to make an honest living."

As he spoke, the forward ranks of the prisoners staggered, groaning, over the rim of the plateau, swaying and lurching.

"This is home, boys. This is the little old summer

resort that'll make you fit and hard. This is the end of the journey, boys."

When they heard this, many of them simply pitched forward and lay still, some on their faces, some turned on their backs in utter exhaustion, arms flung wide, heedless of the boots that stumbled about them and kicked and mauled them. Very nearly all that can be drained from the strength of human bodies had been drained from theirs.

Harriet Wayland, who had made no answer at all to the extravagances of the giant, was busily working at her fire for cookery purposes. As the last of the prisoners came into the camp, big Minder Trent introduced the three rear guards to his uncle and to Wayland.

"They get five dollars a day from me," he explained, "and the best found that you can supply to 'em. There's another fellow down there in the hollow. He'll be up before long."

Then Trent and the worried Wayland drew him to the side. Wayland, shuddering, pointed to the faces, grotesquely ugly in the firelight. Not many of them were handsome by nature. Nearly all had been handmarked by crime, and the exhaustion of this day's work had completed the grim pictures.

"What are these men?" demanded Wayland.

"Fellows who would murder you for five cents," answered Little Minnie with a look of the greatest content as he ran his eyes over them. "That one with the gray hair . . . prematurely gray . . . is a smuggler. Used to run Chinamen over the river. That one close to the fire, stretching out his hands to it, is a dope peddler. The fellow beside him, with his head hanging down, is a well-known yegg. He's taken a fortune out of banks, but not by writing checks. The little pale man with the sad and poetic face . . . that's Charley Legrange, the murderer."

"Murder, drugs, smuggling, robbery!" exclaimed Wayland. "Great heavens, man, why have you brought these scoundrels up here? Is this your idea of a joke?"

"That's the beauty of 'em," answered the big man. "Every man has his own story. Every dog-gone one of 'em. If you get tired of looking at 'em, you can just start in thinking about 'em. A smart fellow could write fifty-seven biographies about that bunch of fifty-seven clever gentlemen. But they'll work in the mine, believe me, and they'll work for two dollars a day a head. I'll see that they work, all right."

"It means that our throats will all be cut," declared Wayland. "It means that we'll all be destroyed. I never saw so many villainous creatures in my life to call men. Besides, I've no doubt that we'll be liable to the law for this."

"I'm a deputy sheriff," said Little Minnie, and opened his coat so that the firelight flashed upon his steel badge.

Jim Trent stared, then he burst into shattering laughter.

"Oh, he's a lamb, this boy," he said to Wayland. "He's started this game, and we've got to let him try to finish it. Maybe we'll all be dead men in three days . . . or maybe he'll rip the mountain open for us with all these workers, and we'll be so far ahead that we can afford to turn them all loose. That's a possibility. Anyway, they're here."

Little Minnie stepped forward and stood close to the fire. The great shadow of him flared and flickered up the rocky face of the mountain behind him.

"Boys," he said, "I've got to talk to you for a minute. Now we've come to the summer resort, and tonight you get bread and coffee and a strip of fried bacon apiece. But beginning with tomorrow, nobody eats unless he's worked. Every man who works is going to have plenty. Those that only do a half day's job get a half ration. Those that try to run away will be chased. We're going to have guards posted night and day. If you slip past the guard, you'll be spotted on your way up or down the cliff, and then you're going to be tagged with bullets. I shoot fairly straight, and so do the rest of us. We have riot guns to shoot you down if you try mob action. We have plenty of rifles to pick you off if you try to sneak away, one by one. And every one of us will shoot to kill. This is a bad game for you, and you're cornered. Play the game with the cards you hold, and you'll be well enough treated. Try to soldier on the job and you'll catch it. That's all I have to say."

He turned to where the girl was busied with her cookery, and without a word he took up a side of bacon and began to cut slices from it rapidly. Then, as the food was made ready, he was the chief hand in distributing it among the exhausted prisoners who had marched so far. And that was only a beginning. All night long he worked, tearing up brush to make into the foundations for beds, and distrib-

Max Brand

uting spare coats and saddle blankets, and even slickers, for covering. He was tireless. But many of the weary rose neither for food nor for a more comfortable bed. They slept where they had fallen.

Chapter Twelve

"The New Crew"

Morning showed, rising in the blare of the early sun, a haggard lot of rascals drawing together in groups, sullenly murmuring, and looking about them with grimly calculating eyes. Plainly it was one thing to have brought them here, but it might be quite another to keep them.

They were roused up by the loud voice of Little Minnie that called: "All hands for the creek, boys. Here's soap, and there's water. We like to see clean faces for breakfast at the mine. Clean faces make bigger appetites, and the more you eat, the harder you can work. No washing, no eating."

They came, but slowly.

The calm voice of Little Minnie reminded them: "The grub may be used up before the last man comes in."

That roused them more than whip and spurs,

and they swarmed rapidly to the waiting soap and the clean run of the water. Still, as they washed, they talked with one another. Fatty Orcutt was the chief center of the most considerable group, and the others constantly watched him, as though they did not feel that so important a man could possibly have gone down unless there were a formidable plan in his mind.

Then they were marshaled for the breakfast. There were now three cooks, and all three were very busy. The head cook, as a matter of course, was the girl. Her father assisted and one Mississippi Slim, tramp royal and man of many parts, had proffered to do his work by the fire rather than in the mine. His services were accepted, and he was proving his genius, practiced in many a tramp jungle throughout the land, at the cooking fire in front of the Wayland shack.

Jim Trent would handle the business of packing out supplies from the town, and Little Minnie would see that the gangs were kept working in the mine. There were to be two shifts, so after the breakfast, which was eked out clumsily because of the lack of eating utensils, the men were drawn by lot, divided into two sets, and the first was taken into the shaft by Buck Penrose. He and Denny Rourke had both worked more than once in mines, and they knew how to direct laborers.

Lew Eastern and Jumping Jack Story acted as general outside guards and lookouts. For it was not beyond credence that some of the adherents of Fatty Orcutt who remained in Sunnydale might sally out and strike a heavy blow to effect his delivery.

In the meantime Wayland, after breakfast, was directing all the work in the mine, and Jim Trent already had departed with the mustangs on the long trek toward Sunnydale.

Little Minnie, when the day was fairly started and when the cursing and raging of the impressed miners had died down under the direct threats of leveled rifles, so that they were now sullenly moiling and toiling at the drills and the sledge hammers and at the shovels, and the hoisting of the loaded buckets of ore or debris to the mouth of the shaft—Little Minnie now stretched himself in the shady side of the shack and went fast asleep with the bare rock for a bed and his rolled-up coat for a pillow. He slept till mid-morning and then sat up quickly.

Nearby him was the girl, peeling potatoes with skilled hands, and dropping them one after the other into the capacious bucket at her side. She kept on working by mere dexterous touch, while she looked askance at the giant.

"Lie down and sleep again, Minder," she said. "You haven't had enough rest."

"I've done enough sleeping lately to last me," he said. "That's where I have it over a camel. He can store up food and water. I can do that, too, and store up sleep besides."

He rolled a cigarette, hunched about until his shoulders were pressing against the side of the house, and then began to smoke. His looks were not entirely for her, but also for the men who were lolling about in the shade of the shrubs or of projecting fragments of rock. But there was no coolness anywhere. The sun was brilliant and shone with a steady, tyrannical force. Even where its direct rays did not fall, its strength was reflected in part from the surface of the plateau. All of these men of Sunnydale were gathered in significant groups, and all of their talking was in low voices. Now and again a head turned toward the big man and regarded him with a wolfish steadiness and malice.

"How long have you ever done without food and water?" asked the girl.

"Five days," said Little Minnie.

"I thought that three days was the limit of human life."

"That's what books say," he replied. "Books weren't written about me. They may be later on, a few."

He grinned as he said this. And she looked askance at him again. The beard he had shaved off in Sunnydale was growing, and the thick gloss covering his face like paint was bluish now but soon to be again the sleek black. There was an outcropping ugliness in this man that would not remain hidden.

"Yes, books might be written about you," she admitted. "How did you happen to be that long without food and water?"

"Oh, it's a long yarn," he said. "Some friends of mine decided that they'd be friends no longer."

"Why?"

"Because I got away with the fat part of a big poker game."

"How much?"

"I had about twelve thousand bucks in my pockets."

"So they did what?"

"They cornered me in a shack . . . eight of 'em. But the quarters were too close for their guns. I threw them out. Five of them got into the rocks around the shack and began to shoot into it."

"What had happened to the other three?" she asked.

He looked at her for a moment before he answered. Then he said: "They stayed behind with me in the shack."

"Were they dead?" she asked.

"No, but they were hurt. One of them was killed later on by the bullets that the five outside were shooting into the shack. Then I sent the other two out crawling, and they got off that way. No advantage to me to have 'em there in the house, starving."

She nodded and kept her eyes to the potatoes. "How did you get away?" she asked. "Posse come to help you?"

"I tunneled out under a side of the house," he said. "It was loose ground. I made frames for the tunnel with timbers from the inside of the shack."

"Did they try to rush the house, ever?" she asked.

"No, they didn't try that. Now and then I came out from the tunnel and took a shot at 'em. They kept discouraged and downhearted. There was a patch of shrubbery twenty yards from the house. They always kept a man posted there, but on the fifth night the ground caved away under him and I came up through the dust. He thought I was a ghost, and ran and yelled. I took his horse and rode away. That was all there was to it."

"Was that all?" she asked.

"Yes."

"You were weak, I suppose?"

"Yes, I was pretty weak. But I managed to get into a house and find myself a meal. They didn't follow me after the first day."

"And you've been a long time without sleep?" she asked him.

"Never more than a hundred hours."

"Let's see. That's more than four days?" she murmured.

"Yes, more than four days."

"How did *that* happen?"

"Why, I was stopping one night with an old friend of mine, a trapper, and a fellow who didn't like me came in and shot me through both legs. I got his guns and things away from him before he could shoot again. And then I sent the trapper for help."

"I don't exactly understand that," she said.

"It was like this," he answered. "That trapper was seventy years old . . . tough as shoe leather, but too old. And I wanted to put the thug who shot me in jail. It's no fun to be shot. So I sent the trapper for help, after I'd tied up the thug. It was only fifty miles to a town. I expected a doctor and the police inside of twenty-four hours. But the trapper didn't show up.

"After a while I had to have the bandages changed, and I had to have food, too. And the fire had to be kept up, because it was freezing weather.

And I couldn't move around to take care of myself. So I reached over and cut the ropes that held the thug. That was the second day. The pain kept me awake the first day. I held a gun on the crook and made him cook and work around for me, but I had to be on the watch every minute because, if I closed my eyes, he'd beat me. He took his sleep when he wanted it, but I never knew when he'd open an eye and see that *I* was asleep. So I had to be on the job all the time."

"Was it very bad?" she asked.

"After about eighty hours it got bad," he said. "I'd been leading a busy life, and I was tired to begin with . . . dead tired. Loss of blood and pain make you tired, too. Along on the fourth day I had to tie a knot in the bandage over the mouth of one of the wounds. When I felt myself getting sleepier, I tied another and a bigger knot. It was pretty bad. It was worse than the five days without food or drink. Finally they came."

"What had happened?" she asked.

"Why, the old trapper had been thrown from his mustang and broke his leg, and the horse ran away. He dragged himself on that spoiled leg for days. Finally he got to the town."

The girl gasped. "How frightful!"

"He was dead game," said Little Minnie. "His leg was never any good after that."

"How did he manage to live then?" she asked.

"He kept house for me for a year, and then he died. He couldn't stand living inside when he heard the wind in the trees outside. That's what killed him."

"And you had a house?" she went on.

"Yes, to make a place for him. I wasn't glad that he died, but I was glad to be on the road again."

"You'll never take to the road again as long as you live."

"Oh, won't I? What'll keep me from it, then?"

"These fellows," she said, and indicated the dark-faced men who lounged in the shade.

Chapter Thirteen

"The Bet"

He followed her glance and shrugged his vast shoulders. "You mean that I'd be apt to meet them, and that they'd have the knife out for me?" he asked.

"I mean that," she answered.

"They'd only be added spice along the trail. But that's not why I'm leaving for the open road."

"What's the other reason?" she asked.

"I'm going to make a home and get married," said Little Minnie.

"Is that it?"

"Yes, I'm thinking of marrying you, Harry."

At this she laughed pleasantly and looked him in the face. "I was angry the first time," she said. "But now I see that you're always having your joke on the world."

"I'm not joking."

Her laughter turned into a quizzical smile. "You're going to pass some time telling me that you fell in love the first moment your eyes found me, is that it?" she asked.

"Not the first time. You had a smudge of soot on your nose that evening," he said, "and that was as bad as a black mask. I couldn't see you, even though I knew that I'd have to marry you."

"What made you know that?" she asked.

"I'd made a promise to myself. A vow, you might call it."

"Go on," she said. "What was the vow?"

"I was beginning to see that someday I'd be too old for the road. Have to settle down. So I swore to myself that I'd marry the first girl I met who could talk clean English and cook at a campfire. You're the first girl, Harry."

She smiled again, turning her head slowly, meeting his glance without difficulty. She said nothing.

"I haven't found the way to get you on my side yet," he admitted. "But I've opened the way."

"Have you?"

"Yes. You like big things. You're cut that way. And I'm big. Big enough to fill your eye, even if I'm not big enough to fill your mind. I'm ugly enough to keep you looking, too."

"I like big things," she admitted. "This country, for instance. But I. . . ." She waited for him to speak again.

"Go on," he said. "Finish off. What don't you like about me? I want to know. Tell me how high the ladder is so that I can climb it."

"Talking is no good, Minder," she answered.

"I know what you want," he told her. "You want a fellow with a college education leaking out all over him, and good connections, a shave every day, trousers pressed, a traveled man who speaks the languages, a man who is known. Isn't that what you want?"

She looked up at the sky, frowning a little. "Yes, that's what I want," she said.

"All right," answered Little Minnie. "You can't have him, because you're going to have me."

"Tell me why I'm going to have you, Minder."

"A lot of reasons will work all together," he said. "Outside of my size, which you like, you'll be grateful when I push this thing through and crack open the mountain and make your father rich. You're fond of him. You pity him."

"Why do I pity him?"

"Because he's one of those nice fellows who generally need help or luck to get to the end of the trail. He wouldn't do a wrong thing, but sometimes he finds the right thing too hard for him to swing. Otherwise he wouldn't have brought you out here."

"He didn't bring me. I came."

"That was fate," answered Little Minnie. "It brought you my way. Every minute I see that I'm going to get you. I think you're weakening right now."

She laughed aloud again. "Go on," she said. "You like to have your own joke, and I don't mind how you talk." Then she grew serious. "Don't you suppose I see what will come out of all of this?" she demanded, her lips compressing as she anxiously waited for an answer.

"Go on," he advised. "I want to know what's going to come out of it."

"I'll tell you, then," she said. "My father and Jim Trent won't see it because they simply don't want to look on the black side of things. But I can see what will be the result of your enormous kindergarten game."

"I'm waiting to know."

"You have three-score of criminals here," she said. "And you have four other criminals, beside yourself, to guard them. My father doesn't count, and Jim Trent can't shoot fast and straight enough to count very much, either."

"I'm fighting fire with fire," said the giant.

"You're fighting fire with foolishness," said the girl sternly. "Before three days are out, those people will have agreed. I can almost pick out the projecting rock that they'll hang you from and build a fire at your feet."

"Have you got second sight?" The giant grinned.

"I have common sense."

"Will you bet on your common sense?" he asked her.

"Money?"

"No. Yourself."

Suddenly she flushed, and her eyes widened. She stared at him. "Don't you think that it's time to play another game?"

"Game?" murmured Little Minnie. Then he held out both his hands in a gesture of unexpressed power that yearned to be free. "You'll see how dead serious I am." He stood up and looked calmly down at her. "You're young and cool and sure of yourself," he told her. "You know what you know, all right, and most of it was learned in school. I've offered you a bet. I'll keep these hounds working for the whole fifty days. If I fail, I'll be a dead man. If I win, you marry me."

"You want me to think that you mean that?" she asked. "You want me to think that without caring I. . . ."

"You can learn to care about me later on," he answered with brutal abruptness. "You're sure of yourself. I'm sure of myself. Now, come across and take the bet or admit that you're a short sport."

She was quivering with intense anger. "I have half a mind to!"

"You have the mind, but not the courage," he said. "You can sit still and calmly foresee things, but you won't back your judgment. I'm backing mine. I'm staking my life on it, Harry. What do you stake?"

She could not speak for another moment, because of rage rather than hesitation. "I'll take that bet," she snapped at last. "But not if I can first persuade my father and Jim Trent to give up this crazy business."

Suddenly men began to pour out of the mouth of the mine.

"What's that?" she asked.

"They've drilled the holes and planted the first charges," he replied. "Now we'll hear the shots."

It was an odd thing to see the laborers as they issued from the mouth of the shaft, most of them looking like condemned souls redeemed. Some of them threw themselves down without waiting to find shade, and others sat down on rocks here and there and looked woefully at their blistered hands. But a considerable portion of the men instantly drew into close groups, talking with fierce faces, their voices low.

"That's the real beginning," said Little Minnie to the girl. "They've had a taste of the work now, and they hate it like the devil. I don't blame 'em. Soft-handed gamblers and confidence men hate the rough grip of a sledge hammer. So do I. Yet my hands are not soft. Now they're talking, and they want to find a way to do the business . . . your business it is now, Harry . . . of smashing me to bits." His great jaw thrust out. "But that's where the fun begins for me, too."

As he spoke, almost as though in answer, the plateau trembled, and the muffled, prolonged roaring of the shots came hollowly from the mouth of the shaft, sounding, through that thin mountain air, strangely dim and far away. To the girl that roaring was as the opening guns of a great battle, but Little Minnie was laughing, with his teeth set hard.

Chapter Fourteen

"Four Men of the Law"

In spite of that ominous beginning, three days went by before a shot was fired, and that shot drew no blood. It was simply that Dick Flinders, trying to escape by worming his way upward among the rocks, was overseen by Buck Penrose. A rifle bullet, clipping the rocks above the head of that celebrated second-story man, instantly made him surrender and come back. His punishment for this attempted escape was very gentle. It consisted, very simply, of twenty-four hours without rations; but twenty-four hours of labor in that sharp, bracing mountain air was enough to torment Dick Flinders severely. He made this attempt on the third day after the prisoners started their work. Another ten days went by before a really serious event occurred.

In the meantime, interesting news was brought back from the town of Sunnydale on every trip that

Max Brand

Jim Trent made to the place for supplies of food and for powder, hammers, shovels, stamps, drills. It seemed that Sunnydale had passed at one stride from a state of black evil to one of almost white-washed purity. The gunmen and thugs were thoroughly in hand. The crooked gamblers had been run out of town, and all at the expense of not a single lynching. There had been merely a few rides on a rail.

There was a new mayor in the town. The sheriff was again limping about his work. The amiable judge, Herbert Loring, had little to do except to pass judgment upon minor offenses, such as breaking the peace. This condition was attributed by all hands to the efficient cleaning up of the leaders of crime of every kind that Little Minnie had performed.

"You don't need to work no more, you lazy hound," said Jim Trent to his nephew. "You could go over there to Sunnydale and they'd give you an income for life. And that's where you'll wind up, sitting pretty, with your face in the sun and your back to a wall."

This might be the opinion of Jim Trent, but at the end of a fortnight two important things happened on one and the same day. The first happening was very pleasant; the second was just as unpleasant.

The first happening was that, in the opening round of shots that blasted down farther along the vein, a chunk of rock was tossed up and lay on the floor of the shaft with a yellow gleam across its face—wire gold! When they cleared out the débris and examined the face of the vein, Jim Trent saw that it had widened suddenly, and in one place there was a pocket of this pure gold—not a great deal, but where it occurs once, it may occur again.

There was no question any longer of barely scraping together from each man's labor a few dollars more than his pay. It was a totally different affair. Jim Trent, after a few calculations, estimated that they were now about to take well over a thousand dollars' worth of metal from the rock every twenty-four hours. At that rate, before many weeks they would have enough capital dug out of the ground to install the proper machinery and handle the diggings in the best modern manner. What profits they would make then staggered even the free and easy imagination of Jim Trent.

It was the happiest day they had put in at the mine, until three o'clock that afternoon, when four men rode up the valley to the foot of the trail, dismounted, tethered their horses, and climbed up the trail to the plateau. Jack Story stood at the top of that trail and covered them with a riot gun as they stepped onto the level.

Lean as greyhounds, hard as rawhide, with gray-blue eyes gleaming beneath sun-faded brows, they looked enough alike to pass for brothers. But it was very plain that they were not brothers.

One of them stood forth before the others. "I wanta see the big man here," he said. "I wanta see that fellow, Little Minnie as they call him at Sunnydale."

"Whatcha wanta see him about?" demanded Jumping Jack.

"About business," said the other. "Where is he? I'm Sheriff Lacey, and I've sheriffs of three other counties along with me."

Jack Story grew a little green about the gills. He shouted, and presently Little Minnie came striding from the mouth of the mine. He stood before the four strangers, looking bigger than ever because he looked more gaunt, and the spareness of flesh brought out the adamantine frame of the man. Constantly for a fortnight he had been watching his mob of laborers, moving among them, studying their faces, keeping them in check, and silencing their muttered conversations by his very presence. His sleep consisted entirely of an hour taken here and ten minutes of dozing there. His eyes were sunk far in his head, and his cheeks were hollow. Yet, there remained in him, still untapped, what seemed an inexhaustible well of nervous and muscular energy.

"I'm Minder Trent. Glad to see you fellows."

"You oughta be glad," said Sheriff Lacey. "We've come to take a lot of responsibility off your hands."

"What responsibility?" asked the other.

"A good many of these crooks that you've herded here from Sunnydale."

"You're going to take 'em off my hands, are you?" asked Little Minnie gently.

"I'm going to take that cut-throat, Dan Binney, for one," exclaimed one of Lacey's companions. "There he is. See him? I eye-witnessed one of his killings, and I've been hankering after him ever since."

"There's Doc Bogue, too," said another of the

quartet. "I want Bogue more'n I want money. I've got enough on him to keep him in jail for the rest of his life."

Sheriff Lacey said: "But there's the real man of the lot. There's the brains. There's the brains that I can hang. There's Fatty Orcutt. Hello, Fatty!"

Fatty Orcutt had lost a pound a day with great steadiness under the régime at the mine. He had proved himself an exemplary laborer, keeping at his task even when his raw hands left blood on the handle of the sledge hammer. Now, as his hands had hardened, he was able to keep pace with all except old and experienced miners. He appeared far less plump now, and he smiled far less. Even when he smiled his broadest, the wrinkles of fat no longer tried to hide his eyes. Those eyes appeared bright and clear and keen. They were fixed upon Sheriff Lacey, and Orcutt waved a hand to him.

"Hello, Lacey," he said.

"You're going home with me," said the sheriff.

"Glad to go anywhere with an old friend like you," said Fatty Orcutt. "But you can't get me away from Little Minnie. Not four like you. You can't handle him, Lacey. He's too much for you, and he means to sweat us for five more weeks in the mine."

"No matter what he means, I'm going to have you," said Lacey. He turned back to Little Minnie. "Trent," he said, "you've done a grand job down there in Sunnydale. It was a great bluff, and it worked. You had brains, and you had a pile of luck, too. Everybody gives you a lot of credit. But now the real law has gotta take a hand in the business."

"What'll the real law do?" asked Little Minnie.

"It'll take the prisoners that it recognizes. I see six men lounging around here that I want. When I look over the gang that's working in the mine now, I'll probably want six more. And the rest of these fellows are gonna want just as many, most likely. That won't leave you many of the crooks to weigh down your hands and keep you awake at night, Little Minnie You'll have all the glory, mind you, but we gotta have the men. It's our business, and the law besides."

"The law's a fine thing," said Little Minnie. "I've got a lot of respect for it, particularly when I see it in the distance. But I don't like to have it bothering me at close hand. You can have all the law in the world, Lacey. But I've got the men, and I'm going to have them here for thirty-six more days."

The head of Lacey lowered a little. "I hope you don't mean that, Trent," he said.

"I mean it," answered the giant.

"I can arrest you on the spot," said Lacey. "I hate to do it, but I can arrest you for interfering with the execution of the law. It's a serious charge, Trent."

"Arrest me?" asked Little Minnie with great good nature.

"We'll have to take you by force, if there's no other way," said Lacey.

"That's all right," answered Minder Trent. "You blaze away and take me if you can. Buck," he called in a louder tone, "keep this fellow, Lacey, covered first. Lew, keep your rifle on the rest of 'em."

From the shadows beside the shack those four sheriffs now made out the gleam of two rifles held at the shoulder by men who reclined at their ease upon the ground. Besides, Jack Story himself was still at hand, with his rifle at the ready.

"You mean it?" exclaimed Lacey. "You mean that you're gonna play the fool and make a fight out of it?"

"Why, Lacey," said Little Minnie, "if you wanted any of these fellows, why didn't you get 'em before? They were running loose in Sunnydale. Nobody was keeping you from getting in there to catch them like rats in your trap."

"You know damned well," exclaimed the sheriff, "that Sunnydale used to be a solid army of thugs! If you touched one of 'em, you got a shock from the whole battery and were knocked stiff. You know that, Trent."

"I know that I broke up the combination," said Little Minnie. "And I brought it out here, and I'm going to keep it going till the fifty days are up. I've got the judge's sentence behind me."

"That sentence means no more'n the barking of a dog," answered Lacey angrily. "Herb Loring wasn't acting the judge then. He didn't follow any three of the forms of law. It was simply a joke, except that he hoped that it would help to clear up that town of Sunnydale for a while. It was nothing but a joke, man. If you try to play it out seriously, it'll land you in jail, and, believe me, I'm the fellow to put you there if you stand in the way. I'm going to take Fatty Orcutt back with me today or know the reason why. Are you ready, boys?" he muttered in a lower voice.

But a long-barreled revolver, a longer one than

Sheriff Lacey ever had seen before, seemed to fall now into the fingers of the giant. It was a gun, in fact, proportioned to his size. And he waved the muzzle of it toward the four men of the law.

"Partners," he said, "this has been a fine little chat. But I'm a busy man, and now I've got to get back to work. I'm sorry to have seen the cards that you were so ready to play. You see that I've got a few up my own sleeve. Lacey, so long."

Sheriff Lacey for a moment gritted his teeth as though he were feeding on his own wrath. Then he nodded. "You've got to have it, man. I see that. You won't stop till you've had it. You're dug in here, and you've got the jump on us, but don't think that this is the finish. We'll be back, and, when we come the second time, we'll come with enough men to pull the mountain down around your ears."

He turned on his heel, paused, and then pointed a quick finger, like a gun, at Jumping Jack Story. "That's Story, too," he said. "I recognize him now. And he's another that I want. You know what for, Jack?"

Jack Story blinked like an owl. He said nothing, but the rifle shook in his hands.

Now the four men of the law slowly, with deliberate strides, as though to sustain the weight of their defeated dignity, passed down the trail to their horses, mounted them, and rode at a trot back across the valley.

"They'll come back, too," said Jack Story, glaring after them. "They'll come back, and bring plenty more. It's time to break camp, Little Minnie."

"If they come back, they'll only break their faces

on the rock," answered Little Minnie. "Let me do the worrying."

But he had a distinct feeling that the end was not far off.

Chapter Fifteen

"Trapped"

There was eager discussion that day. The girl was insistent that the criminal gang should be discharged. Her father wavered, but Jim Trent was equally insistent that the work should be kept going every possible day. They were in bonanza. They were richly in it. And who could tell what the future would deal to them? As for the return of a powerful posse—well, that was the business of Little Minnie. He could take care of that situation.

So the work went on. And bonanza it was, deeper and richer than dreams. For still the vein widened, and the percentage of the gold increased. There was richer ore and more of it and more easily worked and so many hands to perform the labor.

The very crooks who had been swept in from Sunnydale seemed to join in the excitement. Sometimes a few of them raised a song. There were jokes in the evening and yarning about the fire. Always Fatty was the center of the fun.

"Fatty's changed his mind. He may go straight," said Little Minnie.

Both Wayland and Jim Trent agreed, but the girl said: "Orcutt will never change. The more he smiles, the more devil there is in him. I've watched his sleek face."

Anxiety had preyed upon her in the last days, and her eyes were shadowed with purple. They looked gloomily now toward the giant, but Little Minnie merely said: "You're the pessimist, Harry. Things always go better than you suspect that they will."

"I hope with all my might that you're right." And she said it with such a fervor that he lifted his great head and looked rather grimly back at her.

That very evening the blow fell.

It was the rose and golden time of the day, when the sun was down, but the night still seemed far away, that big Minder Trent, in striding through a lounging group of the off-shift, saw something gleam and sparkle like mica in rock. It had shone in the hand of one of the men and was instantly extinguished under a flap of the fellow's coat. But Little Minnie, though he had seen the thing merely from a corner of his eye, knew what it meant. It was death, perhaps, for all of them. For that sparkle of light had been from the barrel of a Colt six-gun. If one of them was armed, others were sure to be. And if they were armed, they were only waiting for the change of shifts at the end of the day to make the outbreak.

He finished his inspection tour of the plateau beside the cook's fire near the shack, and, standing there with his feet spread and his hands toward the fire, he seized a moment when Mississippi Slim was off gathering brushwood for the fire to say to the girl: "You were right, and trouble is about to pop. They've got guns. Somebody's been crooked, and they've got guns . . . I don't know how many."

She looked up in his face and saw his calmness. Her own heart stood still.

He went on: "Your father's inside?"

"Yes," she gasped.

"You and he have got to slip away at once. Get down the trail, find the horses, and then ride like the wind . . . for help," he added as an afterthought.

He turned and went into the house. There he found Wayland, lolling at his ease, reading an old newspaper for the tenth time. He passed him and opened the old empty powder box at the side of the room where all the weapons—rifles, revolvers, and riot guns—were kept.

On top he saw a solid mass of rifles and revolvers, and he sighed with relief. They could not have taken many weapons, then. Only, it was strange that the shotguns, which, of course, were the most necessary weapons for the handling of a crowd, were not on top of the rest. He lifted two or three guns, and a chill sank through him. Beneath that topmost layer was a tarpaulin, and under the black tarpaulin was simply brushwood. That was not all. For when he looked carefully at the locks of the weapons that remained, he saw that every one of them had been ruined dexterously.

What weapons remained? His own revolver and

the six bullets it contained. Jim Trent and Wayland were not in the habit of carrying guns when they mixed among the prisoners for fear lest they might be overpowered and their weapons fall into the hands of that mob. That revolver and the guns of the four guards remained.

He went to the door and glanced out. Yonder, near the group of the loungers, he saw Jack Story, leaning against a rock, his rifle hung carelessly behind his shoulders, while Story joked with the thugs. Lew Eastern was not far away, sitting on a rock, arguing intently with Fatty Orcutt, and Buck Penrose was near by, listening and nodding.

Denny Rourke? Aye, there was Denny, striding up and down along the edge of the plateau, on guard. They never could budge that honest Irish heart, but it was perfectly clear that the others had thrown in with the mob—almost openly they had thrown in.

He heard the voice of Jim Trent, coming from the mine. And he waited for the arrival of his uncle. The latter came in, cursing.

"They got something on their minds," he said. "The whole gang of 'em are muttering and whispering and laughing down there in the shaft. I told Dan Binney to stir along, and he said that he'd stir fast enough to suit me before long."

"They've got our guns," said Little Minnie. "Eastern and Story and the rest have the guns. That's where I was a fool . . . to trust crooks to guard crooks. Anyway, there are only six guns left in that box, and every one of them is spoiled. And there's not one round of ammunition left except what

Denny and I have in our guns. This evening or to-night's the time they'll do it. It's Fatty Orcutt's brain that managed the thing. Harry was right."

Neither Wayland nor Jim Trent was capable of speech.

"Wayland," said Little Minnie, "you go and take Harry off the plateau and down the trail. They won't think much about that. Go down to the horses and ride like the wind to find help. Uncle Jim and I will stay here and hold the fort, along with Denny Rourke."

"I can't leave," Wayland said huskily. "My place is beside the rest of you."

"You can't help here," said the giant. "Go get Harry. Think of her, if you can't think of yourself."

Wayland, without an answering word, went to the girl. She had risen from beside the fire and met him as he stepped through the door.

"Harriet," he said, "we have to go to. . . ."

She shook her head and came on into the shack.

"I made a bet of it," she said, looking at Little Minnie. "And now I'll stay and see it through. I won't leave."

"What good will you be to us?" demanded Little Minnie harshly. "What good, if you're murdered along with us, when you might be riding for help?"

"You know it'll be over hours and hours before help could come," she answered. "I'm not arguing. I'm staying!"

"And I," said Wayland.

Jim Trent began to swear, but his nephew stopped him abruptly, saying: "It's no good arguing with 'em. People like that can't be budged when what they call their consciences are stirred up. They'll only serve to make the mess a little bigger and bloodier. But that can't be helped. The next thing is to get Denny in here."

He went to the door and called: "Hey, Denny! Come in here a minute, will you?"

A sudden volley out of the red of the evening answered him.

Half a dozen shots whistled by the door or crashed into the woodwork. Big Denny Rourke, as he turned to answer the call, staggered, fell upon his side, strove to rise, and then toppled back and lay inert.

Wayland, at that sight, which he could see through the doorway, screamed suddenly in a thin voice, pinched and high, like the cry of a woman.

But his daughter ran to Little Minnie and caught his arm, murmuring: "Did they strike you, Minder? Are you hurt?"

He looked down at her with agony on his face, but it was only pain of mind. Dumbly he shook his head.

Now they saw through the doorway how Lew Eastern—lately a guard—ran across to where the fallen man lay and deliberately kicked him in the face. The long-barreled revolver flashed out into the hand of Little Minnie. He poised the weapon, but he did not shoot.

"Shoot him, Minder!" snarled Jim Trent. "Kill that dog!"

Little Minnie shook his head again. His great chest was heaving with emotion, but he answered: "Every bullet in this gun we save for the time when

121

they're sure to rush the house. They know that, too. We have six bullets in one gun. They have sixty men."

"We'd better charge and break through," shouted Wayland.

"You know as well as I do," said Little Minnie, "that there's only one way off the plateau, and that's down the trail. Even a mountain goat couldn't get down the other cliffs. That's why you spent so much work building the trail. And they've got half a dozen men already there at the head of the trail. You see?"

A cluster, in fact, already had formed there, every man armed with a rifle or a shotgun. The exit was effectively blocked. Now, as the night wind began to blow up cold, and the sky went suddenly dark, a great bonfire was built in the center of the plateau, and around it gathered the men of Sunnydale. They seemed drunk with joy at their liberty. Their shouting, their roars of laughter, were punctuated by two other sounds—the clang of a rifle from time to time, fired maliciously into the shack where the late tyrants now lay prone upon the floor. Still more awful to the ears of those four, in intervals of the uproar and celebration, they could hear the groans of big Denny Rourke, left to die on the wind-swept rock.

Chapter Sixteen

"Minnie's Scheme"

Little Minnie, his face pressed close to a crack between two boards, watched with care the proceedings about the fire. It was plain, through the midst of the general celebration, that Fatty Orcutt was the hero of the moment. His brains must have planned and directed the whole event, the corruption of the guards, the stealing of the guns and ammunition, and the time fixed for the uprising. Now and again closely packed groups gathered around him, and his back was slapped and his hand shaken in congratulation. Even in the distance the firelight shone brightly upon the sleekness of his face.

However, mere noise and laughter were not entirely all in the mind of Fatty Orcutt. No doubt he was now deliberating the best means of putting an end to the four lives of those who remained in the shack, still unharmed. There were various methods that might commend themselves to him. For instance, a steady rifle fire would probably kill all four in time. Or again, there were such interesting possibilities as that of throwing a stick of dynamite into the place, or, even better, letting the wind roll a fireball against the flimsy little building, then shooting down the inhabitants as they scooted for dear life.

Perhaps these and other devices were forming in the clever brain of Fatty Orcutt as he withdrew from the brightly lighted circle and walked slowly up and down in the more thoughtful gloom beyond the immediate range of the firelight. Most of all, how his soul would be warmed if he could devise a scheme whereby he could get Little Minnie alive into his hands.

A similar scheme formed suddenly in the mind of the giant, and he set about its execution. To leave the house, it was hopeless to try to crawl out the door. The riflemen at the head of the trail would cover that point efficiently. There remained almost as simple a way. It was not hard to work loose two boards at the back of the shack, and through this he crawled. The muttered questions of the others he hushed and crept slowly out into the darkness.

It was far from as dark as he could have wished, for now and again the wind tossed up a gigantic arm of flame that sent a shuddering wave of illumination far up the face of the cliffs and all across the plateau. He could only hope that most of the thugs would be so close to the fire that the glare of it would blind them to dimmer objects far away. He moved first straight to the back of the plateau.

Under the wall of broken rocks that fenced it in he changed his direction, rose to his hands, and then to his feet. People would not be expecting trouble from this angle of approach. As for his bulk, he could mask that no little, in this light, by sagging his knees as he walked.

So he made straight for the place where Fatty Orcutt walked up and down with hands clasped behind his back, head bowed in thought—in deep thought. That head raised with a jerk and turned toward the bulky shadow that was approaching when a strong voice, the voice of Jack Story, called from near the fire: "Hey, Fatty! Hey!"

Orcutt turned his head toward the speaker.

"Come here," yelled Jack Story, "and we'll tell you a scheme that'll squirt 'em out of that shack like watermelon seeds out of your fingers."

"Shut up, Jack," answered the leader. "Let me alone while I do my own thinking."

"Leave him alone, Story," said another voice. "Fatty can think for himself, and for us, too."

Then, as Fatty Orcutt turned to resume his striding, the shadow leaped at him. He reached for a gun; he parted his lips to shout for help. But the blow that reached the base of his jaw benumbed brain and throat and hand. A loose weight, he fell into the arms of the giant, and lightly the latter raised that welcome burden and bore it away.

All had been lucky so far, but very strange it seemed, as he made one prodigious stride after another, that those men about the campfire had not seen what was taking place to their chief. No, not until he was within six steps of the shack did a sudden shouting rise and then a clanging of guns.

"Who's that by the shack? Where's Orcutt? What in blazes has happened?' cried the outlaws.

But Little Minnie was running like a deer in spite of the freight that he carried. He came to the place from which the boards had been broken away, and through it he cast the bulk of Orcutt's senseless body. He himself dived after. What did it mean? Even Little Minnie could not tell as yet. He only knew that they had secured one hostage against destruction. How great a hostage, how immensely the crooks valued the man whose cleverness had set them free from this shameful life, they could guess a moment later, when, as bullets began to crash through the little house, emphatic voices yelled to stop firing or Orcutt might be hurt.

Orcutt himself now sat groaning in the dark. His two guns had gone to arm Wayland and Jim Trent. Certainly, if a fight had to come, there was more of a ghost of a chance for the besieged.

Through the door, which they left open, they now saw a delegation of three men approach, bearing a white rag in token of the flag of truce.

The smooth voice of Lew Eastern said: "Little Minnie, the game is all tied up, now. We've got you fellows, and you've got Orcutt. You give us Orcutt, and we'll let any one of the four of you go. Yeah, any two, except you, Minnie. We all want to see a little more of you."

Suddenly the girl's voice answered: "Lew Eastern, we've determined to live or die together. You can have Orcutt . . . but only if the four of us go free

. . . and if we have a chance to take care of poor Denny Rourke."

"Rourke's as good as dead," said the gambler calmly. "But all right. You give us Fatty, and then we'll let you all go."

"If we give you Fatty, you'll change your mind," she said. "We'll have him until you've cleared out altogether. Then we'll turn him loose."

"D'you think," exclaimed Lew Eastern, "that we're fools enough to do that?"

Orcutt himself cut in, still groaning, and his voice was changed by the effects of the blow which had twisted his jaw to the side.

"Do what they say, Lew," he said. "I can trust 'em if they give their word. Little Minnie, give me your hand and your oath."

"Here's the hand," said Minder Trent. "And my promise."

"That's enough for me," said Orcutt. He called loudly: "Boys, it's time for you to march. Get out of here, and get fast. You know what Lacey is. He said that he'd come back, and he will. He'll come with an army. About Little Minnie . . . there's plenty of time to cook his goose for him later on. But if you stay here, you're wasting time. You'll kill me while you're killing them. Besides, they've got more guns now . . . the ones they took from me. Boys, take my word . . . the best thing is to vamoose."

There was no long discussion. They dreaded the return of Sheriff Lacey. So in five minutes they were trekking down the trail, shouting back their last insults, their last promises of revenge to Minder Trent.

127

He waited until the last of them was gone, then out they went with a rush. One armed man at the head of the trail was enough to secure it from any surprise attack. They turned Orcutt free to follow his herd. Little Minnie rushed to the side of Denny Rourke.

To his amazement, the latter sat up suddenly and rubbed his face.

"Denny, Denny," said his friend, "lie back, man. Everything's going to be done for you to. . . ."

"Do nothin' for me but gimme a chance to bust in the face of Lew Eastern," stated Denny. "Did ye think that I was dead or dyin', Minnie? No, but when the guns went off, I played hurt to keep from getting my finish. My throat's sore from groaning, and my face from where the dog kicked me. But that's all."

Sheriff Lacey and his men did not come back to the mountain, after all. More interesting to them, by far, was a certain troop of fugitives they intercepted on the march toward Sunnydale. They caught many; they caught enough to gladden their hearts and fill the newspapers for a week. But Fatty Orcutt evaded them.

There were strenuous days that followed at the mine, for there was money now to buy machinery, and all was installation of engines and steel monsters that baffled the mind of Little Minnie. He had been on the center of the stage for a long time. He had started the machine working, but now it ran beyond his guidance.

Gloomily he sat and watched, on this day, with

his chin resting on his clenched fist, and did not look up even when Harriet Wayland stopped by him.

"Minder," she said, "what trail are you thinking of now?"

"The out trail," he said without looking at her.

"When do you start?" she asked.

"In about half an hour."

"All right," she answered. "I can pack my things in that time."

"Now, what do you mean by that?" he asked her, looking up at last.

"If you were more than a great hulk," she said, "if you were even half a man, you could guess."

He rose and towered over her.

"Don't try to bully me, Minder," she cried.

"Bully you?" he exclaimed. "Great Scott, I can see which one of us is going to need help. But tell me, Harry, when you made up your mind to burden yourself with me?"

"The very first day," she answered. "I saw you needed teaching, because your manners were so very bad."

The Coward

The short novel Frederick Faust titled "The Coward" was sent to Street & Smith's *Western Story Magazine* in late 1922. It was readily accepted and appeared early the next year in the issue dated January 27, 1923. By that time Faust, who was living in New York, was at work on the seven-part serial he titled "Hired Guns," first published in book form in an abridged edition by Dodd, Mead & Company in 1948 under the title *Hired Guns*. Frank E. Blackwell, editor of *Western Story Magazine*, retitled this story "Under His Shirt." For its first appearance in book form here both the title and the author's text have been restored, based on his original typescript.

Chapter One

"The Breastplate"

It was a battered rectangle of steel with the corners chipped off. Undoubtedly it had been enameled, but the enameled surface had been covered with a scroll work, and the uncounted generations in their passing had left it with a strange, half-molded appearance. Underneath it was a placard that read:

A BULLET-PROOF BREASTPLATE OF FINEST STEEL

Joe Daly passed on to the next object, a stack of murderous halberds and cruel-headed spears, but his eyes were cloyed with seeing, and he closed them. Far away, beyond the walls of the museum, he heard the murmur of the traffic of New York. He had not been able to escape from that sound since he arrived in Manhattan, and his only true happiness came to him at night in sleep, when he dreamed of the mountain silences that he had left.

He opened his eyes again, and the oppressive load of ancient armor sickened him. The more he saw, the more bitterly he longed to be back there, to be out of this thick air, this stifling heat, and in exchange to feel the clean and honest burning of the western sun.

TASLET, CHASED IN GOLD. PART OF GOLD-WROUGHT
SUIT OF ARMOR PROBABLY BELONGING TO . . .

He turned away, shaking his head, and went back to the doors of the great museum and stared out into the street. When he saw the scurrying drift of automobiles and buses that roared up Fifth Avenue, his heart sank again. Better this retired gloom of the distant ages and their relics, better the strange-smelling atmosphere of the museum and its sense of death than to mingle in a crowd of which he was not a part. A lump grew in his throat. He set his teeth to keep the tears out of his eyes. Self-pity was beginning to unnerve him.

When he thought of going back to that West for which he yearned, the compelling fear of death stepped in between and warned him back. He saw again the squat and ungraceful form of Pete Burnside, with the long arms hanging at his side. He heard the voice of Pete, ringing at his very ear, with a threat of dire things that would happen if he ever came back.

For six mortal months he had remained away. If he returned, he must face Pete Burnside. If he wished to be able to hold up his head among his own gang of chosen reprobates, with whom he had plundered society for three years, he must face Pete Burnside, the deputy sheriff who had crushed him.

He touched his shoulder and winced. The wound had long since healed. It was not the memory of the pain that troubled him. It was the recollection of the magic by which Burnside had conjured his revolver out of its holster—the terrible and uncanny speed with which he had produced and leveled his weapon. How it had been done, Joe Daly could not understand. But he was at least sure that it would never be in his power to rival that speed and accuracy. So far as he was concerned, Burnside was sure death—as long as he was susceptible to wounds.

Here his thoughts came to a sudden and jarring halt. For there had risen in his mind another vision of what he had seen but a few moments before:

BULLET-PROOF BREASTPLATE OF FINEST STEEL

Bullet-proof breastplate! Then the fire died out of his eyes. He snapped his fingers and shrugged his shoulders in disgust. Of course, this bit of old armor had been bullet-proof only in the days when unrifled muskets had belched forth great, blunt bullets that would thud against armor more like putty out of a sling than a bullet carrying death in its touch. However, he went back to look at it again. It had become fascinating, and he was profoundly grateful, now that the great chamber in which it hung was practically deserted. That loneliness had been driving him distracted a short time before, but now it was a blessing. Was he alone? He began to perceive a hundred muted little whispers and stifled voices. And yonder was an old, old man, with white hair flowing down to his shoulders. He was bent over before a glass case, either copying inscriptions on the armor exposed there, or else writing a detailed description.

Joe Daly scowled and stepped closer to the plate of armor and touched it between thumb and forefinger. Then a thrill went crawling up his spine and into his vitals. For the steel was thick—very thick. There was a padding of time-eaten velvet on the back of it, but even without the velvet the steel was very thick.

Now, his heart thumping in his breast, he turned carelessly away and traversed the gallery in some haste. At the farther end he turned and began to retrace his way with even greater speed, pausing now and then for a last sight of particular relics here and there. When he arrived at the breastplate, he did not even look around him, on the theory there is nothing that calls attention so quickly as the furtive glance of a guilty eye. He picked the breastplate from the peg and dropped it inside his coat, so that the lower part of it touched the upper half of his trousers and was supported there. Then he went on again, with his hands in his pockets and his thumbs raised to support the weight of the steel. He had not dreamed that the stuff could be so ponderous. If a little specimen such as this weighed so much, how could a poor devil, entirely encased in metal, have navigated—how could he ever have got upon a horse, unless a friendly derrick and windlass were used to hoist him? At the thought Joe Daly smiled and continued down the gallery. Not that he left directly, or in haste. No, he paused from time to time, still examining curiosities. When he reached the farther end, he saw a uniformed attendant stride up to the place from which he had taken the breastplate.

Joe waited for no more. He did not pause to learn if the guard had discovered the theft. Instead, one long leap to the side carried him away from the aisle and into a side turning. Here he hastened on briskly. Someone was calling in the great gallery behind him, and he heard the noise of running feet. Joe, turning to the left and then to the right, was presently lost in a maze from which he issued out into the first and main hall of the museum. It seemed an interminable space to the revolving doors. Presently he stood outside at the head of the long flight of steps. Now he hurried down and stood on the pavement. There were taxi cabs nearby. But in the magazine which had diverted him the night before, he had read how criminals are often traced by the taxi cabs in which they had ridden. Such a fate should not fall to Joe Daly.

Quickly he turned and started briskly down the avenue, climbed onto a plebeian bus at the next stop, and presently was rocking along on the way downtown to his hotel. In spite of himself he could not help but glance back over his shoulder and down the street. He saw, from time to time, half a dozen automobiles, recklessly violating the speed laws and nosing swiftly through the traffic. Any one of these might be filled with the uniformed men from the museum. How many such men—stuffy and antiquated figures—would be required to capture Joe Daly?

He pondered that question with some pride and a stiffening of his lower jaw. In due time he was back at the hotel. Instantly he snatched the breastplate from beneath his coat and flung it on the bed. *It was a thick slab, to be sure, and if it were of a particular quality. . . .* He did not pursue this thought. The plate must be tested. There was a loud explosion in the street—a backfire. That gave him his next idea. Instantly he propped the breastplate against the wall on the farther side of the room with a well-wadded pillow behind it. A breastplate on a human body would not proffer the rigid resistance of a wall. Then he took his stand near the window, so that the sound would not echo through the building, but pass freely into the open air. He drew the revolver that was always with him, leveled it quickly, and fired.

The breastplate shuddered and drew back, as the great forty-five slug struck home. It was a snap shot, but beautifully planted. It had landed in the exact center of the armor. Now he ran forward to see the results of the shot, quivering with anticipation. This was the great moment. Behold, when he raised the armor, a cruel abrasion in the surface was exactly in the center, but the hole did not cut clear through. There was still a solid sheet of steel behind. Hastily he concealed gun and breastplate, but no one came with inquiries. No doubt those who were near and heard thought it simply another backfire in the street.

"What a cinch," said Joe Daly, "to bump off a gent in this here town and get away with it."

Chapter Two

"Pete Rides to Battle"

When the news of Joe Daly's return was first carried to Pete Burnside, the deputy sheriff did not believe it. And there were good reasons for his incredulity. Through a long life of battle on the Western frontier, he was well acquainted with what happens to the heart and soul of a man who is once beaten in fight. After the shameful and conclusive beating Joe Daly had sustained seven months before, Pete Burnside would have sworn that the latter could never return and hold up his head among his old companions.

To be sure, Pete Burnside knew that there are some men who can be beaten in battle, shot down in the midst of the fight by a fair foe, and then arise at a later time and crush the once-victorious enemy. These are phlegmatic fighters—*English* warriors, so to speak. But there is another kind, the kind to which Joe Daly belonged. These are men whose muscles are set upon hair-trigger nerves. Their movements in a crisis become blindingly swift. The draw of their gun is like the uncurling of the lash when the whip is snapped. In a tenth part of a second, a single terrible explosion of mental and nervous energy, the bullet is fired, the enemy is dropped, and the battle is over. Or, if it is maintained, the battle, while it lasts, is simply a prolongation of that original conflict. But when such a man is beaten to the draw, he is very apt to lose his nerve. After one defeat he is no account. Joe Daly, as Pete knew, was one of that high-strung type. And the reason that Pete knew so well was because he was himself in the very same category.

He knew that he himself conquered in the same spirit in which Daly fought. There was that resistless union of hysteria of nerves and muscles, working together in great flashes of effort. His life, it might be said, was composed of a scattered series of such flashes of effort. Daly's was composed of the same thing. The chief difference was the use to which they put their abilities to paralyze the efforts of ordinary men. Daly was, as Burnside was practically confident, the leading member of a gang that rustled cattle and in other ways defied the law. But Burnside was a deputy sheriff.

So well known were Burnside's ability with a gun and his dauntless courage in the pursuit and destruction of outlaws, that he might have been sheriff in half a dozen counties. But he preferred to hold a more or less roving commission, going here and going there, striking at random, as the occasion moved him, and always acting as an invaluable coadjutor of the law.

Burnside had trailed Joe Daly and his gang until Burnside was on the verge of cornering half a dozen of them. On that occasion Joe himself had turned back to face and destroy the destroyer. And in that memorable encounter Joe had gone down. The bullet of Burnside had crashed through the shoulder of Joe just a fraction of a second before Joe's own gun had exploded and sent a slug whistling past the head of the deputy sheriff.

No matter how close a call it had been, there was never a truer maxim than that a miss is as good as a mile. The burden of victory rested with Pete. He lifted the fallen enemy and carried him to town. On the way he assured Joe that the time had come when Joe must hunt for better camping grounds, and if he returned in that direction after his recovery, he, Pete Burnside, would make it his duty and his pleasure to call upon him and blow him off the face of the earth. For Pete Burnside was well convinced that Joe was a rustler of cattle, a horse thief, and other things unspeakable. He would never forget the peculiar expression of horror with which Joe had looked up into his face on that day. And in that instant he had known that Daly would never dare to face him again.

He knew that by consulting his own inner man. Concerning himself, he was calmly confident that no human being could ever beat him if the chances to draw were equal at the start. If they were not, that was another story, and defeat would be no disgrace—would mean nothing except death, perhaps, and death was meaningless compared to the glory of being the greatest and most dreaded man-hunter in the mountain ranges. In the meantime, he believed that it was impossible for any other human being to possess that flashing speed with a gun and that deadly certainty in action with which he cultivated and improved by constant practice. But if the impossible should ever happen—if another should surpass him in speed and precision—what would happen to that perilously and finely organized nervous system?

At the thought he shuddered and felt his pride disintegrate. He could feel himself crumble at the prospect. He would sink as low as he had once been high. Such was the thought of Pete Burnside. Knowing what he did, it was no wonder that he blinked and then shook his head when it was told to him that Joe Daly was back in town, more insolent than ever and clamorously announcing that he was ready to meet the terrible deputy sheriff whenever that worthy desired a meeting.

The sheriff himself was worried. He could not send for Pete, because there was no charge against Joe. There was only a huge weight of suspicion. Legally speaking, the deputy had not had the slightest shadow of a right to command Joe Daly to leave those parts and never to return. But in the eye of the public at large Pete had every right. And it had been noticed that after the disappearance of Joe Daly the rustling of cattle, the stealing of horses, the occasional hold-ups through the adjacent hills had, comparatively speaking, fallen away to almost nothing.

What could be a more vivid proof that Pete Burnside, as usual, had been right and had solved the problem for the community? They would have voted him a whole flock of gold watches and chains and huge diamond pins. But gifts were not wanted. Pete lived for the pleasure of battle, and he did not wish to be paid for doing his duty. His salary, he often said, represented living expenses, not a reward for service.

And when the distinguished deputy heard that Joe Daly was returned to the town, he shrugged his shoulders, removed his cigarette from his lips, and blew a cloud of smoke at the moon. "There's sure queer things happening around these parts," said Pete Burnside, and straightway mounted his horse and started for the town.

It was just after twilight when he started. It was eight o'clock when his horse jogged down the main street, knocking up a cloud of alkali dust that stung the nostrils of the rider. He knew where to go, but he did not know what he should expect to meet. Strange doubts had been rising in his mind, and he had pushed on his horse until the poor creature was almost exhausted in his eagerness to get at once to his enemy and settle all doubts with guns. But what had nerved Joe Daly to return?

A chill of terror struck through the deputy sheriff. It was not fear of Joe, to be sure, but it was fear of some power that might be behind Daly. It was fear of fear, one might have said. Something had happened not to the body of Daly, of course, but to his spirit. Something that must have been like a miracle, for he could vividly remember how Daly had cringed before him on the occasion of their last meeting.

Where he would find Joe now was not a matter of question. Daly would be on the hotel verandah. At the coming of the deputy he would rise. They would exchange words, so that both could be said to have received their warning, and then they would go for their weapons of one accord. He who died would be buried. He who survived might be arrested, but, in that case, he would plead that he saw the hand of his opponent go toward the holster at his side, and that he had shot in self-defense. And not the most prejudiced jury that could be brought together in the mountains would convict where there was a reasonable doubt about that plea of self-defense. For, as the good citizens told themselves and one another, how could they tell when they themselves might be in such an encounter? When they were about to fight for their lives, would they wish to know that the law would hang them, should they happen to escape from the bullets of the enemy?

Straight up to the hotel, then, rode Pete Burnside. How would Joe Daly appear, and what would be his manner? The deputy saw even from a great distance; even from a great distance he heard a ringing and loud laughter. When he came a little closer, he saw Joe Daly, tilted far back in a chair on the verandah, with his thumbs hooked into the armholes of his vest, and his hat thrust to the back of his head. His ugly, square face was wreathed with grins of confidence and self-satisfaction.

The deputy hesitated a single instant. Then he

gritted his teeth and made the nervousness leave him. He swung to the ground and advanced. There was a gripping chill in his stomach, and his head was light and empty. His lips trembled; his knees were unstrung. His face was white. Now a great coldness of spirit was translated into a physical chill.

It was fear. But, for that matter, he never entered a battle without being in the hold of this same terror. He fought it away and forced himself up the steps to the upper level of the verandah. This, after all, was the great joy of the battle—to feel himself on the verge of collapse through terror, to fight away that weakness, to summon all his faculties for the great effort, to whip out the gun at the opportune moment, to dash the enemy to the ground with his flying bullet—this was a joy compared with which all else was as nothing. The gaming table had no fascination for one who had taken the chances of life and death in his hand.

Suddenly he stood in the full blaze of the big lamp that lighted the verandah. Joe Daly, he noted, had chosen a distant and obscure corner, where the light fell only with half the radiance that shone upon Pete at the head of the steps. But let Joe have that handicap in his favor. He, Pete Burnside, had ever been willing to take the worse portion in the battle. It made the glory of victory all the sweeter. As he appeared, Daly sprang to his feet.

"Is that the mean four-flusher and lying hound who's been spreading talk about me around these parts?" asked Daly. "Is that you, Pete Burnside?"

Pete pushed back his hat, then remembered that

he must not expose the utter pallor of his face. Now he jerked his sombrero lower, so that its shadow might protect him from the prying eyes of Daly.

"I allow it's me, all right," he said. "I been hearing that you want to see me, Joe."

"I ain't said a word like that. I just sent out to say that I'm back in town. Does that mean anything to you?"

He was working himself into his battle fury, but Pete Burnside hesitated. He had not yet evoked that coldly hostile frame of mind he liked best before he struck. The fear had been pushed to the back of his mind, but it was still present.

"I ain't going to say, 'Welcome home,' if that's what you expect, Joe."

"You know very well what I'm driving at. When I got out of town, you said that you'd come with your gun ready and shoot me full of holes, if I came back. Well, here I am, Pete. And how come that your gat is in the leather still, eh?"

There was no chance to wait after such a direct insult. Pete Burnside reached for his gun. Daly had not waited. No sooner had he hurled his defiance than he jerked out his Colt. And yet the deputy, watching the movements of his antagonist, knew that he had the result of the battle in the hollow of his hand. He could still delay for a thousandth part of a second the convulsive move that would stretch Joe Daly, bleeding and dying, on the boards of the verandah.

Now was the time. Daly's gun was clear of the holster. All men must admit, afterward, that he had allowed Daly to have the advantage in the start of the draw. Then he made his own motion. It was a co-ordination of mind and muscle. The gun was literally *thought* out of his holster, the heavy butt of the Colt struck the palm of his hand, and he fired. It was a clean death to his credit. For that bullet struck straight over the heart of Daly. There could be no doubt about it. Pete saw Daly stagger under the blow, he could have sworn, and yet Joe did not go down. No, amazing though it seemed, Joe Daly stood. Before Burnside could fire again, Joe's gun exploded. There was an ocean of darkness poured over the spirit of Pete Burnside, and he pitched forward upon his face.

Chapter Three

"Red Stanton"

No man ever performed in six months a journey as long as the journey Pete Burnside completed. Men had girdled the globe many times in such a space of months, but Pete Burnside passed from courageous manhood to cowardly and slinking meanness of spirit. He was completely gone. There was nothing left to him. If it had been a shot fired at a longer range, or if he had shot with a trifle less surety, it might have been well enough for him. But he had seen the bullet drive home, he could have sworn. Having seen that, and also how Daly failed to fall, it was all over with Pete.

He himself had been the first to realize it. He had heard other beaten men tell with pitiful eagerness and certainty how they had really won—how their bullets had landed—and how only a miracle had saved the other fellow and enabled him, instead of falling, to strike down the other man instead. The bullet had struck Daly in the middle of the breast, or a little to the left. Daly should have died. Instead, he had staggered and dropped his man, the bullet grazing Pete's head. Indeed, he was even wrong about the staggering. For it appeared afterward that Daly had been absolutely uninjured, and he had walked away from the spot, whistling, a moment later.

It haunted Pete and pursued him like a living thing, the horror of that moment. His spirit began to crumble and decay, just as he had known it would do in such a case. Finally, when he was healed of the wound he had received, there came the showdown he had dreaded.

A big cowpuncher went wild with moonshine whiskey one evening, and Pete was summoned to quell the disturbance. He went with dragging feet to perform the task. He faced the big man and ordered him out of the room. Instead of going, the 'puncher had reached for a gun. After that, Pete tried not to remember. For when he thought of it, perspiration rushed out on his forehead, and a wave of sickness poured through him. But Pete knew that, when the big cowpuncher, Stanton, came at him, and he had tried to get out his own gun, his fingers had been paralyzed, and he had heard the weapon of Stanton explode. The bullet flew wild. The 'puncher was too drunk to hit the side of a barn at ten paces. All the strength had run out of Pete's body, and his knees sagged. He cowered in a corner and begged Stanton to let him live.

That had been the nightmare as it actually happened. One thought of it was enough to turn the former deputy to a ghastly gray-green. Most of all, he remembered the sick faces of the men who had come to him and raised him and, with voices full of scorn and disgust and pity, bade him go back to his bed, because he still must be sicker than the doctor knew.

That night he had sneaked out of the town and never went back. He carried with him what possessions he could take conveniently, but he dared not stay to sell what else belonged to him. He dared not meet other men and face their scorn. First of all, he fled straight south. He went as far as San Antonio. Here he lived for a month and established a new circle of friends. Just as he began to make a name for himself, a man came in one day from the north, saw him, recognized him, and told the story. Pete Burnside fled from San Antonio by night, with horror of himself choking him. Then he dipped into Mexico, but it made no difference. Wherever he went, there were men who had seen him in his old home town, men who had watched that awful scene of degradation.

There were two paths open to him. Either he must put an end to his respectable life with a bullet, or else he must put an end to that life by sinking out of sight of all his fellows. He made the latter choice and became a vagrant. In four months he drifted to the four corners of the country. He saw Vancouver one week and Los Angeles the next. He wandered to New Orleans and thence to New York and from New York to Quebec. But eventually the pull of home will draw men back, as surely as the old instinct guides the carrier pigeon.

Pete dropped off a train in the mountain desert, a scant two hundred miles from his home town. He had left the train just outside a small village, and, near the place where he had left it, he found a gully covered with low scrub and brush and with a small stream trickling through it. It was an ideal place for a hobo jungle, and he began searching through for the assemblage place. He had not been wrong. He came upon a clearing on the flattened shoulder of a hill. In the midst were half a dozen men in various stages of raggedness and now busily at work on the preparation of a great stew. The huge wash boiler, that some hobo of another generation had stolen from the village and presented to the jungle—black with a hundred coats of soot on the outside—was a perfectly satisfactory dish to contain enough stew to supply the appetites of twenty voracious eaters. There is not in the world a set of gourmands equal to the great American hobo. He has a hump like the camel. He has to live a week on nothing, and he makes up for seven days of starvation in one heaven-astounding attack on victuals.

Pete, being broke, sniffed the preparation from afar. Then, as he drew closer, he was asked if he had money to "pony up" for his share. He admitted that he was broke, but he offered to buy his share with some newly purloined cigars. The cigars made the mouth of more than one tramp water, but they were obdurate. If he had not the money, the rule was that he must procure his share of the edibles.

So he turned back toward the town, a mile and

a half away. It was dusk when he reached it, and in the dusk he slipped quietly into a hen roost, removed a fat hen from her perch, and with that prize stole back to the charmed circle around the fire. He was greeted with acclamation. For the meat end of that mulligan was not altogether satisfactory. They had gathered enough potatoes and some cans of corn and tomatoes. They had secured greens. Someone was frying bread over a little adjacent fire. And at another blaze a great can was half filled with seething coffee. There were some bits of pork and a few pounds of beef in the stew, but the chicken was a blessing sent straight from heaven.

There was a breathlessly short interval spent in cleaning and plucking that fat hen. Then it was tossed in to join the rest of the stew. And the hoboes sat back to regard the steaming result of their united thefts. They contemplated one another, too, not with direct and insolent stares—for there is no courtesy so consummate in some respects as the courtesy of derelicts—but with secret and furtive glances. They estimated one another with the greatest cunning.

Pete Burnside, as usual, was wretched so long as he was forced to be in the company of his fellow men. For one among them, even among these tramps, was liable to know what he had been, and how he had fallen. Nay, worse than that, of late he had sunk so low that men had begun to get at the craven truth about him by simply using their observation. However, it seemed that the half dozen worthies whom he had joined on this occasion were a great deal less formidable than the majority

153

of those whom he had met on his unending pilgrimage. They were all rather old. That is to say, they were past fifty. And when a man on the road reaches the age of fifty, his back begins to stoop. He has crammed too many years into a short space, and he begins to pay up his penalties.

Among such as these, Pete felt himself to be certainly secure. He began to stir around with a slight air of authority, such as might be forgiven in one who had brought in the choicest portion of the evening meal. He fetched some more wood and stood over the fire and fed it with fresh pieces. He looked into the dark and simmering mass of the stew and sniffed its contents—the dozen blending odors that made it so pleasantly attractive. Altogether he bustled about as one who has a little authority and who is anxious to make it appear more.

Not one of them needed to be told when the moment had arrived to serve the stew. They had risen as of one accord and grouped themselves about the caldron. In a moment more, the first huge helpings had been ladled forth. And now they sat around in a loose circle and devoured their rations in utter silence. There was only the whispering of the wind and the loud snapping of the fire.

So intent were they on their feast that they suffered themselves to be surprised by the advent of a new arrival.

"Hello-o-oo!" thundered the newcomer. "What sort of gents are you to leave me here starving?"

They looked up in amazement, each crowding an extra bite down his throat for fear that he might not taste the remainder of his meal. What they saw was a towering giant, large enough in fact, but made still larger by the manner in which the shadow and firelight shook in turn across him. A great sombrero, half of whose brim had been torn away, was pushed back to expose a densely curling crop of red hair, hair so flamingly red that it might have seemed on fire. He wore a ragged coat so much too small for him that it was apparent one serious exertion would tear it to bits. Around his hips sagged the cowpuncher's cartridge belt, with a Colt in a battered old holster, and he wore on his feet the cowpuncher's riding boots, though there is no known gear so inconvenient for walking. His huge hands, doubled into fists, were now planted on his hips, and he looked down upon the circle of veteran hoboes very much as a man of ordinary stature might have looked down with surprise and amusement and some mischief upon a circle of fairies, dancing in a ring.

Pete Burnside looked up to the intruder with a speechless horror, for he saw in the hairy-handed giant no other than that final instrument of his downfall, Red Stanton himself.

Chapter Four

"The Playful Giant"

Yes, it was Red Stanton, sunk at last to the level of a tramp. Indeed, he had long been headed in that direction by a love of drink and a detestation for work. He was newly come into the world-old order of vagrants, however, as his cowpuncher attire testified. In another month this would be exchanged for a more comfortable outfit.

The big man looked about him, made sure of his people one by one, and finally rested his steel-blue eyes upon Pete Burnside. He strode straight across the circle. He stood above Pete and, looking down at him, laughed. It was long and loud laughter, and the gorge of Pete rose. Then he dropped his head and submitted. What was the use of resistance? Once before, when he was closer to being a man, he had been beaten by this huge monster of a man. How could he hope to stand before Red now that he, Pete, had sunk so far into degradation? But the shame that took hold on Pete was less hot and stinging than he had felt a thousand times before. It was at least some mitigation of his misery that those who witnessed his humiliation should be fallen men, though they had not fallen quite as low as he.

Not fallen quite as low as he? He looked around upon those wretched derelicts. He saw their scornful, sneering faces turned toward him. Yes, the worst of these was a better man than he. The worst of these would have made some feeble resistance of words, at least, before he would submit to being laughed at.

Red Stanton turned away and stood at one side of the steaming wash boiler.

"I was thinking that I wasn't to eat tonight," he said, "but I see where I'm wrong. You boys got this all fixed up just in time for me. Gimme something to eat with, Burnside. What are you sitting there for? Ain't you been stuffing your stomach all this time, while I been starving? Ain't you got the manners to lemme have a spoon?"

So saying, he leaned and snatched from the hand of Pete the spoon with which he had been eating. He dashed this through a can of water that was steaming close by. He seized upon the inside of the stew pot.

"Well, boys," he said, "looks to me like there ain't any more than one man-sized meal here."

He flashed his glance of defiance around the circle. And Pete Burnside returned that glance with a curious interest. He was seeing in imagination what he would have done in the old days. This loud-mouthed ruffian he would have silenced with a word, and if a word were not sufficient, there would have been the sure speed and accuracy of his gun play to fall back upon. But his gun had been rarely needed in the days of his glory. There had been in his bearing an unconquerable air that imposed upon the most daring. In his eye there had been a straight look that went through and through the heart of a bully and warned him that battle and destruction lay just ahead.

But that day was long since past. His very soul had shriveled in him since the day when he had seen his bullet strike home in the body of Joe Daly—when he could have sworn that he saw Joe stagger in his tracks—and yet Daly had failed to fall. How could a man be sure of anything in such circumstances? The world was in confusion, and the strength of Pete Burnside was sapped at the root.

So Red Stanton reached into the deeps of the pot and brought forth a spoonful of the stew. At the sight of their food gone to waste on this tyrannical giant, there was a stir of angry feeling in the six tramps. Not a man among those hoboes but had been in his prime a gallant fighter. Many an heroic tale could have been told of their prowess. Now, to be sure, time and hard weather and harder usage had unstrung their muscles and stiffened their joints, but the spirits within them were not altered. They were as keen-edged as ever. They could not attack him in hand-to-hand battle; that was obviously foolish. Their united valor and physical power banded together would not have made enough opposition to give him meager exercise. In those burly hands of his was power enough to have crushed skulls. Instead of fists, they fell back on other weapons. A gray-haired man, stiff, straight—his face red with weather and anger—stood up from the relics of his meal.

"Look here, you double-stomached bull, you can't bust down the fences and get in at our feed like that. Lay off, will you?"

Red Stanton looked around at the speaker from behind another heaping spoonful. He grinned, then stowed the contents of the spoon behind a bulging cheek.

"Very good," he said. "That's a good joke. Are you meaning to argufy with me, son?"

"Don't it sound that way?"

"It *sounds* that way, but you look too plumb sensible to be talking fool talk."

"Boys," said the other, "it looks to me like we got to get rid of this baby. Are you going to gimme a hand?"

His doubts were soon set at rest. Each in turn rose and shook himself. Upon their hard features appeared smiles of joy, as when some stiff-legged war horse hears far off the whining of the battle horns and lifts his head from the rocks of his pasture. So they stood up, and each man reached for the weapon that was most to his choice. One man, as he got up, took a large, ragged stone in either hand and advanced with these formidable weapons. Another pushed himself to his feet by means of a cudgel with a knotted end, a section of a small sapling that had been burned off in the fire. The others caught up sticks and stones, or else produced from their pockets long-bladed knives, quite capable of inviting forth the soul of the strongest man from between his ribs.

As they came on, Red Stanton hurriedly stowed another spoonful of the stew in his cheek and then blundered to his feet. Pete Burnside watched him sharply. Even a veritable hero would have been apt to flee from that assortment of rocks and stones and knives. He had a revolver, to be sure, but the first shot, that might drop one man, would be answered with a volley from which he could hardly hope to escape. Yet Stanton threw out his arms and laughed thunderously in their faces.

"Come on, gents," he said. "I ain't had no exercise but breaking up a couple of shacks to bits today. I don't get no pleasure out of food unless I can work for it. Come on, old sons!"

His confidence abashed even their iron hearts, and they paused an instant to permit their only ally to join them. But, though Pete dropped his head under their accusing glances, he did not rise from his place. He dared not.

"No good waiting for him, boys," said the giant. "He ain't going to look for no more trouble with me. He knows me, eh?"

Stanton's laugh rolled and bounced across the clearing. It was the last blow. Surely now the fallen spirit of Pete would rise. He felt the first hot pricking of anger stir in him. He waited with joy and thankfulness for that wrath to increase to a hot fury, but the cold wave of fear returned and drowned the last embers of his courage. He could only sit there with his head down like a whipped cur and watch the fight in the distance.

There was a snarl of disgust and rage from the six hoboes. Their glances promised annihilation to Pete, should they have leisure to deal with him a little later. Then they swept suddenly forward to the attack, as though they dared not delay, lest the shame they had just looked upon might unnerve them.

Forward they plunged, and three ragged rocks shot at Red Stanton. Suddenly he began to move with a celerity that amazed Pete. He was amazed for two reasons: the first being that Red apparently had no desire to use his revolver; and the second reason was that the big man was able to weave about as deftly as a football player or a dodging boxer and so avoid the missiles. Another volley could not be entirely avoided. One rock just grazed his head, and he staggered drunkenly. Before he could straighten and his brain clear, another big rock knocked him back, gasping for breath.

The six saw their advantage and with a wild whoop rushed in to pull down their victim. But Red Stanton, though badly hurt, still had fight in him. He had staggered back until his shoulders struck against the upper rail of an old fence that extended through the trees down to the edge of the water below. Red, with a roar of satisfaction, caught hold on the board that had arrested his fall. He tore it away from the two posts to which it was nailed. He swung the big timber around his head with as much ease as, in another age, a stout English yeoman might have twirled his quarter staff on thumb and finger.

Into the circle of that swaying engine the six hoboes would not have been eager to run, but they had started forward so fast that they could not stop themselves. The blow crashed upon them just as they strove to stop. The result was ruin. One went down headlong under the blow, his knife spinning in a bright arc from his hand. Another stumbled, staggered, and fell flat. Two more dropped to their knees, and only one of the men was left standing.

This worthy jumped forward with a yell that was more fright than battle courage. He was met in mid-air, as he sprang in with his knife poised and murder in his eyes, not by a shooting fist, but by a most unromantic weapon. The great boot of Red Stanton swung out and up. His toe and heel landed at the same moment into the breast and stomach of the veteran. There was a gurgling cry from that fellow, and he shot back, struck the earth with a soft thump, and lay flat, as though with a great weight crushing him down.

In the meantime, however, there remained four men ready and unhurt, capable of getting to close quarters with the big man. As for the fence rail, that cumbersome weapon had been knocked into splinters at the first blow, for it was more than half rotten. Red Stanton was now empty-handed. Even in this crisis, though, he did not draw his revolver. Moreover, he refused to give ground, and with a roar like the bellow of a wounded bull he plunged forward at the vagrants.

Stanton was too much for them. They had tasted

the strength of his hand, and it was more than enough for them. They turned their backs and fled at the top of their speed. Yet all their speed was not enough. Three of them were allowed to get away, but the most rearward laggard, limping as he ran, was caught from behind, and, while his shriek rang through the air, he was whirled and then sent hurtling down the slope toward the water.

It seemed to horrify Pete Burnside that the old man was surely no better than dead. He toppled down the slope, hit the water with a crash, and finally dragged himself slowly out on the farther shore. Red laughed until he staggered, and amused himself by heaving stones at the battered fugitive. Luckily none of them hit him, and under cover of this distraction the man who had been knocked senseless by the blow of the fence rail now dragged himself to his feet and crawled away. He had disappeared in the shadows of the distant brush before Red Stanton ceased his laughter and turned back from stoning the last fugitive.

Chapter Five

"The Lay of the Land"

Now there remained only one of the six. This was the man into whose body the boot of big Stanton had been driven. He lay where he had fallen. He had not stirred so much as a finger in his prostration.

"Hello!" thundered the victor.

Pete Burnside jumped to his feet.

"You through dreaming?" growled Stanton. "Then pick that gent up, throw some water on him, and bring him over here. I got to ask him some questions."

Whereupon he calmly sat down and resumed the meal that had been interrupted by the battle. Down the side of his head, where the rough edge of a stone had grazed him, ran a crimson trickle. It reached his collar and then ran down slowly over his shirt. Pete stared in fascination. This was not courage; this was simply the absence of fear. It made him feel more horror than admiration.

It was impossible to resist the command. Ah, yes, time had been when he would have smiled to hear such words from any man; time had been when death was nothing, and honor was all. But now he had seen a miracle—he had seen his bullet, he could have sworn, strike a human body at twenty paces or less and do no harm. Pete went obediently to the fallen man and brought him to the firelight. The man seemed dead, and dead Pete Burnside thought him at first glance. But when a handful of water was thrown into his face, he recovered almost at once. He sat up, groaning and grunting, clasping himself around the body with both arms and swaying himself back and forth. At length he managed to gasp back his breath.

"Kick the skunk over this way!" bellowed Red Stanton through a gust of laughter, for the sight of the hobo's contortions had made him roar with glee.

Accordingly, Pete attempted to help the injured man to his feet, but the latter pushed aside such assistance.

"I don't need no help from you, you rat!" he snarled at Pete. "You sat back by the fire and let us do the dirty work. Yaller . . . you're yaller, you hound! And when I get shut of this here mess, I'll find you again and open your carcass for you and let in the sunshine."

Staggering to his feet the man went to the big man.

"Sit down!" barked Red Stanton.

He reinforced his command by hurling a chunk of wood at the head of the tramp. The latter attempted to dodge, but he was much too weak to move with any celerity. The flying missile struck him across the chest and the arm he had thrown up to protect himself. With a thud he went down and fell flat on his back.

"Sit up!" thundered Red Stanton. Picking up a coal from the fire at the end of a stick, he tossed it so deftly that it fell near the face of the prostrate man.

Pete Burnside groaned with horror, but the scorching fire quickly brought the unlucky tramp to his senses. Brushing the lump of coal out of harm's way, he sat up, but said nothing. He watched his captor in silence. His rat-sharp eyes admitted defeat, admitted that he had endangered his life by the attack in which he had joined upon the giant. Whatever came his way was no more than his due.

"Now, Dad," said the giant, "you and me are going to have a little chat . . . understand?"

The other nodded, but said not a word. Pete Burnside, watching, tried to moisten his dry lips. What would he have done in the same case? With what courage would he have been able to bear up against such brutality?

Such was the feeling in him—and a base fear set him shaking, for he knew that he would have whined and begged. There was not a courageous fiber left intact in his whole being.

"Now, look here," said Red Stanton, "I ain't much of a hand for traveling around and getting the facts about a country. And I want to know what's what in this here range. You've been around here quite a spell, I take it."

"This is a poor country for a 'bo," said the tramp. "There ain't any worse. These cowpunchers that ain't got any sense about giving away their time and their money, they sure hate to see anybody around that ain't working steady. They'll ride ten miles and swim a river to rope a 'bo and get him on the end of a rope, so's they can have some fun with him. And what they call fun is plain torture. Nope, I sure would rather batter the doors of jails for handouts than try to get anything out the kitchen of a ranch house. They ain't even got any work to do, unless you can ride and rope and such stuff. But I take it that you know all about that as well as me." And he glanced significantly to the cowpuncher's outfit Red Stanton was wearing.

"Look here," said the latter, "you been around. Tell me what's what. I ain't much of a hand to ride the freights. I don't get on with the shacks, and the shacks don't get on with me. I've cleaned up on about a dozen of 'em in the last couple of weeks, but before long a dozen of 'em will start to clean up on me. They're getting to know me, and that means the finish. They'll bean me and roll me off a train that's hitting up fifty per. And that's all. So what I want to do is to work in on some graft around here . . . me and my friend."

Here he raised his head and stared at Pete with a brutal grin that promised the latter he was by no means through with his hard time.

"I don't get your drift," said the tramp.

"Ain't there nothing stirring around these parts?"

"Nothing that a gent could take a hand in," said the hobo. "The only easy money that's loose is for them that know the country and got hosses and kin ride and shoot. There's a gent named Daly that's cleaning up big, rustling cows and hosses up yonder."

"Huh?" grunted Red. "Might that be Joe Daly?"

"Yep, his name is Joe. Is he a friend of yours?"

"He's a friend of a friend of mine," said Red, and he grinned again with great meaning at Pete.

"Oh, he's cleaning up big," said the hobo. "He's up yonder, somewhere in them mountains in the third range."

"Around Mount Sumner?"

"I guess that's the name of the mountain . . . that one with three heads."

"Right."

"What this Daly does is pretty rich. He gets his boys together and starts in running cows. He gets a pile of coin ahead. Then he starts working the game both ways. He comes down to the ranchers. He points out that the sheriff ain't been able to do no good . . . that's a regular hole-in-the-wall country, so's a sheriff and a posse ain't got no chance at all . . . and he offers to furnish a sort of irregular police . . . if they'll pay him something tolerable fat."

"That sounds queer," said Red Stanton.

"Well, the point was that the news got to spreading around that somebody was running off cows in them Sumner Mountains, and a lot of other gents come along and started following the good example. What Daly wanted to do was to get rid of the competition. And he's done it pretty well. He's got a gang of mighty hard riders and hard fighters, and he ain't no slouch himself. I've heard tell that he cleaned up on Pete Burnside himself, but I guess that's just talk."

"Might be that it is," said Red, grinning again.

And Pete, hanging his head, wished that he were dead, indeed. Even now his broken spirit could not rally, for fate had spoken against him once, and it was folly to go against her dictates.

"Go on with Daly."

"What he does is to collect something pretty fat from some of the ranchers, and he keeps them all free and clear. They never lose so much as one calf in a whole season, you see? And every once in a while Daly rounds up some of the smaller gents that are rustling. He gets 'em and hangs 'em in a row on a tree and drives back the cows to the ranch that owns 'em. But some of the ranchers ain't going to pay no money for a tax to a gent like Daly. That's mostly because old Doc Peters keeps his head up and says it's a plumb disgrace if they got to pay blackmail. Well, those gents have a pretty bad time, because them are the ones that Daly makes his own special picking, and he works 'em right down to the bone. That's the only game that I know around here. If you want to try your hand at something pretty big, you can throw in with Daly. But it sure means a whole pack of hard riding."

"I hate riding," said Red with a sigh. "I ain't got no comfort in the saddle." He looked down gloom-

Max Brand

ily at his great bulk. "How long has Daly been running things?" he asked.

"I dunno . . . three or four months, maybe longer."

"And don't nobody know what he's doing?"

"Everybody guesses that he's robbing some and blackmailing others, but they ain't sure."

"How long will he last?"

"Until the gents up in them parts get together and make an army and clean out the hills. If you want to get a fancy job and a salary, you can go up to old Peters's ranch and hire out as a plain cowpuncher. He can't keep no hands, because Daly just cleans out his men as quick as they come."

"How's that?"

"Lays for 'em in the hills and gives 'em a run whenever they get far away from the ranch house. Tied one gent up in a tree, and he stayed there three days. He was nutty when they cut him down, and he ain't got his sense back yet, they say."

"What would Peters pay?"

"Mostly anything."

"Well," said the big man, "I guess this talk ain't been wasted. Now . . . get out."

The hobo rose.

"And if you sneak around and try to get back at me, I'll tear you in two!"

But that thunderous voice was not needed. The hobo shrank back to the edge of the shrubbery. There he glared at the conqueror with keen, glittering eyes of fear and hatred. A moment later he had melted into the background.

"Well, Pete?" asked Red Stanton, turning on the latter. "How does it sound to you?"

"What?" gasped Pete, hardly daring to guess what the big man intended.

"How does it sound to you to go up to Peters's ranch and get a job, being a sort of a garrison in the fort, eh?"

Pete Burnside drew a long breath. It was too terrible to have been inspired by anyone except the devil himself. Go to the Sumner Mountains? Run the risk of encountering that rock of his destruction, Joe Daly himself? He felt the blood rush out of his brain, and he was sick at heart.

"Red," he said heavily, "I can't go."

"Can't go?" thundered the giant. "Can't go? Ain't I got to have somebody to go along and take care of me? Sure you're going, and don't forget it."

Chapter Six

"Doc Peters"

Only a man with a powerful imagination could have looked upon the site of the Peters ranch and seen its possibilities. No part of the ground was level, no part of it was without a surfacing of rocks that grew out of the soil. But, in spite of precipices and rocks and hills and ravines and thundering avalanches and snow slides in the winter and quick-shooting, noisy water courses in the spring season of the melting snows—in spite of all these things, hardy cattle could make a living, and a good living, among the Sumner Mountains. For, among the rocks, the soil was rich and the grass, where it grew, was thick, long, and nutritious.

But civilization in its westward course had split around the Sumner Mountains as around a rock. It was not until Doc Peters came into the Sumner Mountains that any man conceived its possibilities.

Doc Peters backed his judgment with his money. In ten years, twenty men had followed his example. The Sumner Mountains were filled with odd ranches, in the center of which huge mountains shot up above timberline. But the important thing was that there was plenty of grass for cattle, and cattle multiplied and grew fat.

In ten years, Peters had become a wealthy man. He himself did not exactly know how wealthy. What he understood was that, when he wanted to buy anything, there was always money with which to buy it. What he understood was that he could give his daughter, Miriam, all that her heart desired. When the first crash in prices came, Doc Peters was as one bewildered.

Calves that had been selling for fifty-six dollars were suddenly selling for six. On all sides, ranchers were ruined in a single season. Then prices began to climb slowly toward normal, and, just as they reached a level at which the ranchers could again make money, rustlers appeared in the Sumner Mountains. There could not have been a better resort for such a business. There were innumerable cuts and cañons, hills and mountains. There were stretches of forest into which ten thousand head might melt and disappear for the time being. And so the rustlers stole here and stole there and waxed fat. If they were pursued, they could generally dodge the pursuers and keep the cattle. At the worst, they could abandon their stolen gains and make good their own escape.

That is, they could do all these things until Joe Daly appeared on the scene, as a sort of enforcer extraordinary of the law. Then, to be sure, rustlers were captured right and left, and captured sections of herds were restored to their rightful owners. Every man who was willing to pay tribute—and fat tribute—to Joe Daly went free. So confident became that gentleman he actually guaranteed to pay for any loss in stolen cattle out of his own pocket.

Doc Peters, however, preferred to take his losses in cattle rather than to fatten the bank account of that consummate rogue. Rather, it should be said, that Miriam objected. She had left her school to help on the ranch. In the space of a single month she had transformed herself into a cowgirl. She had supplied the good will that carried her father cheerfully through that first terrible season of losses. And she was still with him, now that the ranch had begun to climb toward prosperity again, only to be stopped halfway up the ladder by the depredations of the rustlers. Then it was that Joe Daly came, offering his protection. Everyone knew his game. He had begun the entire rustling operation in the Sumner Mountains. Now he was choosing this novel means of freezing out his competitors. And he himself would prey on those who refused to pay him tribute for protection. It was a great game. But, though everyone saw through it, no one knew how to avoid the wiles of Joe Daly. While Doc Peters was gravely conferring with this smiling robber, Miriam herself appeared on the scene. She went to work upon Joe Daly with a speed and effectiveness that bewildered the cunning ruffian. Every word she spoke was a crushing blow to him.

"Mister Daly," she said, "I've heard your talk with Dad. You offer to protect us with your men. I want to be sure that you *have* men."

"There ain't any doubt of that," Joe Daly grinned. "Everybody has seen my boys around. And they're a hardy gang. Eh, Doc?"

Doc Peters made a wry face and nodded.

"Most of them have been with you ever since you came into the mountains?" asked the girl.

"More or less."

"Then what have they been doing to make a living, Mister Daly?"

"Eh?" he grunted at her.

"You haven't a ranch," she answered sharply. "How have you managed to support all those men during these months?"

Joe Daly swallowed hard. "Oh, just doing one thing or another," he said.

"Hush up, Miriam," her father said in pity for the humiliation of Joe.

"I will," she had said, "when I've told him what I think everybody in the Sumner Mountains guesses about him. They all say, Mister Daly, that you've been making your living by rustling cows. But, whether you have or not, we'll pay no money for protection. We have a sheriff for that job. We'll hire some deputies for him, but you'll get nothing out of us, Mister Daly."

Joe Daly listened to this outburst with a wicked smile, and, when he left the ranch, he vowed to wipe it clean of livestock.

Industriously he set to work to accomplish this object. Time and again droves were herded away.

175

Time and again the men on the Peters place vainly rushed into the mountains or down the cañons in pursuit. Once or twice they had come close, but they had been repelled by a rattling volley from half a dozen repeating rifles. One such warning was enough. They fell back and waited until another day. But the day never came when their force to pursue was nearly as great as the force of the thieves in flight to defend themselves. On the whole, there could not have been a more hopeless war. And so it was that Doc Peters sent away to the far, far south and brought up a terrible man of battle, Dan Bunder. The price Dan Bunder charged for his services was high, but he was worth it.

His sharp instinct for trouble led him into it before he had been on the ranch twenty-four hours. He came upon a lone horseman in the hills, challenged him, and was answered with a bullet. That bullet flew wide, for the ample reason that the slug from Dan's own gun had smashed through the body of the other. He took the man to the ranch house where he died from loss of blood, refusing to the last to tell his name, or his errand in the hills, or who, if anyone, was connected with him. Nevertheless, it was known that he was one of the gang.

After that first signal victory, Dan was not quiet. He scouted abroad again, hunting for scalps with all the joy of any Indian. He came on three of Joe Daly's best men engaged in running off a few young steers for the larder in Daly's camp. There followed a terrible battle. One of Joe's men was mortally wounded. Another was shot twice through the body, and he was brought back to Daly's camp to die. The third member of the party had been shot through the left arm and nearly bled to death on the trail.

There was a muster of forces among the rustlers and a review of what had happened. They found that three of their men had been killed and one had been wounded by this man-slaying demon from the south country. Various means of getting rid of him were suggested, but the chief himself made the most appreciated suggestion. He declared that he would ride down to the ranch, wait for the coming out of the new manhunter, and have it out with him as soon as they were beyond sight of the ranch buildings.

Daly was as good as his word. The next day Dan Bunder was found dead among the hills, near the ranch house of Doc Peters. There was this peculiarity about the affair. It was found that Dan had fired twice before he died and at an enemy who, according to the prints of the horses' hoofs, had not been far away. And yet they could find no trace of the effects of his bullets. There was no blood trail, nor was there anything to indicate that a wounded man had spurred desperately away from the place. Instead, there were ample tokens that he had come up to the dead body, had examined the pockets and wallet of Dan Bunder, and even lingered to smoke a cigarette at the spot. All this was seen, and it was considered a miracle that so deadly a shot as Dan should have actually fired twice without inflicting the least apparent injury upon his opponent.

But there was a greater catastrophe for Doc Peters, following immediately upon the heels of the

Max Brand

death of Dan Bunder. The tidings of his exploits had made it possible to hire a full quota of cow-punchers for the ranch work. But now the new hands left in a sudden panic. Where Doc Peters should ordinarily have had ten men, his force was limited to five, and these were all such old and decrepit fellows it was apparent that only the knowledge of their age gave them the courage to stay on the ranch and face the dangers of Joe Daly and his gang.

Such was the situation when on this dreary night, as Doc Peters sat quietly opposite his silent daughter in the living room of the old ranch house, there came a heavy knocking on the door. When Doc opened it, a red-headed giant was seen, standing outside in the night.

"I hear tell," he said, after they had exchanged the usual greeting, "that you want hands?"

"I sure do," said Doc curiously. "Come in and set down."

There entered a monster with intolerably bright and steady blue eyes that roved leisurely around the room. Beside him and a little to the rear was a companion who was quite dwarfed by the comparison, a rather bowlegged man who stood with hanging head.

As Doc Peters said later to his daughter: "A man and a half and half a man makes two men, so the new hands will do pretty good."

Chapter Seven

"Miriam's Wonder"

"My idea," said the big man, who by removing his hat had showed a great mop of red hair, "is to get some of the boys together and go hunting Daly and his crew. What d'you say to that, Doc Peters?"

"You won't get a crew around here," asserted Doc Peters. "The boys ain't got any stomach for fighting or trailing Joe Daly. They say that bullets don't even make no dent in him."

Pete Burnside shuddered.

"Well," declared Red Stanton, "I'm one, and my partner here, Pete, is another that'll take the trail. Eh, Pete?"

Here he clapped Pete on the shoulder, and the latter winced. Pete fought with all his might to stand straight and nod a cheerful answer. He strove with all his force to appear at his best before this bright-eyed girl who was watching so intently. But

he could only cringe. The very name of Joe Daly
sent water instead of blood through his veins. Sickness took hold of the very heart of him. From the
corner of his eye he saw scorn pass like a shadow
over the face of the girl.

Suddenly she stepped to Red Stanton and shook
his hand. "I have faith in you," she said.

And it sickened Pete Burnside to see her lift her
head and smile up into his companion's brutal
face.

"I have faith," she repeated. "I know that you
can't lose."

"Lose?" roared Red Stanton. "I ain't ever started
a fight yet that I ain't won. I dunno what it means
to get licked. Ask Pete, here. He'll tell you."

Red winked with brutal meaning at the rancher
and his daughter. He could not see the shadow of
disgust that darkened their eyes for a moment. But
here was an ally too powerful to be turned away
simply because he seemed to be a bully and a brag-
gart.

They sat down with the two newcomers. They
placed them at a table where there was more food
than even the tremendous capacity of Red was
equal to. And, while the two travelers ate, they were
given in detail the history of the struggle against
Daly, and in particular the feat of Dan Bunder in
killing no less than two of the Daly gang, as was
known, and three, as was conjectured. But since
Dan had been killed in single combat with a man
who must have been Joe Daly himself, no one in
the mountains could be induced to take service on
the Peters Ranch, with the exception of a few fight-

ers made half worthless by their great age. It would be a problem of the very first water to get even a handful of willing men together to attack such an enemy as Joe Daly had demonstrated himself to be.

Here Red smashed his great hand upon the table with such force that the dishes chimed. "Leave that to me!" he said. "Lemme offer 'em money. Lemme go to town to get 'em, and I'll come back with men enough."

It seemed impossible that he could do as he promised. But the next morning he mounted the only horse on the ranch capable of bearing his tremendous bulk with any ease or speed. On this mount he made the journey to the village on the eastern edge of the mountains. He entered in the late morning. He went straight to the combination general-merchandise store and post office. There he emptied his six-shooter to the accompaniment of a wild whooping that brought every inhabitant out and ready for action. Afterward he harangued the crowd.

It was a good speech. He declared that he had come down for men. They were to get three dollars a day and their keep. They were to get good chuck. And there might be a small ration of moonshine whiskey at the end of each day's work, if all went well. Also, their hours were to be short, and their work during those hours was to be light. They were not going to ride the range all the day. There was to be no wearisome wandering along a fence, repairing the breaks and lifting the sagging wire. No, all they were to do was to join in a manhunt.

He paused and surveyed his audience with a

growing enthusiasm. He would himself lead in that manhunt. He would ask no man to go where he, Red Stanton, did not first lead the way. He would ask nothing impossible of any of those who happened to serve under him. Not only did he make these promises, but he also declared that the number he could take was limited. Some men, he knew, would have been glad to take fifty men to do the work he had at hand. But Red Stanton would admit only an even dozen men in the hunt. And he reserved the right to pick that dozen to suit himself from all those who flocked in to volunteer their services.

It was a master stroke, that limitation of the posse. It did what the promise of fat wages could not do. It put a distinguishing badge upon all who should be so fortunate as to be chosen to take part in the expedition. Money, indeed, could never have induced them to come forward. But, since it was to be a measure of merit, that to be sure was quite another thing.

Red Stanton got a room at the hotel and spent two hours there, interviewing men who clamored for a place in the ranks. It was not until he had each man closeted in the room that he confessed the object of the expedition was to be against no other person than Joe Daly himself. They heard it with abashed eyes and a scowl, but they would not take a step backward, once they had engaged their honor. Before the two hours were passed, Red Stanton had sifted out twelve of the hardiest men in Casterville. Of all the rough towns in the Sumner Mountains, Casterville was the roughest, and of the toughest inhabitants in Casterville Red Stanton chose the worst. He chose them by instinct; he recognized his brothers in heart, if not in blood. And, by an odd coincidence, when he had finally chosen all his worthies, it was found that there was not one of the twelve who had not passed some days of his life in a prison.

Such were the men with whom Red Stanton returned to the ranch of Doc Peters. They filled the old bunkhouse with a thunder of drunken merriment that night, for Red Stanton had lived up to his word and had procured some moonshine whiskey of innocent and watery appearance and terrible potency. But when the morning after the revel arrived, these hardy souls merely doused their faces in water, shrugged their shoulders, and prepared for the work of the day.

That work began at once. Red Stanton was thrilled by the praise and the wonder of Doc Peters, when the latter saw the troop of heavy cavalry that had been rallied to his cause by the ruffian. He was thrilled, more than by the words of the rancher, by the smile of Miriam from the background, and he started as soon as they finished their breakfast. He took with him Josh Tompson, the only one of the cowpunchers then on the place with nerves steady enough to make him of any use. Josh had many ideas about where the headquarters of the rustlers might be, and he was willing to point out what he knew to the warriors, though he warned them every step of the way that they were apt to be shot—to the last man—by a hurricane of rifle bullets that might pour down at them at any moment.

While preparations were being made, Red Stanton lingered at the ranch house. He wished to state his self-assurance once more for the delectation of the rancher and the rancher's daughter.

"But they'll get the start on you, Red," said Doc Peters.

"My hoss will be ready with the rest of 'em," said the giant. "Pete does my saddling for me."

"Is Pete your slave?" asked Miriam with sudden interest.

"Pete's a no-good one," said the other in a large manner. "He ain't worth much. You'll watch him start out with the rest of us this morning, but he won't keep up with us. Nope, his hoss'll go lame . . . or something. I know! He'll have to drop behind and. . . ."

"The hound," snarled Doc Peters.

"Why do you keep such a creature with you?" asked Miriam, shuddering as though she had been hearing of some unclean thing.

"Well," said Red Stanton, "he's pretty handy for saddling the hosses and making the fires and patching the clothes and such like. Besides, I ain't got the heart to turn him loose where other gents can kick him around. I'm sort of used to him and sorry for him, lady."

Here his horse appeared, saddled and led by Pete Burnside.

"I'm with you, Red," called Doc Peters. "I ain't going to stay behind here."

"Don't be a fool," growled the giant. "Ain't you going to keep a guard here at the house on all your chuck . . . and your hoss feed . . . and your family?"

He leered winningly at Miriam as he spoke. But, no matter how offensive his manner, it was perfectly apparent that he was right. A guard must be kept at the ranch house, and the rancher himself must take up that duty. So, frothing with impatience, Peters watched the expedition take to horse and thunder away down the slope to an accompaniment of yells and curses. In the rear rode Pete Burnside. After him the girl pointed.

"Do you see that?" she cried to her father.

"Yes," he nodded.

"What's wrong with the man they call Pete?"

"I dunno," answered her father. "When a gent is yaller, there ain't no way of explaining him. He's just plumb wrong all the way through."

"But that man, Pete . . . ," said the girl. "I can't explain how he haunts me. He did last night in my sleep, after I had seen his face for the first time. He fascinates me. He seems to be always in torment."

"Because he always knows that he's yaller," said her father, "and he's afraid that somebody's going to find it out."

"I'll wager," she answered after a little interval of silence, "that he finishes the ride with the rest of them today. I'll wager that, if there's a fight, he fights as bravely as any of them."

"Miriam, you're talking foolish. A dog can't act like a lion, and he's just a plain hound with no heart to him."

"Don't say it," breathed the girl. "It's too horrible."

"He ain't the only coward in the world, honey."

"But I keep thinking. . . ."

"What?"

"I keep thinking that he's been a brave man once, and that he's trying to be brave again."

"Miriam, quit your dreaming. Take a ride right over the hill, and you'll find him somewhere pulled up just the way that Red Stanton said you'd find him."

She followed the impulse that had taken hold on her. In five minutes she was in the saddle and heading into the sharp wind that was blowing out of the northeast. An elbow twist around the pointed shoulder of a hill brought her suddenly in full view of her quarry. Not fifty feet away was Pete Burnside. The wind that blew from him to her cut away his chance of hearing her, and his back was turned, cutting off his chance of seeing her. She jerked her neat-footed pony behind some saplings and peered out curiously into the hollow.

Pete Burnside she had seen in the act of stopping his horse. Now she saw him drop limply out of the saddle. She saw him crouch down on the ground. She saw him take his head between his arms. She saw his body racked and tormented and quivering with pain. Never had she seen a man act like that before. It was as though a bullet had torn through his vitals. The horse from which he had thrown himself sniffed curiously at the bowed head of his late master and then turned away to pluck at some grass nearby. And still Pete was curled up in a knot.

Then she understood, and the understanding sickened her. Fear, as her father had said, had stopped this poor renegade and made him stay out of the group that was riding toward the mountains.

Now the bitterest shame was making him writhe in an agony. She watched with horror and with awe. And then suddenly she turned the head of her horse away, as though she had been eavesdropping where she had no right. And, when she came back to the house of her father, she said not a word to him. She kept what she had seen to herself, as though she had entered upon a part of the shame.

Chapter Eight

"The Captive's Saddlebag"

Old Josh did not content himself with pointing out the way toward what he was sure was the main rendezvous of the rustlers. He stayed with the riders all the day. Fourteen strong, they journeyed deeper and deeper into the Sumner Mountains. In the late afternoon they started back, fifteen strong, for the Peters ranch house.

They had picked up one man in their journey, and with that man they came to Doc Peters at the close of the day. They described how they had taken him, and how they had questioned him. But he would not return an answer. They wanted to know whether or not he had formed a part of the gang that operated under Joe Daly. They demanded to know where the rendezvous of that gang might be. But the prisoner would not speak. In vain they had tried every persuasion on him.

They had tried to corner him by showing their knowledge that the very horse he rode was known to be the favorite horse of Joe Daly, but still he could not be induced to speak.

Then Red Stanton had tried other measures. The muzzle of the unfortunate man's own six-shooter had been heated and pressed into his flesh. He had fainted, but he did not speak. They dragged him down to the ranch house, reeling in the saddle, but with his jaws locked together. The pain of his torture, and the weakness that followed it, were on his forehead, but his eyes were still strong with defiance. They brought him into the ranch house. When they dropped their hands from his shoulders, he stood, swaying from side to side before Peters.

"Now," said Red Stanton, grinding his teeth with fury because the man had held out so long against him, "now it's your chance, Doc. You've got something ag'in' this gent. You can make him talk out. All you got to do is to make him tell you where we can get at Joe Daly, and your job is finished."

"D'you mean torture it out of him, boys?" asked the rancher slowly.

"Dad!" cried Miriam.

To Red Stanton in the morning it had seemed that nothing was more important than to win the favor of the girl. He could have sworn that the happiest man in the mountains was that man who could make her smile. But since the morning another nature had risen in Red Stanton, his true self. Now he swung around on the girl with his muscular arm outstretched, pointing. But it was almost as though he had struck her down.

"You," he said, "what are you doing in here? Ain't this a man's place to hear man talk? Run along and sit in a corner. You ain't wanted here."

She shrank away from him, but she kept her head high.

"Dad!" she pleaded. "Do you permit one of your men to talk to me like this?"

"I'm telling her to keep away from this sort of a job," explained Red, a little more mildly to the rancher. "Ain't I right?"

"You are," said Peters. Inwardly he was boiling with rage at the insolence of the big man, but he was forced to admit that Red had been of great service to him already and might be of still more value in the immediate future. "Miriam, you ain't needed here."

His voice was drowned by a roar of beast-like violence from Red Stanton. "Look at the yaller-hearted hound," he thundered. "There's Pete. Look at him, boys. Look at him come creeping in. Why, I got a mind. . . ."

He gave over words for a more direct and effectual expression of his emotions. He caught up the chair that was nearest him. Though the chair was heavy, and though he used only one hand to swing it, yet he sent it whirling across the room with such terrific speed and force that Pete Burnside had not time enough to dodge. He was struck by the flying missile and sent crashing into a corner. And when he staggered, half stunned, to his feet, he was greeted with a huge burst of laughter. Even Red

Stanton dissolved in mirth. He had pacified himself in the joy of seeing poor Pete, tumbling head over heels. Now he laughed, and laughed again, swaying his great bulk from side to side, but Pete strove to cringe away through the door.

"Stay here!" thundered the bully.

Pete paused.

"Come back and stay here till I tell you to go. I dunno, I might have a job for you to do."

Miriam watched the white and working face of Pete, watched it until shame and grief choked her and made her stare down to the floor. It was as though she had herself stood in the flesh of this craven and tormented man.

Suddenly all attention was focused on Peters. "Red," he said, "if you try a thing like that ag'in, I'm through with you . . . understand? I don't care what you can do for me, I'm through with you."

"Sorry, chief," said Stanton, "but when I seen that sneak and remembered how he'd ducked out of the trouble that we'd been hunting all day . . . when I seen that sneaking face of his . . . why, I couldn't help sort of busting out." He went on hastily to change the subject. "But there's something to be got out of this gent, boss. Ask him what he's doing with this, will you? We tried to get him to talk, but he wouldn't say a word to us. He wouldn't do no explaining."

As he spoke, he drew out of a saddlebag that he had been carrying a rectangular object blunted at the corners. It was backed with a heavy quilting, and the upper surface of it was armor steel finely chased and engraved.

"I found this here thing in his saddlebag," said Red. "He wouldn't do no talking, but I figure that maybe this means something. Maybe this scrawling stuff is a code."

"I'm sure I don't know," said the rancher in mild wonder. "I can't figure what. . . ."

Miriam came suddenly forward from the corner where she had remained after the outbreak of Stanton. She took from the ruffian's hand the object he had been holding.

"Dad," she said, turning her back on the rest, "there's no need to ask him what it is. I know."

"Well, Miriam, what is it?"

"A breastplate . . . an old piece of armor."

"What the deuce would a gent be using armor for? That ain't got sense, Miriam."

"Don't they still wear it . . . a regular coat of mail . . . don't men wear it in Mexico and along the border when they expect that they may get into a knife fight?"

"I know that," replied her father, "but this here thing ain't mail. Who'd wear a thing that heavy to keep from a knife?"

"Why not from bullets, then?"

"What you mean?"

"I say, why not wear that old breastplate to turn a bullet?"

"Honey, a rifle bullet would go through that like it was a piece of cheese."

"Yes, a rifle bullet has penetrating power, but what about a revolver bullet . . . a big, soft slug of lead? Would that go through?"

The Coward

"I'll be durned," gasped the rancher. "I never thought about that."

"It's an idea, sure enough," muttered Red Stanton. "We'll try it out."

Catching the steel plate from the hand of the girl, he propped it against the wall at the side of the room. He stood back, whipped out his Colt, and pumped three shots squarely into the center of his target. Then he ran across the room, while the echo of the last shot was still humming in all ears, and picked up the little slab of steel.

"Well, dog-gone my hide!" roared Red Stanton. "Not a one of them slugs went through. Look here . . . I didn't no more'n put a dent in the surface. And here's other places. Look here, partners, and here. There's pretty close to twenty dents, much like the three I've put into her. I tell you what, this ain't the first time that this here thing has been shot at!"

They crowded around it, clamoring with wonder, and from the farther side of the room arose Pete Burnside. His square jaw was set, and his face was white, and there was an almost maniacal light in his eyes. He was drawn nearer and nearer to the center of interest. His movements were like those of a sleepwalker.

In the meantime, the talk turned back to the stranger from whose saddlebag that steel plate with the quilting down the back had been taken. The controversy raged hot about him. Should all that he knew be torn out of him? Should they torture him until he was glad to speak?

They even forgot about the old breastplate. Pete was allowed to pick it up. He seized it in trembling hands and retired to a corner of the room. There the girl saw him bend over the plate and study it with a wild interest, a passion so consuming that he seemed to be trying to tear a secret out of the very steel.

Chapter Nine

"Nothing But a Big Joke"

During the night the prisoner stirred and suddenly sat up in his bed. It availed him little to sit up, however, for his wrists were chained together, and one wrist was fastened in turn to one of the posts of the iron bed. They had taken no chance that he might escape, as though there could be strength in his fever-stricken, tormented body to make even the effort. Now he listened with starting eyes to a faint sound at the door to his room. Could it be that the incarnate devils were coming back? Could it be that Red Stanton, furious because he had not been permitted by the rancher to torture his victim in the evening again, as he had tortured him during the day, was now coming back to claim the helpless man for fresh brutalities? There were many ways of inflicting the most exquisite tortures. One might light a match and hold it close to the flesh of a man who was so bound that he could not move.

Darkness swam before the eyes of the prisoner at the very thought. Yes, he was weak, he was very weak, and his nerves jumped and twitched. He could not endure torture again. He would break down. The secrets would tumble from his lips before he knew it.

Oh, it was true. Someone was opening the door to the room in which he lay. Not that he could see anything, no matter how he strained his eyes, but a strange sixth sense made him aware that they were close to him. Now the door closed with the softest of clicks, and someone was stealing closer to him. Oh, horror of horrors! Heaven only grant that he might die like a man rather than shame himself. If only he could see the door by the light of the day, but this stifling blackness of the night— he set his teeth and forced away the faintness. His mind was clearing. Presently he heard a whisper from the darkness.

"Partner, there ain't nothing for you to be afraid of. Keep your nerve plumb steady."

A delirious joy ran through the weak body of the victim. It seemed that he could not stand this sudden thrill of hope which rushed through him.

"Who is it?" he gasped. "Joe Daly, it ain't you yourself?"

There was a little silence, as he turned cold again. Could it be that this was only a trap to trick him into admitting that he knew Daly?

"I ain't Daly," said the whisperer in the blackness, "but I'm one that'll do you no harm. Will you believe that?"

"Yes. But who are you?"

"I'm the gent that they call Pete."

The prisoner sank back on the bed with the faintest of groans. He remembered, now. What could be either feared or hoped for at the hands of such a craven?

"I've come up here to have a talk," went on Pete. "Partner, I want to find out who wore this here breastplate that they got out of your saddlebag."

"What good would it do me to tell you, even if I knowed?" asked the prisoner.

"I got a key to these here locks that are holding you. I swiped it just now from Red Stanton. . . ."

"That devil . . . I'll tear the heart out of him if I live to get a square chance at him."

"You'll get that chance if you talk to me straight."

"About this here piece of steel?"

"Yes, I want to know who wore it."

"What could that mean to you?"

"I'm just curious."

"Well, I'll tell you. Charlie Burnet got this thing to keep for. . . ."

"That's a lie," said Pete Burnside. "Charlie Burnet ain't the gent that used to wear it."

"If you know, what are you asking me for? And even if I should tell you, how can I be sure that you'll be able to turn me loose?"

"You got my word of honor, and something'll tell you that I mean what I say."

"How could it mean anything to you to know who used to wear this?"

"It means more to me than a million-dollar gold mine. I been lying awake, thinking about it."

"The devil you have. Well, it's sure queer to me what makes you so interested in it, but I'll tell you the fact and no kidding. Joe Daly himself has been wearing this right around his neck and under his shirt."

"Thank the Lord," broke in Pete Burnside. "Thank the Lord I know that now."

"And your promise . . . ," cut in the prisoner.

"I'll keep that."

Instantly the key dropped into the first padlock, and it clicked open. In another moment the prisoner stood on his feet.

"And now Red Stanton?" he snarled softly through the darkness.

"What?" asked Pete Burnside.

"I'm going to get that hound and carve the heart out of him."

"Wait till you got daylight, and he's awake."

"Did he give me any fair chance when he caught me? No, he mobbed me, and then he tortured me. . . ." His voice choked away to nothing as he recalled the horror of that long pain.

"You'll start riding now with me," said Burnside.

"*You* ain't got any call to love him!" exclaimed the man of the gang. "Ain't I seen him talk to you like you was a dog? Ain't I seen him knock you down with a chair?"

"You've seen that," said Pete Burnside.

Suddenly he was laughing, but the sound of his laughter made the flesh of the rustler creep. "I'll have a little accounting for him for all that," said Pete, "but I got another job now."

"What's that?"

"I got to ride up to see Joe Daly."

"Eh?"

"I mean it. You and me got to ride up to see him."

"I'll never show you the way, Pete."

"Let's get outside, and we'll talk more about it."

He led the way to the window. It was ridiculously easy to get down. Pete tied one end of a blanket around a nail, and then the rustler climbed down. He had scarcely reached the ground, when Pete landed beside him.

"Now we'll get our hosses and start," said Pete, and he led the way to the corral behind the barns.

They secured their mounts. Pete did the roping and then the saddling, for the whole right side of the rustler, including muscles that must be strained if he moved his arm, was terribly inflamed from the manner in which that burning steel had been thrust against his flesh. Nevertheless, he was able to climb into his saddle. He fastened his teeth to keep back a groan. He asked of his companion: "You got to show me a reason why you should be brought up to see Joe Daly. Are you wanting to join his gang?"

"Well, tell me, man to man, ain't he got a need for new hands?"

"He sure has. There's three gone that ain't going to come back. And he needs a lot more'n five to do his business."

"Well," said Pete, "he'll be mighty interested to see me."

The other coughed. "How come you to let Red Stanton walk over you that way, partner?" he asked in a cold voice.

"I had to play a part. I've had to keep after it for month after month while I been sick"—his voice raised a little—"but I'm sure done now. I'm through with that game, and I'm ready for something new."

"I dunno that I understand," growled the rustler, his horror and contempt growing as he recalled the scene he had witnessed in the Peters house between Stanton and Pete.

"What you understand don't matter a lot," returned Pete. "What amounts to something is that Joe will understand when I meet up with him."

The rustler turned in his saddle and stared at his companion. There was no possible doubt that this was not the same man who had been abused by Red Stanton in the Peters house. His flesh might not have altered, but there was a new and braver spirit in him. The rustler drew his breath in wonder. If ever a man had been changed, this was one.

"Look here," he said. "Let's talk straight. You want me to show you the way up to where Joe Daly is hanging out. Now, how can I tell that you ain't going to. . . ."

"To what?" asked Pete. "D'you think that maybe I'll clean up Joe and his whole gang?"

The rustler laughed. "Oh, that sure sounds foolish," he chuckled. "But. . . ."

"What d'you think I *would* do then?"

Again the rustler pondered for a time. "You've turned me loose," he said at last. "It sure looks like you were a friend of Joe's. I'll take the chance. Come along, partner."

They started out at a rocking canter, the rustler

twisting in his saddle so that the torment of his injured side might be lessened. So they went on until they came to a steeper grade, where it was necessary to bring the horses back to a walk.

"I'd like to know one thing," said the rustler.

"Fire away."

"What did it mean to you to know that that breastplate belonged to Joe Daly?"

Pete was silent for a moment, then he answered: "I'll tell you the straight of it, partner. I been up here in the mountains, trying to find out something that Joe would be as much interested in as I am. And it wasn't till I heard about him owning that breastplate that I knew. D'you see?"

"Something important, eh?"

"Sure it is, but if you look at it another way, you might say that it's nothing but a big joke." And, as the humor of it seemed to strike him, he broke out into loud and ringing laughter.

Chapter Ten

"Between the Eyes"

There was blackest gloom in the gang of Joe Daly, gloom so utter that he himself felt the shadow to some degree. But they made one great mistake in which he did not share. They felt that because three old and trusted members of the gang had recently died, their loss could not be replaced. Joe knew this was not true. Now that his fame had grown, he had only to give a call, and he could take his pick of a hundred desperate men. In fact, he could assemble fellows far more formidable than his present outfit. The others could not appreciate this fact. All they knew was that from eight men they had shrunk suddenly to five, and that very day one of the five had been torn away from one of their most secured haunts. It reduced them to four and the chief, Joe Daly himself.

He was now in his most favored and least used

retreat—the old mine that had been sunk into the side of the mountain. But, instead of occupying the deserted shaft itself, he had insisted on bringing them, this night, to the shack that stood at the mouth of the mine, ready to collapse with age and weather. In this shack he recklessly showed his lanterns as though there were nothing in the world to fear. To be sure, one of the men kept guard before the shack, but it was not because they might be captured. The real danger was simply that this excellent hiding place might be located, and every hiding place that was discovered narrowed their resources for escape and hiding when they should next be pressed by the manhunters. And it seemed that from now on they could never have any surety of peace. If one rancher could by his own unassisted efforts cause so much havoc and distress, what could not be done by a league of ranchers, each with his hired posse, and each working with a wholehearted desire to end the rule of the rustlers?

These thoughts were in the minds of the most careless of the men, but Joe Daly was unperturbed. Perhaps he had come to believe in his destiny. All great criminals come to that point, sooner or later. Such good fortune had favored Joe that it was little wonder if he felt some kindly deity presided over his affairs. He dated his good luck, in fact, from that day in Manhattan when he had discovered the bullet-proof breastplate and stole it away to his room. That was the strange foundation on which he had built.

When he had found it, he had been a poor exile,

hungry for his home country, and kept from it by the mortal dread of terrible Pete Burnside. With that bit of armor he had dared the most famous gunfighters time and again since his battle with Pete, and he had always been victorious. His fame had spread. There was no man in his band who dared to raise hand or voice against him. He was considered on all sides a hero of the first water.

In the meantime, he had outgrown that breast-plate. It had saved his life, to be sure, but it was by no means all that it should be. Fine steel it was, or it would never have turned the slug from a Colt pistol fired at close range. But it was by no means the sort of steel that had been invented later on to turn the cutting noses of armor-piercing bullets. And the outlaw determined that he must make a change for the better. So he had sent away to have a new piece of body armor forged for him. Far away in Philadelphia he had a friend who executed the commission and saw that the corselet was made. And it was far more safe than the original plate. That slab of steel had insured him against the slug of a revolver fired at any closeness, but the new corselet, made of the very finest quality of armor steel, with a diamond-hard surface, weighed hardly any more than the breastplate, but it was so much larger that it fitted over his entire breast and abdomen and then curved under his arms. There was another very clever contrivance also: a steel lining for his sombrero that was strong enough to turn the slug from a Colt revolver. So equipped, he felt that he was the only man who had ever lived with so many enemies, and with so much surety of triumphing over them all.

With three of his men he sat this night in the crazy little shanty, playing poker, sipping throat-scorching moonshine from time to time, and listening to the singing of a rising storm through the boards of the shack. The old cast-iron stove, so sadly cracked that it spouted smoke and filled the cabin with a blue-white vapor twisted in wisps about the card players, they packed with wood until it roared with a crowding mass of flames. It shivered and shook with the rushing of the draft, and it managed to keep the windy hut warm enough for comfort, assisted by the moonshine whiskey.

Not much of that whiskey, however, was passing the lips of Joe Daly. His glass was often in his hand, and he pretended to drink to every man who made a winning, but in reality few drops of the liquor found their way down his throat. Daly needed a clear head for his business.

In reality, the poker games in his camp were the most important source of his revenue. Out of them he drew the many thousands that went to recruit his bank accounts. His scheme was admirable. He gave his men a very large portion of the proceeds of the crimes he planned and organized. He was not one of those who took a third or a half of the profits as a return for the brain work he expended on them. Instead, he merely took two shares, and out of his own shares he paid for the food, the guns, and the ammunition of the entire party.

What could have been more generous? It was plain that such an open-handed leader was working as much for the happiness of his men as for his own fame and profit. At least so thought the followers of the bandit. The other side of the picture was never exposed to their eyes. But had they kept track, they might have found that what they made in their raids, they quickly paid back into the pockets of the leader at the poker games. For Joe Daly was no common manipulator of the cards. He did not know many tricks, but he had his own system of marking the cards with his fingernails, a method ancient as the very hills and a million times discovered, but it was never discovered by Joe's gang. It never occurred to the worst of them that anyone could be so base as to cheat the very men with whom he had been adventuring that same day, perhaps. But Joe was not bothered by the scruples of an active conscience. Indeed, as time went on and his bank accounts swelled and he saw himself becoming a rich man, he decided that it was as good to have an armor-clad conscience as it was to have an armor-clad body.

Daly had just won five hundred, and, seeing his left-hand neighbor take in a wretched little bet of thirty dollars on the next hand, he poured generous doses of the moonshine into each of the tin cups.

"Here's to Harry, boys," he said. "Old Harry sure ain't had his luck tonight. Here's where his luck changes."

Immediately the cups flashed up to do the proper honor to Harry. Before they went down, there was a clamor of voices outside of the cabin.

"Nobody's got a right . . . you must be crazy to bring him up here where. . . ."

"Shut up! He's an old friend of the chief's. Don't you suppose that I'd be sure of that before I went this far?"

On the heels of this outburst of noise, in came the guard on a rush. "Here's Bud come back," he began.

"Bud got loose from 'em?" shouted the gamblers, springing up in joyous forgetfulness of their game.

"And he's brought up a stranger."

Bud himself here pushed into the cabin.

"Come on, Pete," he said. "Step up and meet the chief, and see if he ain't glad to see you."

"Hello, Joe," called Pete Burnside, pausing at the door of the cabin.

At his voice there was a gasp from Joe Daly. The rustler leaped away from the table until his shoulders crashed against the wall. At the same time the other members of the gang crowded back so as to make a passage that would be clear from one of them to the other.

"By guns," breathed Daly, "it's you . . . Pete."

The men of the gang turned in utter bewilderment to their chief. They found that their hero had turned the gray of ashes and was staring at the square-jawed man in the doorway as though the latter were a ghost.

"I come to pay you a call, Joe," said Burnside.

"Pete . . . ," began the other.

"Well?"

"I got something to say to you."

"I ain't come up here just to talk."

"You dunno what you're saying, partner. All I want is to try to explain to you. . . ."

The rustlers gasped at one another. It could not be that they were hearing aright; it could not be that their dauntless commander was knuckling under to this stranger. And Bud, with the picture of Red Stanton and the Peters house, was the most astonished of them all.

"Joe," said the other, "I got something to say that the rest of 'em might as well hear. Boys, my name's Pete Burnside."

It sent a shock through two of them who had heard of that not obscure name.

"I was the gent that run Joe out of the mountains last year. He went away because he was afraid to face me. Then he come back all at once and sent out the word that he was just waiting for me. When I went to meet him, I got my gun first. I sent in the first shot . . . I could have swore that I seen him stagger . . . but he sure enough didn't drop. Like a sneaking hound he was wearing this right over his heart!"

Pete tossed onto the floor of the cabin the breastplate. It landed softly on its quilted back, and the rustlers stared down at it. Every one of them knew about the strange method their chief used to make himself invulnerable. They only wondered how he could endure dressing in iron during the furious heat of the summer or the biting cold of the winter. Yet, it had not seemed to them that there was anything particularly dishonorable in his proceedings.

"Boys," said Pete Burnside, "when he'd stopped two of my bullets with this here plate of steel, he got his own gun on me at last and sent me down for the count. When I got well, I was a no-good hound. Bud, here, will tell you what I was. I didn't put no trust in myself. I'd seen my bullets go right into the mark and miss. It took all my nerve. I wasn't no more good than a hound dog." He paused, his face white, breathing hard. "Then all at once I found out what had happened. It hadn't been my fault. I'd shot straight, but that hound was wearing armor when he sent to ask me to fight. When I heard that, I got my nerve back. I come up here with Bud, letting him think that what I wanted was to join the gang. But what I really wanted was to get a crack at Joe Daly. Understand, boys, I ain't up here to spy on you. I don't have no care what you do in rustling cows. I want to rustle Joe Daly. Joe, are you ready?"

The face of Joe Daly was a study. The certainty of death was before him. But in another moment his courage returned. Like a traitor Bud had told that his chief at one time had worn the breastplate, but he could not have told about the new armor for the simple reason that Bud did not know of it. Pete had come to strike down a man whose unfair advantage was removed; he could not know that a still greater advantage was still on the side of the chief of the rustlers. And, as the surety returned to Joe, he laughed aloud.

"Pete," he said, "I'm ready when you are . . . get your gun."

As he spoke, he went for his own with all the speed at his command. But slow, slow was his fastest motion compared with the sudden flash which brought the Colt into the hand of Pete Burnside. And the breast was not the target at which Pete fired. The muzzle of his revolver twitched higher than that, and the bullet drove squarely between the eyes of Joe Daly. He spun around and dropped on his face. Then Pete leaped aside and backed through the door.

They followed him at once. In vain he shouted to them that he would do them no harm if they would let him alone. They rushed out through the door. The bright shaft of the lamplight illumined each one as he came. And the revolver spoke—and spoke again and again, where Pete Burnside had dropped upon one knee in the dark and emptied his six-shooter.

Chapter Eleven

"Enter the New Man"

"If I have to see him again in our house," said Miriam, "I won't answer for what I'll say to him."

Her father smiled at her.

"I mean it," she declared.

"But," said Doc Peters, "you sure got to admit that Red Stanton has plenty of nerve."

"He has courage . . . of a sort. He knows that he's stronger than other men, and, of course, that makes him confident. But that brute sort of bravery doesn't mean a great deal."

"You don't mean that, Miriam."

"But I do. And it sickens me to see his great red face and watch his insolent rolling eyes, as he stares at me. He acts as though he were paying his suit to me."

"That's nonsense, honey."

"I tell you, it's in his stupid head. He thinks that

he's saving us, and therefore he can make any demand he wants to make."

"Well, Miriam, he *is* saving us."

"I tell you, Joe Daly will smash him and all his gang. What have they done? They've captured one poor rascal who got away again, and. . . ."

"He didn't get away. He was turned loose by that pleasant friend of yours."

"Dad, you're simply trying to be aggravating."

"I'm talking facts."

"I haven't spoken a dozen words to that poor fellow, Pete."

"Poor sneak thief."

"Is it right to say that?"

"I'm staying with the facts still."

"You call him a thief because he turned the rustler loose."

"What would *you* call a thing like that?"

"I know why he did it."

"Tell me if you can."

"Pete had been used to torture. I know that. He had been broken with pain . . . he has been crushed by it. And that was why his heart bled for the poor rustler. I pitied him myself . . . and when I think of that unspeakable beast of a Stanton branding the man with a hot iron . . . oh, it sickens me when I think of it."

"He was trying to tear the truth out of the rascal, and cowpunchers don't figure rustlers to be real men . . . they're just sort of snakes in the eyes of a 'puncher, Miriam. You'd ought to know that."

"Oh, he wasn't trying to tear the truth from him. Little he cared about the truth. He was torturing

The Coward

that man to make him break down. He wanted to hear the rustler shriek for mercy. He wanted to make the rustler crawl the way poor Pete crawls. Oh, I can't even talk of it."

"I know," nodded her father.

"If Red comes into this house again, I'm not going to be here."

"Honey," said her father slowly, "I know how you feel. Red Stanton ain't a pretty thing to look at. He's got the manners of a hog and the nature of a wildcat. But I can stand bad manners, and so can you. There's only one thing that counts in all that you've been saying about him . . . if he really has been making a fool of himself in the way he's been looking at you, I'll fill him full of lead, or else just kick him off the place."

"But don't you see, Dad, that's the horrible part of it? If he finds out what we think of him, he'll go mad with spite and hatred. He'd burn the house over our heads and never think about it twice. What are we going to do, Dad? Can't you ask him to go into the bunkhouse with the other men after supper?"

"He thinks it's his right to be here. Remember, Miriam, that he hired a dozen men to do work for us. And we couldn't have gone out by ourselves and hired two. You can go to town until this job is finished."

"I'll never leave you here alone with such a man."

Doc Peters shrugged his shoulders and smiled. His rather tired old eyes lifted and looked past the bright head of his daughter and into the stormy past. He had seen his share of trouble. He had

213

taken his part in battles enough. Now he smiled at this touch of solicitude on the part of his girl.

That night the crew of cowpunchers and Red Stanton's wild group of hired men crowded into the dining room and filled the place with uproar. When they had finally stamped their way out again, Red, as usual, tilted back in his chair and drank extra cups of coffee. All the while he was keeping his eyes fixed upon Miriam.

Peters had been wondering how it was that such a worm of a man as Pete had managed to find the courage to defy them all and set the prisoner free.

"But you don't know that man," said Miriam. "I'll wager that there's still courage in him. I'll wager that he was once brave."

"Brave?" echoed Red Stanton, eagerly seizing upon this chance to win the favorable attention of the girl. "Say, lady, maybe you dunno what his whole name is?"

"What is it?" she asked on fire with eagerness.

"Pete Burnside," he answered pompously.

Here Doc Peters jumped up and ran across the room, though he was a man who was rarely much moved. "You mean to say that's Pete Burnside?"

"I mean that."

"Miriam!" cried the rancher, turning on his daughter. "Think of that?"

"I don't think I've heard about him," she said wretchedly.

"Never heard? That comes of taking all that time to go to a fool school in the East!" exploded her father. "But you remember about the train robbery four years back, when the robbers blew up the guards in the mail coach simply because there was nothing worth taking in the safe? Five men done that trick."

"I remember that horrible story," said the girl.

"Well, Pete Burnside was him that went on the trail of that five. The posses couldn't get 'em. The five was too strong for a few men and too fast for a whole mob of hossmen to follow 'em. They'd have got clean away and melted off into the mountains somewheres, if Pete hadn't got onto their trail. Then it was a yarn that would make your hair stand right up on end. Dog-goned if Burnside didn't keep on their heels until he dropped one of 'em. Then the other four found out there was only one man behind 'em, and they turned back and cornered him. They got around him, and then they rushed the pile of boulders where he was lying."

Doc Peters paused and lighted his cigarette.

"Hurry, Dad," cried the girl. "I can't breathe, I'm so excited."

He threw away the match.

"Well, when the smoke cleared away, two of 'em was dead, and two of 'em wished that they was dead. But Pete stayed up there and nursed 'em back till they was strong enough to travel. About six weeks later he come down with his two prisoners . . . yes, sir, he'd stayed up there a whole six weeks with them man-killing hounds."

"Oh!" exclaimed the girl, "how perfectly wonderful, Dad."

"Ain't it?" said Peters. "I tell you, there ain't another man in the mountains that's done the things that Pete Burnside has done. And when he come

down with those two gents, he'd got so fond of 'em
that he went all the way to the governor and come
in and sits down, and he tells the governor that
these two gents ain't really as bad as the newspapers makes them out, and that, if they get a year in
prison and then get pardoned, that he'll go bond
that they don't ever turn wild again. And will you
believe me that old Governor Parks listened to Pete
and took his suggestion? Yes, sir. It sure spoke well
for Pete, and it spoke well for the governor, too.
One year them two was in prison, and then they
was turned loose. And ever since then they've just
settled down and lived like white folks and ain't
give no trouble to nobody."

"Why, Dad," said the girl, "he's not a manhunter,
then. He was a maker of men."

"Maybe you might call it that," nodded her father. "But, any way you put it, I'm sure glad to hear
that's Pete Burnside. And I don't care what sort of
a man he's turned out to be lately, he's been man
enough in the past to suit me. If he ever comes back
to this here ranch, he's going to be treated like a
king."

"Yes, yes," agreed the girl. "Oh, Dad, he surely
deserves everything that good men can do for him."

Here big Red Stanton, who had listened to the
story about Pete Burnside with a restless indiffer-
ence, now rolled himself about in his chair until it
squeaked and groaned in every joint.

"Look here," he said, "I ain't going to have you
spoiling him for me."

The rancher and his daughter looked at the giant
with disgust and some surprise. In the little silence

that spread through the room they could hear far away a resonant baritone raised in a song that carried far across the night. Perhaps one of the new men in the bunkhouse was entertaining himself and his companions.

"I ain't going to have you spoil him," continued Red Stanton. "He's no end useful to me. Does all my darning and patching and saddles my hoss for me . . . and does so many things that I dunno how I'd get along without him. Why, if you started treating him like he was a man, pretty soon *he'd* think that he was a man. And there ain't no sense to that at all. What he's cut out for is to keep me comfortable. The more comfortable that I'm kept, the quicker I'll get at Joe Daly and his crew. Ain't that good sense and plain sense, Peters?"

The rancher looked upon his guest with a strange eye. "Maybe you're right," he said, "but there ain't much to worry about yet. There ain't much likelihood that he'll come back."

Red Stanton threw back his head and laughed. "You dunno him," he declared. "You dunno him, but I do. Oh, he'll come back."

The two stared at him, utterly fascinated.

"But what makes you think so?" asked the girl. "What could make him come back when he knows . . . ?"

"When he knows that he'll get a beating from me soon as he shows up?"

The lip of Miriam curled with horror and scorn, but she could not answer directly.

"I'll tell you why he'll come back," went on Red, as the singing grew a little louder and a little nearer. "First off, when he gets off by himself with the rustler, he'll begin to think that it's a pretty good thing to be free. But as soon as he runs into somebody that talks loud and has a handy pair of fists, he'll begin to wish that he was back under cover. I dunno how brave he used to be, but I know that I never heard tell of a gent that was half as yaller as he is now. He'll be wishing that he was back where he didn't have nobody to cuss him, but someone that he knowed. He'd begin shaking and trembling the way I've seen him do when strangers come around. That's him."

He laughed again. Miriam dropped her face into her hands.

"What's the matter?" growled Red. "I tell you that he *will* come back, and partly because he'll figure out that, if he comes back quick, he won't get as bad a licking as he will if he stays away a long time."

"Let it drop at that," said Peters. "We'll talk some more about him some other time. Who's that, Miriam? You expecting somebody?"

"Yes, Nell Hotchkiss said she might come over for the night. . . ."

She ran to the door and threw it open. Then she fell back with a shrill, faint cry. As she retreated, Pete Burnside stepped forward into the room.

Chapter Twelve

"Burnside Is Himself"

But what a different man was this. Pete Burnside seemed a full two inches taller. The sullen droop of his mouth at the corners was gone, and a faint smile played there. His square jaw was thrust out a little more than usual, and the very color of his eyes seemed changed now that he stood so erect, and no shadow fell from the brows across the pupils. And the bearing of his body, at once erect and easy, made him seem ten years younger and three-fold stronger.

Indeed, with all the stories attached to his name, and with his hardy appearance, he might have passed for thirty-five years of age. But those who knew declared that he had managed to cram all the events of his life into less than thirty years. He now closed the door carefully behind him and looked about upon those who were in the room. In his left hand he carried a saddlebag that seemed very heavy, and that clinked when it struck against his knee.

"I'm sure sorry that I give you a start," he said to the girl.

"*I'll* be the one that'll change your manners, son!" roared big Red Stanton. He pushed the cuffs of his coat away from his hairy wrists. "I'll be having a lot to say to you, you gutter rat, you soft-headed fool, turning loose the men that I capture."

The right hand of Pete Burnside raised, and the forefinger indicated Red Stanton, like the snap and drop of a revolver upon its target. "You, over yonder," he said, "be quiet. I'll attend to you a little later on."

If he had struck Red over the head with a club and stunned him, he could not have changed the expression on the other's face more completely. With sagging jaw and with mouth agape, the giant leaned forward and stared at him with dull eyes of wonder. Surprise had utterly unnerved Stanton.

"But I've come to give you my report first," said Pete, turning to the rancher and to Miriam.

Doc Peters was combing his mustache with furious speed, first to one side and then to the other side. Now he seized the hand of Pete and gripped it hard.

"I didn't know you before," he said. "I'd seen pictures of you, too, but I was a fool and didn't recognize you. While you were gone, we heard that you're Pete Burnside."

Pete lifted his head and looked across the room

at Red Stanton, and the giant blinked stupidly back at him.

"That's my name," he admitted modestly. "And I ... I come up here to try to work this here case...."

"That's a lie!" roared Red Stanton. "I had to drag him up here. He sure enough begged me not to take him up into these mountains, where there was so much trouble and...."

"Be quiet!" snapped the rancher, turning suddenly upon Red. That sudden reproof shocked the giant into another silence.

"I turned that rustler loose," said Pete in his quiet way, "because of me figuring that maybe he'd show me the way to get at Joe Daly. And I was right. He took me all the way up to Joe's camp."

"You don't mean to say ... ?" began the girl.

"What I mean to say," said Pete soberly, "is that there won't be any more trouble from Joe and his crowd."

He turned the saddlebag upside down.

"There's their guns ... six guns. There's their wallets ... six wallets, I guess. You might take that as a sign that they ain't going to bother you or nobody else for a while." He could not help smiling his triumph into the face of the girl.

"Burnside," said the rancher, "it sort of staggers me. Say it over again. Tell me the straight of it. You mean to say that you got all six of 'em?"

"They piled out the door at me ... they stood in the light of the lamp, and as they come out one by one...."

"All lies . . . all lies!" thundered Red Stanton. He had risen and strode toward them.

"You," called Pete Burnside, "get out and stay gone. You hear me, Red?"

As he spoke, he slipped his revolver from its holster and fired. The Colt was jerked from the hip of Red by the tearing impact of the bullet, sent to its mark with an uncanny accuracy. Red's big gun dropped heavily to the floor.

Red, disarmed by miracle, so it seemed, stood wavering an instant. He staggered, his arms stretched out, as though on the verge of lunging either forward or back. And then, clutching at the place where his revolver had been, with a sudden yell of terror he plunged through the door and raced into the night.

Pete Burnside, from the open door, fired into the dirt behind the fugitive. There was a hoarse shriek of fear, and the other bounded out of the lamplight. And so he disappeared swiftly into the blackness, like a nightmare disappearing from a sane mind, it seemed to Pete.

The rancher was laughing uproariously, and Miriam was clinging to his arm and looking out through the door at the renegade. Pete Burnside did not so much as smile. Indeed, he had lost the habit of smiling forever.

Slumber Mountain

Frederick Faust's original title for this story was "The Man of Slumber Mountain." It was changed simply to "Slumber Mountain" when it appeared in Street & Smith's *Western Story Magazine* in the issue for July 8, 1922. It was published under the byline John Frederick, in part because an installment of "The Shadow of Silver Tip," a six-part serial by Faust under the byline George Owen Baxter, was running in the same issue. The same month "Alcatraz," a five-part serial, was also running in a slick magazine, *The Country Gentleman*. This latter serial would be filmed that year as *Just Tony* (Fox, 1922) starring movie cowboy, Tom Mix, and his horse, Tony. "Slumber Mountain," appearing here for the first time in book form, has all of the fine qualities of the storyteller's art and is especially memorable for the poignant creation of Alice Woolwin.

Chapter One

"The Print of a Paw"

Halting his mule, Woolwin turned into the wind, lifting his head a little like one who listens to music with critical ears. There was a faint, but certain, odor of musk in the air. It was like the scent that the musk plant gives forth from damp ravines. But at this time in the fall there was no musk plant growing. No, it must be that the muskrats were swarming again in the string of shallow ponds and lakes that stagnated in the Rinwash Valley. He hesitated. Had he been mounted on a horse, he would have taken the detour without hesitation. But today he had taken out old Baldy, the mule. The gait, the temper, and the speed of Baldy were as far from desirable as possible. But his sure-footedness was wonderful among the mountain rocks. Since Woolwin intended an excursion through the difficult crags of Slumber Mountain, he had taken the savage veteran for his riding.

Finally, shaking his head, he determined to continue in his originally chosen direction, straight for the upper reaches of the great mountain. Baldy carried a burden of great traps that might clamp over the leg of a timber wolf and hold the powerful animal safely. For Woolwin was out today not for pelts, but for scalps with a bounty upon them. If he wanted to set those traps and get down the mountainside before dark, he must hurry. Not even Baldy was absolutely safe on the staggering downtrail along Slumber Mountain.

Straight toward the noble mass of Slumber Mountain he directed the mule that pegged along with short, jerky steps, its head nodding, its long ears flapping, its pendulous under lip stirring loosely, as though muttering in revolt against the tyranny of the rider. And now and again the ragged tail of Baldy was switched swiftly, two or three times in succession, and his little eyes glanced savagely from side to side, as though he turned over in his mind the prospect of trying to throw the master. But always that thought was sullenly dismissed. Revolt had been tried before; revolt had always failed. Buck he could, like a very devil incarnate. The fifteen bitter winters and the fifteen burning summers through which he had lived and labored did not seem to have noticeably impaired the agility of the long limbs with which he flung himself into the air and literally tied himself into knots before striking the ground again.

But for all his skill in bucking, and for all the

savage cunning and hatred that sustained him in such efforts, he had long before recognized in John Woolwin his master and had submitted to him. For where a horse has more heart than brain, a mule has distinctly more brain than heart. It constantly thinks. It thinks, indeed, far too much for the well-being of its owner. In the meantime Baldy, who got his name from the absence of hair on his black forehead, was dreading and loathing the thought of the laborious climb that lay before him, and at the second touch on the reins he stopped in the middle of a step.

For once more the scent of the musk had blown to Woolwin, and he turned with something between a smile and a curse. There had darted into his mind the picture of a sharp little black nose, cutting the surface of stagnant water, and of an umber-colored body beneath the surface, barely visible, so closely did the color of body and muddy water blend. That picture of the muskrat made Woolwin turn Baldy at once into the east wind that was blowing up the odor from the flat below. For half an hour they climbed swiftly down, Baldy with one ear pointed forward in joy because they were going down instead of up, and with one ear laid back because they were not taking the trail toward home. But Woolwin was following the irresistible urge that stirred in his trapper's heart. He was by nature a hunter, and not a hunter with guns, but a hunter by superior cunning, superior patience, tricking animals into his traps. It was that instinct, rising hot in his veins, that made him leave his ranch so often and his house at the town of Shawnee, below in the lesser hills. Had he stuck close to his own cow business and to farming, of which a large portion of his land was quite capable, he would have been prosperous. But now and again he felt the call, tingling to his very fingertips, and then he would leave the village, leave the ranch, and head up toward his cabin in the upper lands. This was the center from which he struck in all directions for prey. What matter if, while getting a hundred dollars' worth of pelts, work on the ranch went to rack to the extent of a thousand dollars? He could not help that. The trail had lured him. His motherless daughter had many a time wept in the pauses of her housework, seeing the ruin toward which her joyous, big-hearted father was tending.

Now the trail carried him out into the flats of the Rinwash, and he dismounted, threw the reins, and in addition secured Baldy by pouring out a torrent of prodigious threats and mighty curses, in case he should take it into his vicious head to wander homeward. Then Woolwin started through the rushes of the swamp and walked careless of noise, for noise hardly disturbs the foolish little muskrat. Yet he made a sufficient disturbance to attract the attention of a flock of ducks. They were out of sight, beyond a low knoll and on the surface of the next lake. He heard the rush and flapping of their wings, as they rose and gathered headway. Then in another direction they poured into view, scurrying east with incredible speed, with necks thrust forth and small wings, working furiously. That clatter and whir of wings having died out and the original silence descending upon the Rinwash, Woolwin found himself standing on the half-submerged, half-rotted wreck of an old log by the edge of the water. Before him lay the unrippled lake, brown in the shallows, black in the depths, with highlights of blue struck out by the sunshine. Now the wind scooped a strong scent from the very surface of the lake and whipped it into his nostrils. Yet nothing was visible. His quick eye darted here and there.

Then, at last, he saw what he was looking for, a little bow wave, spreading on either side of an invisible bow. The mysterious prow approached the end of a branch that projected just above the surface. Instantly above the water appeared a rat-like head. Then a webbed forefoot hooked over a branch. Woolwin could see the eager, quick working of the whiskers and the glitter of the little eyes. Then, taking alarm for no cause, the muskrat slid noiselessly back into the water and dived out of sight, just the tip of a long tail showing as it did so.

Then Woolwin began to work his way along the side of the marsh, keeping ankle-deep in ooze in spite of his care. After a time, looking down among the short, thick reeds, he saw many diminutive trails, now flung apart, now weaving together. They led him close to a little dome of mud pushed above the water. That was the round top of the muskrats' wattled house, he knew, and by the trails he guessed that the muskrats were thicker than ever before in his experience of the Rinwash. Woolwin nodded wisely to himself. He would make a special trip down here before long, with some three or four dozen little traps and strong pomatum to bait them. With that resolution definitely taken, he turned around and went reluctantly back to Baldy. In the saddle he turned again and looked back to the wind, shivering among the reeds, then he faced Slumber Mountain once more.

A mid-afternoon mist had gathered around the mountain, not enough to befog its outlines, but pouring the hollows and the sharp-sided ravines full of softening blue. Indeed, all the storm scars were completely covered. The mountain rose with an apparently solemn and placid dignity, sweeping up in such lazy and reposeful curves that one could tell at a glance why it had been termed Slumber Mountain. But Baldy, knowing the truth of the jagged rocks and the in-and-out tangle of ravines along the sides of Slumber Mountain, snorted and hung his head when he faced the new ascent. Woolwin himself frowned. It would be dark before he set the last of his traps, it seemed. Should he venture up among the rocks toward the three peaks that made the treble summit of the mountain, or should he turn back and call the locating of the muskrats a day's work?

He looked to the sky with a dubious frown, and there in the east, transparent as a blown shred of cloud, was a rising half-moon. Mountain moonlight would give enough light for the descent, he told himself, and pressed on at the fastest pace that he could draw from Baldy. That pace was by no means satisfactory. The mule was utterly disgusted with the wrongheadedness of the master. Neither spur nor laboring quiet could rouse him to a round trot on the level, nor a fast walk up the slope. When the ragged rocks began, Baldy slowed almost to a walk, though picking his way with the most consummate deftness of foot.

Woolwin, resigning himself at last to a late return and a very late supper, dragged his belt closer around his abdomen and prepared for the fast by filling his pipe with shaved and hand-crumbled tobacco from his plug. With a fragrant cloud of blue smoke blowing around his head, he went on in higher and higher spirits. After all, it would be a pleasant experiment. For two years now the district had been plagued from time to time by the advents of a plundering band of lobos. Even a solitary loafer wolf can do enough damage to cause a bounty of from forty to a hundred dollars to be placed upon its scalp. But now from six to a dozen wolves ranged regularly under the leadership of a huge gray veteran, wise in all the methods of hunting, wary beyond credence of traps.

From time to time he swept away to other regions with his band, but it seemed that they broke up their partnership as soon as they departed, for the crew of deft murderers was not known in other places. But around Shawnee, Silver King was as notorious as any two-gun badman. The average lobo is so light a gray that it stands out like a ghost in the evening as it runs through the hills. But Silver King was pale even among his kind, and therefore his name. Silver King had ranged through the mountains with his crew, killing at their will and never returning to old meat. It was not strange that the cowmen around the town of Shawnee and raisers of horses, maddened by finding the partially eaten bodies of their finest stock day after day, had pushed up the bounty upon the heads of Silver King and his gang until it had reached the truly remarkable sum of one thousand dollars for the prime murderer, and no less than one hundred and fifty for every one of his assistants.

But though Silver King had been hunted with packs of fine hounds and by determined hunters, time and again though he had been sought with trap and with poison, the cunning old veteran still led his band with impunity and mocked the efforts of his enemies. So it was that John Woolwin had worked out a theory of his own, which was that the wise wolf had established as a rendezvous and place of retreat, after the commission of a depredation, the lonely rocks at the summit of Slumber Mountain. That idea had occurred to no other person, and the chief reason was a simple one. Namely, that Slumber Mountain was too far away from the usual scenes of the Silver King's crimes.

For though a man may know that a loafer wolf can travel a hundred miles a day without great effort, still it is difficult to believe that the colt that you find dead at dawn was killed before midnight by an assassin who now lurks in the blue of a mountain thirty or forty miles away. They combed the lower hills with their hounds, but the scents usually ran out before there had been much travel over the rocks of Slumber Mountain. So they gave up the chase and turned back. But to John Woolwin the inspiration came along with the certainty that he would find the wise wolf yonder, near the treble peaks.

Beyond the fame that would be his, if he succeeded, there was the matter of money. It meant a thousand dollars in hard cash if he got the pelt of the grim leader. It meant more if he could capture a few of the others. And never in his life had he needed money as he needed it now.

The story of a mortgage is an old story, but it is never a dull story to those who lie within the danger. Six hundred dollars was not a great deal of interest to meet. It could be borrowed, one might say. But John Woolwin was one of those who lend and borrow with equal ease. As long as he possessed money, he was perfectly willing to share it with the first who asked. He parted from his coin without pain, and the result was that he could not understand those who clung to their dollars as though they were vital nerves. In the first part of his life he had been the creditor always. But when the ready cash that his father had left him was gone, he began to be consistently the debtor, and during the past half dozen years the story had been rather monotonously the same. The good nature of a Westerner is proverbial, as is his trust in men he truly knows. But the persistent borrowing of John Woolwin wore them out, and a week before he had learned with a shock that his credit was absolutely gone in his home town. The discovery sickened him. Then he cast up his accounts—mentally and inaccurately—and decided that the world was using him very ill. It was out of his desperate need for that six hundred that the inspiration to go trapping for the Silver King on Slumber Mountain came to him.

Here he was, toiling toward the nearest crest in the golden light of the late afternoon. He regarded that beautiful light anxiously, where it softened the shining surface of a slab of quartz. For the yellow light meant the approaching end of the day. And he had many a trap to set before dark.

He turned back from his hasty squint at the westering sun and, as men do after they have faced that blinding light, he looked straight down at a sandy depression between two rocks. It was a dark sand, smoothly packed and leveled by the action of flooding rains. Exactly in the center, as though stamped there on purpose, as on the most perfect spot on the mountainside, was the print of a paw as large as the palm of a man's hand, even the palm of his own hand.

John Woolwin with a stifled shout—stifled for fear the great wolf might overhear and understand—flung himself down and leaned over the mark. There was no doubt about it. No wolf, even loafer wolf, that he had ever seen was capable of leaving an imprint as large as that round blur. It was the track of the Silver King, and he had been right in his guess.

Chapter Two

"Red Mouths and Lolling Tongues"

In half of a feverish hour he had discovered far more than he could have hoped to discover. Between the arms of the two southerly peaks of Slumber Mountain that lifted still another five or six hundred feet on either side of him in a drift of light sand he found a regularly beaten trail, thick with the sign of wolves, and here he began to lay out his traps with the greatest care and speed. For the great wolves would begin ranging, beyond doubt, as soon as the first shadows of the evening began to gather on the plain below. Already it was almost the sunset time.

His plan was both simple and cunning. Instead of leaving bait to attract them, he planted four strong traps in close succession along the trail. If the wolves came down the familiar and worn trail in single file, one of them was certain to spring a trap. The others, of course, would leap away. They would not dream of continuing along that treacherous path. But they would form in a circle and sit down and look at their unfortunate companion. And for exactly this had John Woolwin provided. He planted a thick circle of traps along the central four. When the rim had been completed, he stepped back, anxious to leave at once. For the last red rim of the sun had just winked out of sight below the western horizon. But there remained a single trap. Had it been old, smeared with oil-blackened rust, he would have left it. It showed its clean teeth like a savage dog and seemed mutely to promise that its grip should never be evaded, once it was fixed upon a victim. Woolwin spread those yawning jaws, and the strength of the spring was too much for him. He determined to lay this trap, also. It was strong enough to hold a grizzly.

In a few moments the place for it was excavated, just below the fourth trap in the path. The ground cover was strewn carefully above it with the exact appearance of wind-blown sand, and with a nod of self-approval Woolwin rose.

He had remained crouched so long, however, that the circulation was stopped in his left leg, and the moment he put his weight upon it, the leg gave way. He staggered, and there was a sudden clink of iron. The bright new teeth of the last trap had closed strongly upon his left leg, biting well above the ankle.

The shock completed his fall. He pitched to the side, reached out his arms to save himself, and jammed his left hand into the jaws of another trap, this time in his circle. Cursing with surprise and anger, he turned on his stomach to fumble for the chain that secured the trap to the roots of the nearest shrub, but he found to his horror that the pinioning of his foot so shortened his reach that he could not come within ten inches of the place where the chain was fastened to the stout trunk of the shrub. In fact, he was stretched out almost stiff, with barely enough slack to permit his turning upon one side. This he did, for he must call to Baldy and try to persuade the stubborn mule to come close. For that was one trick the old mule had permitted himself to learn. The trouble was that he rarely cared to remember what he had been taught.

Not fifty feet away walked the veteran mountain climber, tearing up shreds of hardy grass, but he pretended not to hear a voice Woolwin purposely kept pitched low lest it might warn away the wolves. For at any time, now, they might begin to come out. Before that happened, he must get at his pack on the mule and draw his revolver from the low-hanging holster. He blessed the habit of keeping the saddle holster low before his knee, for it meant that he could now easily reach the butt by raising himself upon one elbow and stretching up his free arm. Gloomily he decided that he would have to raise his voice to a shout that would certainly bring Baldy, but that would as certainly warn away Silver King and his followers. As he came to this conclusion, he turned his head and saw, black against the red west, the silhouette of a great wolf, sitting upon a rock and staring down with a lolling tongue.

It was Silver King! There could be no doubt, considering the size of the brute and the light color of the fur. While he had labored over the traps, the marauder had watched from a safe covert. As soon as the traps had closed, he had come out upon the rock in insolent full view. And the very heart of John Woolwin came up in his throat with yearning for his revolver. Before he had wanted it to shoot away the spring of the trap that held his left arm helpless. He wanted it now to send the first bullet through the head of the great wolf. For the monster was within easy range of the long-barreled Colt.

But the obstinate mule would not come. Half turning his head toward Baldy, but still keeping the wolf in view from the corner of his eye, Woolwin called again more loudly. At the sound of Woolwin's voice Silver King did not stir. Well he knew that the traps were doing their work. But Baldy, the old rascal, kept his head down and tore steadily at grass Woolwin was sure was half imaginary. His long ears were flattened along his neck, and that was a sure sign that he heard the voice of the man he hated and feared. Would nothing bring him?

Woolwin raised his voice to such a shout, half roar and half yell of rage, that at last the head of Baldy was brought up with a jerk. The next instant it was flung high with a snort of terror. And, despite his own alarm, Woolwin almost laughed at the sight of the dismayed surprise of Baldy. But at least the sight of the wolf served one good purpose. It brought Baldy toward his master at a rapid trot. No matter if that trot were also bringing him straight toward the great wolf that lay beyond and above on the rock, with his red tongue lolling. No matter for that. By old experience Baldy knew that the speed of the fleetest horse was not sufficient to stand off the rush of a wolf, far less to distance one in a long race. There was only one way in which he could be saved from death, and that was by staying close to the master and the master's death-dealing hand that spoke with smoke and fire and thunder all at once. So Baldy came swiftly, but hardly had he progressed ten yards, when he swerved to one side with a squeal of terror and then bolted for Woolwin at full gallop up the hillside.

The cause for that panic was at once revealed. Two gray forms rose from the rocks. Rather, they dissolved from the gray rocks into which they had been melted before. Now they floated toward the mule, racing with that singular and gliding gallop of a wolf. There was no chance for poor Baldy. For every foot he traveled, they covered a yard. They slunk in from either side. One of them leaped, and, as he shot past the rear legs of the mule, his great red mouth opened, with its deep fringe of teeth shining white. The slashing stroke hamstrung Baldy. He staggered, recovered on three legs, and lurched clumsily ahead, his tongue thrust out. But now the other gray demon left the earth in a long leap, his teeth flashing exactly as the teeth of the first assailant had flashed, and Baldy sank to the ground. The two wolves were at his head in an instant. Woolwin, with a yell of horror, threw a rock at the murderers. But the thrown rock and the shout only brought a momentary snarl from them and a momentary halt. Then they closed. There was a spring and a flash of teeth, and the throat of Baldy was slashed wide.

Disgust and rage made Woolwin turn from that spectacle, disgust and a strange chill that had taken possession of the small of his back. He whirled around in time to face the noiseless rush of the pale gray monster. Silver King had left his rock and stolen toward a human victim, while the terrible face of the latter had been turned toward the diversion his two companion wolves were making toward the mule. But, as Woolwin turned, Silver King swerved out of his straight course and, avoiding the circle of the traps, veered away to the body of the mule.

He was ashamed to be balked of his charge, and so he had pretended that his goal from the first was Baldy. But Woolwin, plucking out his long hunting knife, was shaken with shuddering, and his skin prickled. He knew how narrow that escape had been.

Moreover, the false charge had awakened a new fear in him. He had never before heard of the wise loafer wolves when in good flesh, attacking a man, woman, or child, no matter how defenseless they might be. To be sure, wolves were strangely bold and seemed to know perfectly when the eternal enemy was without firearms. But never had they ventured, so far as he knew, upon an actual attack unless desperate hunger drove them.

There was no hunger in the band of Silver King, however. Woolwin saw them appearing, now one in one direction, two in another. And presently they sat down in a wide circle around him, ten enormous loafers, each capable of striking down the mightiest bull on the range. The awe of man still held them, but how long would it be before they closed?

Chapter Three

"Woolwin Waits for Death"

The handle of his knife was wet with perspiration. He dried his palm hastily on the sand, and then refreshed his grip. At least, he determined, thrusting out his jaw, he would die fighting—he would account for one among their number. Strange that he, a man, should feel such a savage satisfaction in the thought of striking down a beast and paying a death for a death. But would he be able actually to kill one of them? The thick, loose hide was admirably adapted to make the tooth of an enemy slide from the chosen mark, and it was tough enough to turn all but the keenest edge. Beneath that wire hair and the loose, rolling hide, there were stone-hard muscles and strong bones. Only by luck, no matter how strong his arm and how sure his thrust, would he be able to cut through to the life in a single stroke. And more than a single stroke, he well knew, he could not have. Before he could strike twice, those deadly teeth would be in his throat.

Yet the nerve of Woolwin was the nerve of iron. He was in extremity. Only the wildest of chances could save him. Yet he kept regarding the circle of enemies with a deliberate observance. Six of the ten were markedly larger than the other four. Their heads were wider and more bearish in appearance; the fur around their necks and shoulders was deep and wiry. Plainly these were the males. But even the she-wolves were of a noble size and with singularly intelligent faces, broad-snouted, with a great width across the eyes, a high forehead jutting up, and the eyes surmounted by dark marks like brows, giving a singularly arch and inquiring expression. And there were other dark lines between the eyes, like the wrinkles of a thoughtful frown. Altogether there was a strangely human cast to their faces.

Each wolf exhibited a different demeanor from the rest. Some regarded the man to whom they were so close with the most marked dread and horror. Others, particularly the females, were eagerly observant and seemed anxious to press in toward him. But not one of the entire group showed an actual savagery. There was something actually kindly in the expression of the great, bright eyes. But when Woolwin raised himself with a start and a shout to drive them back, they merely flattened their great heads to the ground and bared their teeth.

That glimpse of the teeth made him forget the

thoughtful brows and the kindly eyes. Under the hide each was an incarnate fiend of destruction. They were clever enough to know that he was helpless. And still they hesitated. It seemed, in fact, that they would have pressed in to destroy him before, but there was a controlling spirit present that would not yet permit an attack. When one of the females lurched forward, a low, harsh growl from the big leader made her shrink back into her place.

Then Silver King showed why he had delayed the attack. He began to go the round of the circle, just outside of which the wolves lay. One by one, working with the most consummate caution and practiced skill, his big, scarred ears pricking sharply, Silver King exposed the traps Woolwin had just set, and one by one, in a manner the trapper from his position could not discover, the traps were sprung and closed with a clang that never failed to send a shudder through the wolves, as they heard the sharp sound of iron on iron. When he had finished exposing the entire circle, the monster wolf resumed his position, facing the captive, and the female, crouched nearest him, raised her muzzle, flattened her ears, and sniffed at him, as though striving to convey some idea of the adoration with which she regarded him.

The next instant she was off the ground like a supple little tigress and launched at Woolwin. But, as he flexed his arm and raised the knife for the desperate stroke, he saw that she was not striking truly at him. Instead, she flicked past, just below his feet and just outside of the sweeping circle he made with his knife, and her teeth closed purposely and loudly in the empty air.

She was gone lightly into the group of her companions on the far side of the circle. The other wolves lay where they had been before, lolling out their red tongues and staring steadily at the man. They were merely tormenting him with deadly expectation. The time would come soon enough for them to strike home and end the game. In the meanwhile, another wolf, this time a big male, shot through the air, landed with a horrible snarl close beside Woolwin and, flinching from the light that glimmered on the pale knife of the man, leaped away again and back to the spot from which he had come.

Then the whole circle shrank. Each wolf had dragged itself forward a few inches. And still Silver King regarded the center of the heavens and the black peaks on either side and looked everywhere except at his victim to be. No doubt this increased his pleasure. Anticipation was the sauce of his enjoyment of the torture.

The sunset light had faded to a mere ghost of color in the west. In the east the moon had not yet brightened to the full of her strength—at least the eye was not yet accustomed to depending upon her light alone. In between there was a dull dark moment, and, in that moment, the third wolf, another female, leaped to torment Woolwin. Just beside his feet she landed, and there was a dull thud and shiver of iron as one of the traps he had been buried in the path closed upon her hind legs. She whirled upon it, gnashed the iron with her teeth, and then flung herself out at Woolwin's throat. The loose chain gave her some leeway, but in mid-air the chain drew taut and jerked her to the earth with stunning force. Before she could stir, Woolwin drove the keen hunting knife to the hilt between her ribs. She thrust herself back upon her feet, swung her head around to slash his arm with her teeth, and dropped dead. The knife must have pierced fairly through her heart.

Woolwin, straining up on his arm, saw that the whole circle of wolves had shrunk again. More than that, it was continuing to shrink. Inch by inch, slowly and surely, they were dragging themselves forward. The scent of the blood that had gushed from the body of their companion was maddening them, no doubt, to be tearing at the soft throat of the fallen man.

Suddenly he tossed back his head. There was a savage snarl and the shrinking of a flattened body behind him, where a wolf had slipped up the moment his eyes were turned away. When he raised his head again, he saw that a huge pale form had come out before the rest of the circle, immediately confronting him. Scorning to take advantage of the opportunity for a rear attack, Silver King was delivering his assault face to face.

It seemed impossible to John Woolwin that there could be another response from his tortured nerves. But again the wave of cold horror swept over him, as he caught in his nostrils for the first time the reeking scent of the wolf pelt.

Silver King lowered his head and bared his teeth. He had tried no such threat before, and Woolwin felt certain that the end was come. He freshened his grip upon the handle of the knife again, set his teeth, delivered up a silent prayer that death might be mercifully short, and then cast his mind back, for a single terrible instant, upon the thought of his daughter.

It seemed to him, as he lay there in the sand on Slumber Mountain, that a picture of the interior of his house as it would be at this hour was drawn for him, all the depth of shadows behind the black windows, and then Alice, lighting the first lamp of the night, and the glow of light flooding softly up over her bright face and hair. But he thrust that picture away from his mind and turned, though with a shaken nerve, to face the inevitable.

It was only seconds away now. The other wolves were holding back, desisting from taking any hand in a kill the leader had plainly marked down for himself. Woolwin saw the big forepaws separated more widely and buried in the sand, as he gripped for a hold. Then the gaunt hindquarters sank. The whole body of the big animal was a tensed, flexed mass of muscle ready to drive the great teeth at his throat.

Then a gun spoke on the mountainside to the east. Oh, blessed sound, with a ring of the steel of the revolver barrel sweeter in the ear of John Woolwin than the ring of an angel's voice in song! A gun barked, and another gun exploded in quick succession. A wolf from the inner circle shot high into the air, turned a somersault with a yell that was almost human, or like a human madman dying, and struck the rock with a loose thud. Another wolf received the second bullet, spun around like a top, and then darted away, snarling.

Woolwin saw, dark and indistinct against the moon, but with the light glimmering on the two revolvers he held, a man who seemed to him, as he came down the mountainside, greater than a normal man in size and walking with prodigious strides. This was the first two-gun man Woolwin had ever seen in his life in effectual action. To be sure he had known braggarts who loaded themselves down with a brace of heavy guns, but every one of them was better off when he had only one Colt to handle. This man, however, was doing execution with either hand, and from both guns a swift stream of bullets poured, and the fire spurted without ceasing from both muzzles.

He saw this, and he saw and heard great Silver King turn with a snarl of hatred upon the newcomer. Then the senses of Woolwin gave way. Blackness did not roll gradually upon him. It fell from the heavens. It was as though he had been struck down with a club. Yet there was a last flash of perception before he fainted, and, in that flash, he saw the magnified body of the rescuer with the fire leaping from either hand, and a wolf's body, black against the moonlit sky, as it leaped up with its death wound.

Chapter Four

"Alice Advises"

He wakened with the moon almost straight above his head and shining in his face. For a moment he was too numb to feel or think. Then the pain in his left wrist and his left leg made it seem that the traps still clung to him. Last of all he started upon his feet as he remembered the coming of his rescuer. But he found that there was no other living creature upon the side of Slumber Mountain.

Around about his feet lay five dead wolves. Down the mountain was the heap that was the last of poor old Baldy. But of the man who had walked down Slumber Mountain, looking so huge against the sky and dealing death with marvelous speed and skill from either hand, there was no sign. Perhaps the stranger had disappeared for the moment behind one of the nearby rocks, for, taking into account the distance which the moon had raised in the sky, he was sure that it could not have been more than five or six minutes since he collapsed.

A cold possibility occurred to him that the stranger might have thought him dead instead of fainting, and so gone off. But that was incredible. The man had loosed the traps that held him, and he must certainly have told by the warmth of Woolwin's body that he lived, no matter how deep the swoon. Why had the stranger disappeared, and why had he not set about scalping wolves, the least of which meant one hundred and fifty dollars in hard cash? This was a mystery. But when he paused to think of it, there were other odd things in this affair. For instance, what was the man doing on the top of Slumber Mountain? Certainly he was not hunting, for whoever heard of a man going out on foot to hunt, armed only with two revolvers? If he was not hunting, what could he be doing on the top of Slumber Mountain? Some of the gratitude for his life that had been warming the heart of John Woolwin went out of him and left him a little chilled. Who, indeed, could this man of the mountains be? Money he certainly despised, if he did not intend to take the scalps of the loafer wolves. Or might it be that he did not know of the value those scalps possessed? This could only be the case with a man who was a complete stranger in the district.

He went down the slope to poor Baldy. There he examined, as carefully as he could by the rather unsatisfactory light, the contents of his pack, and he found that everything was as he had left it, with one exception—the little pack of food he always had strapped beside his saddle when he rode out on a long trip was gone. It had not been cut away by the wolves. The straps that secured it had been carefully untied and the contents taken. But there was still a second loss. The strange sense of lightness suddenly made him aware that the cartridge belt had been stolen from about his hips.

Here John Woolwin cursed softly with astonishment. A man, who had saved his life from the most horrible and the most imminent peril, had retreated before receiving a single word of thanks and had taken with him, not property that belonged to him and was worth sixteen hundred dollars, but a loaded cartridge belt and a few morsels of food that would hardly comprise two hearty meals for a hungry man. There was only one conclusion to come to after this, and that was that his rescuer was a man who dwelt in solitude because he dared not let his face be seen, not even by a man whose life he had saved. Such a man could only be either a madman or an outlaw. A madman that consummate gunfighter could not be. Outlaw he well might be.

Here John Woolwin ceased pondering about the mystery of Slumber Mountain and devoted himself whole-heartedly to the labor of skinning Silver King. It was a fine pelt. He tore it quickly from the body of the wolf and then contented himself with the scalps of the other four. This bundle, rolled and tied, he slung across his shoulders, securing it with a thong that passed across his breast, and then he started down the trail toward his hunting cabin.

It was a weary dawn, but also a happy dawn when he reached it. There he hastily made himself a pot of coffee, drank it with some bacon and hard tack, and then swung onto the bare back of his horse and started toward the mountain. He reached it well before noon and found all exactly as he had left it, saving for the work the buzzards had done. He worked the saddle off the body of Baldy and cinched it upon the horse, trembling and uneasy at the sight of all this dead flesh. Then he hastily completed the skinning of the four bodies and turned back on the home trail.

He left behind him the entire remnant of the supply of flour and of sugar and coffee he had taken up with him from his cabin. If food was what the man of the mountain wanted, food he should have to the extent of the ability of John Woolwin to provide it. But since it was certain that he did not want comradeship, Woolwin, like a very wise man, did not attempt to force it upon him.

It was dark before, by the straightest and the swiftest trail, he reached the town of Shawnee and rode into the yard of his house. At his call he saw the shadow of Alice run across behind the kitchen window, and she came dancing out to greet him. It was an unexpected pleasure. She had not expected him home for another week at the least. She was full of chattering comments and questions, while he dragged off the saddle and sent the horse galloping off through the gate and into the corral.

"But where's Baldy?" she asked at length. "Have you gone and left poor old Baldy up there by himself?"

"Baldy is gone where better mules than him have

gone before," said her father, with a grin to mask his sententiousness.

"What!"

"Yep, Alice, Baldy's dead."

She was walking at his side in the darkness, he with the saddle draped over his arm. Now she caught at him and drew him strongly into the shaft of light from the kitchen window. He found himself looking down into her pretty, anxious face. "Dad!" she cried. "What's happened to you while you were away . . . and . . . ?"

Here her grip shifted to his left wrist, and he tore himself away with a shout of pain.

"Why . . . why . . . !" exclaimed Alice.

It's where the trap closed on me," said Woolwin. "Now close up the questions and wait till we get inside."

Inside the kitchen he slumped into a chair, a mortally weary man. There he showed her his bruised and lacerated leg and told her the story from beginning to end. His conclusion was: "He sure is some gunfighter. He made those guns talk just the way he wanted them to. I never seen anything like it. He had both gats working faster'n I could work with one, and they was both shooting a lot closer to the mark than I could ever shoot. But who could he be? I dunno that I've ever heard of a gent that would fit in with the description of him. But when I tell the boys in town, some of 'em may be able to place him. A gent that can use a Colt like he can ain't apt to be very obscure."

"Tell the men in town?" queried Alice, "You surely won't do that, Dad."

"Why not? Ain't I got to tell them how them wolves got killed?"

"If you tell what you know, you'll have every man in town starting up to Slumber Mountain to see the stranger, if none of them has heard of him. And that's just what he doesn't want. He saved your life, but he wouldn't even let you see his face. You're not going to send half the people in town to him, are you?"

He agreed that this could not be done, but at the same time the pelts had to be accounted for.

"Let the pelts rot," said Alice sternly. "They don't belong to you, anyway."

Her father writhed. "I could plumb hear you say that," he declared, "while I was riding down the trail to home. I knew that you'd find fault with me some way or other. But I ask you, Alice, is there anything wrong with borrowing the bounty on them pelts for a while?"

He appealed to her better judgment seriously, stretching out his right hand, palm up, as though she could pour it full of religious wisdom. The girl leaned against the kitchen table, with her eyes wrinkled and half closed in thought and her chin propped in her hand. This was an old matter between them. Rough-minded from a rough life, John Woolwin had not always done exactly as the letter of the law bade. The young wife, who had loved him fervently and feared for him for half a dozen years, had striven to keep him to the straight and narrow path of virtue, but she knew his weakness. It was his inability to hew to the mark when he was confronted with a temptation. He naturally argued, and argued with some cleverness, on the side of carnal comforts. When she lay on her death-bed, she had commended him to the ministrations of their little daughter, and with all his might the trapper and rancher had striven to keep the prom-ise he had given his dying wife. He saw now that he had puzzled Alice. He followed up his advantage with all of his might.

"If I can't borrow part of that money for the bounty," he said, "we lose this house over our heads and. . . ."

"That doesn't count," said Alice absently.

"Doesn't count!" he cried, and then submitted with a sigh. "Well, who does get the money? Some folks might say that I had a right to a good half of it anyway, because I was the bait that brought them to bay, wasn't I? Would he ever had got such a good chance to blaze away at 'em if I hadn't been up there?"

"Father," said Alice softly, "you don't mean that. After he saved your life, you wouldn't take credit . . . ?"

"Dog-gone it," groaned her father, "I dunno what's coming. Everything I say seems to be all wrong some way. But suppose I just take these skins down and show 'em to the sheriff? He'll see that the money is brought out. And when they ask me about how I got the skins, I won't say nothing. I'll just let 'em do their own thinking. Ain't that fair? And the man of Slumber Mountain, if he ever comes and wants that money, I'll give it to him. I'll give it to him if I have to go and sell my own hide to get it for him. But tell me, what's wrong in using that money for a while?"

"Did he seem like quite an old man?" was the rather surprising answer of Alice.

Her father looked up sharply at her and saw that she was staring dreamily toward the window. "I dunno. Young, old, or middling, he might be any one of the three," he declared. "But what's that got to do with whether I got a right to . . . ?"

"Why could he be up there? What crime has he committed? And . . . oh, Dad, think of a man like him up there lacking food . . . the man who saved your life."

"Hmm," said John Woolwin, and he rose to his feet. "I'll see that he never lacks for food again."

"Yes, yes, Dad. I know you'll do that. We'd both work our hands to the raw for the sake of the man who saved you. We have that much good in us, I hope."

"But nary a bit of provisions can we buy for him unless we have the money to pay for it, can we?"

"I see," said Alice at last. "The only thing for you to do is to turn these pelts in and, since he won't claim the bounty himself, tell the sheriff that you shot the wolves yourself."

Deeply it thrilled the heart of her father. And yet there was a sense of what was almost horror.

"Why, Alice, that would be a lie," he said, and he watched almost breathlessly, while she shook her head and answered with perfect calm: "If it helps him, it will be a good lie, I know. We mustn't hesitate about that. Sixteen hundred dollars? That will keep him in food for years, if he's careful."

"It will pay our interest, too," muttered her father, but he said it very softly to himself.

He fell into a happy dream. He saw himself in the sheriff's office. He heard the exclamations of wonder when he unrolled the bundle of pelts. And, last of all, he heard the veritable shout that would be raised when they saw the wide-spreading skin of Silver King himself. He roused from that dream to hear his daughter murmuring: "I wonder if I shall ever see his face?"

"What I'm seeing," said John Woolwin, "is the face of that rat, Morris, when I walk in and give him his interest. He's been making all his preparations for moving right into our house, he was that sure we couldn't pay." He added, more to himself than to her: "But what will the boys say when they find every one of 'em shot through the head clean as a whistle?"

Chapter Five

"The Mossback"

What the boys thought was neatly expressed in the phrase of the gray-headed sheriff the next day when the pelts were unrolled for his inspection and identification: "John, the gent that done that shooting certainly was good with his gun. I figure that I've seen you shoot, John. Who gave you these skins?"

There had lingered in the back of Woolwin's mind a somewhat guilty hope that, if he simply kept silent, the good men of Shawnee would attribute the killing to his prowess, but the speech of the sheriff pricked the bubble of his bright hopes. Thereafter during the day men flocked around him thick and fast to speak of the great hunt, but most of their questions were: "Who did the shooting? All five shot square through the head . . . who did that shooting? Who nailed five loafer wolves one after the other before they could scatter out of revolver range?" To those questions he could only reply with a solemn silence. He would neither claim the feat for himself—his awkwardness with weapons, comparatively speaking, was well known—nor could he place the credit where it belonged. But when he simply said: "Here are the scalps and the skins that go with 'em. Where's the bounty?" they had to find the reward and pay it to him.

"But," the sheriff warned him, "if the real gent that done the shooting turns up, ain't times going to be kind of hot for you, Woolwin?"

John Woolwin merely shrugged his shoulders. He separated his money into two parts. One part of six hundred dollars, meant for the payment of his interest, he put in the one side of his wallet. The other moiety of a thousand dollars he placed in the other half to be kept sacredly there until he met the slayer of the wolves and the saver of his life, face to face. Eventually he would be able to repay the six hundred he was appropriating to his own uses. So it was, while he walked down the street, swelling with the warm gratification that comes with a danger escaped, and while he was breathing deeply with relief and the prospect of his home saved to him for another year at least, he met the man whom in all the world he most wanted to meet. It was the rat-faced Ebenezer Morris who owned the mortgage on the house.

Of late, as the time for the payment of the interest approached, the expression of Ebenezer became more and more dour. And he could hardly look at the trapper-ranchman without a gloomy frown and a shake of the head, as if to say: "There walks a man bound for ruin." But today his demeanor was abruptly changed. He crossed the street at almost a run, and he caught at the big hand of Woolwin in his own claw-like fingers and wrung it.

"I'm glad to hear of your luck, John," he cackled. "It sure warms my heart to hear that you got all that fortune dropping into your hands, like this."

"Well," said Woolwin, grinning in spite of himself, "it was luck. But you got to admit that there's something in hunting, after all."

It had always been the contention of the money-lender that only careful attention to his land would extricate Woolwin from his debts. The cow business, he had ever declared, could never prosper on so restricted a range, and trapping was a downright sinful waste of time. Therefore, Woolwin was astonished when the old fellow said with great heartiness: "I'm an old man, John, but old as I am, I can change my mind now and then, and this is one of the times when I ought to change. Speaking in general, I feel just the same about trapping, except where a man has the art of it. And I got to say that you have the art of it, John. You stuck by your guns, and, by the Lord, you've won out."

Woolwin, unable to believe his eyes, stared critically at his companion, but the sincerity of Morris showed in his gleaming eyes, so it seemed, and instantly the heart of Woolwin melted. He was not one of those who bear malice in their hearts for offenses committed in the past, and he forgave in a trice all the elaborate trickery and cruel cunning with which Morris had lured him into expenditures and loaned him the money for them simply so that he could secure the mortgage and a leverage over the rancher. That leverage he had used to force poor Alice into an engagement with his son. Of this Woolwin was sure, and he knew that his daughter had more than once wavered on the verge of accepting young Charlie Morris. For his own part, his mind had always been made up. He would not purchase security and immunity from the debt by such a surrender. He had only been afraid that Alice, constantly made aware of the pressure by old Morris in the interest of his son, would give way to their arguments.

For that matter, he had to admit that Charlie Morris was a fine fellow. The only wonder was how he could be what he was, both physically and mentally, when he came from such a stock as that of Ebenezer Morris. His broad shoulders and upright carriage carried no similarity to the bent and scrawny form of Ebenezer Morris. Instead of almost craven caution, he was inclined to a reckless wildness. Instead of deadly suspicion of everyone, he seemed filled with an honest trust of his fellows. Altogether he was a fine fellow in every way from the viewpoint of a Westerner. The single stain upon him was the fact that his father was the miserly money-lender and land-grabber of Shawnee village.

How much money old Ebenezer had out at interest no one could guess, but there were some who calculated the amount of cash working for him at close to half a million. Even allowing that this was a most generous estimate, yet his possessions in land and in stock, scattered in quarter and half interests here and there, more than made up the sum. Before he died, he would be a millionaire, and he was rising to this height from the zero start of an orphanage. His way had been beset with obstacles from the beginning. He had fought step by step toward the victory he had achieved. And big John Woolwin, looking down into the dark face of the man of money, felt a warming of his heart. He clapped his strong hand upon the skinny shoulder of the other and felt the bone grind into the muscles of his palm.

"It does me good to hear you admit that," he told the other. "I see that you're a good loser as well as a good winner, partner. But here I am with that six hundred. It'll be due you in two days. You might as well take it now. It will be as much good to you now as it will then, I guess."

So saying, he took out the wallet, opened it, and rather ostentatiously exposed the closely serrated edges of the bills, taking out the thick wad of greenbacks that were the portion for Ebenezer Morris. The latter took the money in a trembling hand and laid his other hand over it. His expression was that of an anxious parent, greeting a returned wanderer. Yet the money was not placed in his purse at once. Instead, he remained with his hands stiffly thrust out and his body shaken by a battle of the emotions. What was passing through his mind, Woolwin could not imagine. And he was literally staggered when the old fellow said: "Here, John, keep this money until it's due. It isn't mine until the day comes."

"But all this talk you've been making . . . ," began Woolwin a little harshly.

"Tush," said the other. "It was just to scare you into getting the coin together. You're a free spender, John, you know. I have to warn you, if I'm going to make you into a businessman. I had to start late with you, Woolwin."

And he actually pressed the money back upon the trapper. The latter took it, not because he wanted it, but simply to test the miser. The eyes of the money-lender literally turned green, as he watched the disappearance of money that had actually been in his hands. But finally Woolwin snapped the wallet shut over the money again.

"As you say," he said, "the money ain't yours till the day after tomorrow, and it might do me some good in the meanwhile."

"Sure," replied Ebenezer Morris. "Now you come along with me, and we'll have a drink at Hopton's."

The trapper blinked. He did not know that Morris ever tasted liquor, far less the illegal moonshine that was served in Hopton's place since Prohibition. But without a word he followed the bent figure across the street and into the dingy, shadow-blackened room where Hopton did the business that had once flourished in the long, noisy barroom, since dismantled and turned into a blacksmith shop to Hopton's lasting anguish. The proprietor was astonished past speech at the sight of the money-lender; but silently he served them and took the money Morris, with an unwilling hand, shoved onto the table.

"It's like drinking melted gold . . . a price like this," gasped Morris, as he sipped the fearful mixture that masqueraded under the name of whiskey in Shawnee. The trapper, more wise, tossed off his drink at a gulp and followed it quickly with a chaser of water. Morris in the meantime was seized with a fit of coughing, but he gritted his teeth and fought away the tears that clouded his eyes. The next moment he further astonished both Hopton and Woolwin by calling for a pack of cards.

"Why," he said in answer to Woolwin's uncontrollable exclamation of surprise, "I ain't such a mossback as you might think, John. I've seen my times. I've played cards, too, with the best of 'em. That was before I gave up play and started to work for money."

As he spoke, he broke the pack and mixed it with the smooth skill of an expert, and Woolwin in deep amazement watched the stiff old fingers grow suddenly young and swiftly supple. Could it be that at card tables in the distant past Morris had laid the foundation of the fortune he had so sedulously nursed since that time? He dismissed that thought in the conviction that once a gamester always a gamester. And then pity took possession of him. No doubt there were some elements of kindliness in Morris. He was honestly glad of the good fortune of the other man. He was attempting to break the ice that had formed for thirty years and show himself capable of good fellowship.

He had shown that good fellowship by refusing

the money until the actual date when it was due. He was showing it again by risking his money on stud poker. John Woolwin, a little grimly, decided that as long as the miser wished to risk his coin to prove his good nature, there would be nothing essentially wrong in plucking him well for taking the risk. In fact, the more he thought of it, the more he was convinced that this was a chance for him to make a fine stake. Out of the money-lender's fortune a few thousand would hardly be missed. But the same sum would mean everything to a poor rancher, sorely in need of a little cash to buy stock and machinery for his acres.

Accordingly, as soon as the game was under way, he pushed the stake up to a stiff figure almost at once, while Morris grunted and groaned, as the money slipped through his fingers. In fifteen minutes five hundred dollars passed into the possession of Woolwin. Then he was changed. He became like a beast of prey on a trail. He saw before him visions of actual wealth, passing into his hands across this table. The more so because the older man seemed to take his losses less bitterly after the next few moments.

"The luck's bound to change to my side pretty soon, Woolwin, don't you think so?" he would ask. "I can't quit now that I'm five hundred loser, can I?"

"You play your own game," Woolwin told him with what he felt to be a fine honesty. "You play your own game and do what you please. I ain't going to tell you one way or the other. But it certainly appears like you got five hundred in this here game, all right."

He would have five *thousand*, Woolwin felt, before the game had progressed very much further. For the old man was betting with the craziest lack of system, wagering a hundred on the turn of a card, apparently attempting to outguess the pack.

At length he won. The winning seemed to go to his head. He placed the five hundred on the next deal. And again he won, cutting Woolwin's stake to the amount with which he had entered the game, but the trapper was not abashed by the loss. Blind chance might favor old Morris for a time, but in the end these winnings would simply draw him on to stand greater and greater losses. But Morris was scaling what were to the rancher dizzy heights. He plunged with five hundred on the next bet, and he won again.

In two minutes more the entire six hundred dollars and the thousand dollars behind the six hundred had left the wallet of John Woolwin and had journeyed across the table to the crooked, trembling fingers of Ebenezer Morris. Now he was crouched, with his bony fingers encircling his spoils and his little eyes burning, as he stared at the big man.

Knowledge sometimes comes to us like the opening of a door that lets in light. In such a flood of insight Woolwin all at once knew that he had been trapped and tricked and cheated by the other. He had been allowed to win until his appetite was whetted. Then, in the space of a dozen hands, he had been stripped not only of his winnings, but of all his capital. In place of the lean, pale face on the far side of the table, Woolwin saw in a flash of apprehensive fear the huge, shadowy figure that had stalked down the mountainside, with a gun spitting fire from either hand.

What would happen when, as was bound to be, the man of Slumber Mountain came for the money that belonged to him? Then his vision cleared. He saw that Ebenezer Morris was slowly rising, grinning faintly, and stuffing the money into his wallet. The smaller and older man glided toward the door and, opening it, stood a black silhouette against the light of the outer day.

"Remember," he said in a voice full of ominous promise, "the day after tomorrow you owe me six hundred. Remember that! Because I, John, won't forget."

Suddenly he broke into a hearty, but noiseless, laughter and glided away, closing the door behind him.

Chapter Six

"The Fall of Zachary"

Woolwin was roused from torpor by a melancholy and wailing sound in the distance that fit in oddly and accurately with his thoughts. Presently he recognized the voice of his dog, Zachary. Zachary possessed a character as well known as the character of any of the men in the village. No one, for instance, would have dreamed of referring to the animal by a nickname or shortened to Zach. His name was always given in full. The reason was that Zachary, a strange mixture of breeds with the breadth of a mastiff and the height of a greyhound and the blind savagery of a starved bulldog, was a creature so wholly terrible that men did not easily bring themselves to face him. He was of use to Woolwin as a watchdog, and he was allowed to range the house after the lights were put out, because he would not harm the only two persons he knew, Woolwin and his daughter. Even these he only tolerated. His shortness of temper had grown as he advanced in years, so Woolwin had of late been constantly on the verge of selling the ugly brute. The difficulty with that was he could find no purchaser. Zachary, well nigh strong enough to give battle to a puma, could probably never have been brought to the trail of one of those ravagers. He would have been too eager to fly at the throats of the men and horses who accompanied him.

For it mattered not to Zachary what living thing approached him. Without a warning growl, stealthy as a soft-footed panther, the big beast would steal near and then launch himself at the throat of the stranger. These were his methods, time out of mind. Even the hardiest storytellers in Shawnee did not care to relate what had happened when, on a time, a thief had broken into the house of John Woolwin. There had not been a sound to tell of the struggle. Indeed, the struggle had been horribly short. One champ of the mighty jaws of Zachary had ended the battle. In the morning they found the man dead.

It was the voice of this monster, wailing at noon because of his utter hatred of the world and all that was in it, that roused Woolwin from his stolid mood of self-contempt. He had felt rage at first and a desire to go gunning for Morris, certain that the old fingers of the latter had nevertheless retained enough supple cunning to cheat him at the cards. He had been too cocksure to watch the old fellow, never dreaming that the money-lender would prove a crooked gambler, also. But thinking back he had been able to see many strange slips of the hand in retrospect. Now the terrible voice of Zachary came like the voice of his own fury to inspire him to action. He started up with a wild curse. But, when he tossed the door wide, and the blinding white sunshine beat against his face, he felt the truth of what he had done rush upon him like a bullet, tearing through flesh to his life.

He had thrown away the money of the man who had preserved his life. How could he face the quiet voice and the terrible justice of Alice when he had such a tale as this to tell? In despair, he shrank back from the door and the honest daylight. Like a thief he sat in the darkness of Hopton's back room all the day, drinking, but drinking less than he intended to do. He wanted to dull his mind to such a point that he would not be aware of what he had done. But so full was he of his gloomy thoughts that, when the darkness came, he rose to go home, miserably sober.

As he went, he strove to muster up his spirits against Alice. It was wrong, he told himself, for a father to dread his own child, as he dreaded Alice. But when he gathered his wrath for a thunderous outbreak, he remembered the face of her quiet dignity, and he heard again her gentle voice, and his resolution of fierceness was dispelled like a mist before a morning wind. It was in her silences, he decided, that she was most terrible to him. Her mother had been a little apt to point a moral with a stinging word, but Alice used a smile instead, and the effect was torture to the soul of poor Woolwin.

When he arrived at the house, though by this

time it was very dark, there was no sign of lamp-light in the windows, and Zachary was howling like a lost soul, and his chain was chinking and clanking in the back yard, while he threw himself again and again against the restraint of it. In one thing Zachary was trained, and that was never to leave the house between dark and dawn when he was unchained.

Therefore, to quiet the infernal yelling of the dog, Woolwin went around the house and approached slowly, speaking to Zachary as he came and presenting his revolver at the raging shadow of the monster. For he was never quite sure when Zachary would forget even his master and fly at his throat. Only Alice could control the big dog with surety and ease. He jammed the cold muzzle of the revolver into the ribs of Zachary, while he fumbled for the snap on his chain, found it, and released him. Zachary at once rushed for the watering trough at one side of the house, reared, and began to lap eagerly. Woolwin frowned and shook his head. This had been the cause of the howling. Evidently his pan of water had been overturned, and Zachary had been informing the world of his disaster. What had possessed Alice to leave the dog without water the entire afternoon through the heat? It was enough to ruin the temper of a better dog than Zachary, almost enough to reduce that savage beast to madness.

The darkness in the house now began to take on a newer and a stronger meaning to Woolwin, for it seemed to mean that Alice was not there. Otherwise, she would have come out to the howling dog and would have discovered what was wrong with him. Could this mean that she had learned from the cunning money-lender what had happened to the sixteen hundred dollars belonging to the man of Slumber Mountain? And learning that, had she, in utter disgust, left the house and him for good and all? Why he should have suspected this, he could not tell, for certainly she had never threatened him with such a thing. But it was the mute acknowledgment in Woolwin of the superiority of soul that he felt to be in the girl.

He stumbled into the house. Zachary brushed past him and went whining through the dark rooms, but presently he returned and began to snarl savagely at the feet of Woolwin. Plainly he had not located the mistress. Woolwin, his heart sick with dread, lighted the lamp, as though he needed that light to make his misery clear to him, but, as he did so, he heard the crunching of a horse's hoofs outside and then the cheery, musical hail of Alice. He ran out to her with a groan of thanksgiving and relief. She was already off the horse and working at the straps of the cinches.

"Poor Dad," she said, "have you been nearly starved? It took me a lot longer than I expected."

"I haven't been starved, but I've been near mad, worrying about you. Where have you been?"

"Didn't you see my note? I left it as big as life on the kitchen table. I've been up yonder . . . I've been up Slumber Mountain."

She waved toward the north and west, where the treble peaks of Slumber Mountain were shadows in a shadowy sky. Then, thought the trapper to himself, she had not yet learned of the loss of the money. He hardly knew which was a bitterer trial, to have found her missing because she already knew the whole story, or to have the burden of the telling of that story rest upon his own shoulders.

"If we could pay off the interest money," she said, "I decided that he ought to have the use of part of that thousand dollars that is left, right away. So I bought as much provision as the horse would carry at a good gait, and we went up Slumber Mountain. I saw the bodies of the wolves, Dad. And I saw the circle where the traps were buried. A hundred yards away from that circle I left the food, and then I started back for home. But when I got around the corner of the mountain, I sneaked off the horse and went back to watch from among the boulders. I waited for an hour, but no one came. Finally I made up my mind that he would not come down so long as I stayed there. So I got into the saddle again and came home."

"Good girl," said her father joylessly. "Did you charge the stuff that you got to him at the grocery store?"

"Yes. I told them that you'd pay tomorrow."

He decided to tell everything at once. It would be easier than facing her in the light of the lamp in the house and watching her eyes change as he told the story.

"Alice," he said wretchedly, "the thousand dollars is gone and the six hundred on top of it. I lost it all at cards to old Morris."

Then he waited for a fierce outbreaking of scorn or of sheer denunciation. But, instead, there was only a breathing space of silence, then she said: "I've saved up a little . . . enough to pay for the groceries that I took up Slumber Mountain today. If we lose the house to Morris on the mortgage . . . why, we're both strong, and I'm young . . . and you have a young heart, Dad. We can go out and start over again, just the way you and mother did all those years ago."

He was stunned by the gentleness of her voice, and the touch of her kindly and consoling hand upon his shoulder was like the falling of a great weight upon his spirit. He was weighed down with the bitterest remorse.

"Ah, Alice," said the poor trapper, the memory of all his sins flooding upon his thoughts in a single instant, "what have I done to be worth having such a girl as you? You ought to have been sent to a good man with money, but me, I'm a spender. I can't save. I'm just a weight pulling you down. I've wasted my life, and now I'm starting to waste yours."

She stopped his mouth with the palm of her hand. "You mustn't talk like that," she said. "Why, Dad, it isn't true. You've led a happy life. Then it isn't wasted. And I've been happy . . . I'm happy now. No matter what's ahead, you and I can laugh at what's coming . . . but not if you begin to hang your head. Why, Dad, you act like some man had licked you. And that hasn't happened . . . that'll never happen."

"But I've double-crossed the man of Slumber Mountain . . . ," said her father. "Him that saved me, I've double-crossed him. Even a yaller dog wouldn't have done that, girl."

"Hush up," said Alice almost fiercely. "A man like he is . . . why, Dad, there couldn't be anything small about him. I stood today up there in the hollow, with the three peaks around me, and I could almost see what sort of a man he is . . . big and strong and free-swinging. No fear . . . no. . . ."

"If he's afraid of nothing, why is he up there?"

"Because there's some mistake," she said promptly. "That's why. Some day he'll be free to come down. Some day he'll sit right in that room with us and tell us how he lived on Slumber Mountain."

She pointed toward the window of the dining room where, if a lamp were burning, it would have illumined the photograph of Woolwin's father on the farther wall. But her attitude and her words were so full of vigor that the wraith of the man of Slumber Mountain was suddenly placed within that imaginary circle of the light, it seemed.

"But if we have to lose the home, Alice?" asked her father humbly. "You sure enough think that you can stand it, girl?"

The tight clasp of her hand in his was her answer; and after that she refused to speak again about their moving. Let the place be sold, for it might bring in enough to pay off all their debts.

"And think," she said, "what a wonderful thing it would be to be free, really free. As long as we're in debt, we own nothing. Even our time belongs to the people who have loaned you money."

Woolwin suspected that her gaiety might be a

hollow pretense. For his own part he could not even pretend. All during supper he sat brooding and forgetting to eat. For he was seeing, in a sadly happy review, pictures of Alice in all the stages of her childhood and her young womanhood. He saw her laughing and playing in every corner of the old house and in every corner of the yard around it. And the ghost of her mother, too, lived here. To Alice it must seem as though that dim, but unforgotten, figure now and again moved through the rooms, or leaned above the flowers in the garden that she loved to tend. That passion for gardening had descended upon Alice, and sometimes it had seemed to the trapper, as he watched the girl at work, singing in the garden, that she was cherishing all that was beautiful in the soul of her mother, not merely the blossoms. All the strange happiness and all the penetrating melancholy would be gone. All the little sacred places in the home would be deserted and desecrated. It would not be merely the loss of the old memories; it would mean the destruction of them. For surely the memory of the girl's mother could not haunt a house inhabited by strangers.

No wonder that meal was a dreary one. But when it ended, Woolwin betook himself to his pipe and a solitary hour of even sadder silence, until at last he went up the stairs and to his room. There he paced the floor until he heard Alice come up to her room, and after that he stole down the stairs and went out for a brief walk. He returned with a heart fortified by a sight of the bright stars and his lungs filled with clean air. After all, it might not have been merely talk, that courageous speech of the girl, when he had told her the full details of the disaster. Perhaps she had meant what she had said.

When he reached the upper hall in the house on his return, he paused in front of her door. It was outlined by a penciling of light. She was sitting in her bed, then, reading; and, if that were the case, she was happy, indeed. With a great lightening of the heart he slipped to his own room and, hungry for a glimpse of her face, perhaps for the sight of an unconscious smile, he stood up on the chair and looked in over the transom—for this was a luxury upon which her mother had insisted in the building of the house. He could easily look inside under the half-lifted transom, and what he saw was Alice, sitting up in bed, indeed, but with no book spread open before her. The bed before her was littered with a tangle of faded, broken toys that she had resurrected from the closet. Her head was so bowed that he could not see her face, only the pale hands that lay, unmoving, across the old play things.

John Woolwin got down from his chair and went hurriedly back to his room. There he closed the door and staggered to the window and leaned far out, thrusting his face into the cold, refreshing current of the night wind. For it seemed to him that he was on the point of stifling. At length he sat down and rested his elbows on the sill of the window, his face in his hands.

Out of such bitter thoughts no solution comes. But, at least, it could be said for Woolwin that he did not turn his sorrow into rage at another. He did

not finally divert his attention to hatred of Morris
and a will to destroy the man who had ruined him.
Instead, he took home to his heart a full realization
of his own sins and all the evil that he had done in
the world.

So midnight found him—when he was roused
sharply from his brooding by the crash of an overturned chair and then the wild howl of Zachary's
attacking—a howl that was cut short in the middle.
The scuffle ended in the room below, and once
more there was perfect silence.

After the thoughts that had tortured him, danger,
no matter how mysterious, was nothing to John
Woolwin. He went down the stairs with a lighted
lamp in one hand and a revolver in the other,
though he well knew that the lamp would make
him a target for any marauder. He stepped into the
dining room. One chair lay upon its back, and just
under the window lay the body of Zachary. Woolwin leaned to examine it. He found that a knife had
been plunged deep into the throat of the beast and
then wrenched to one side, making a ghastly
wound that must have killed almost instantly.

Chapter Seven

"Gold Dust"

He leaned out the open window, but to his eyes, blinded by the nearness of the lamplight, the outer night was a solid wall of darkness. Then a whisper of cloth on cloth from behind made him whirl with a stifled exclamation. But it was only Alice, standing in the doorway, her white dressing gown drawn together high at her throat, her figure raised against the black hallway behind her.

She came toward him, her face alive with excitement, but she made no outcry. It was one of her qualities that she could pass through the most trying events without a storm of words. Now she merely leaned over the body of dead Zachary and made sure at a glance of what had happened. Then, without a word at the horrible flow of crimson that had even reached to her slippers, she stepped back and faced her father.

"Who can have wished to break in here?" she asked. "What under heaven have we that anybody could wish to steal? And there's something he's left behind him." She paused to point to the table upon which there was a little bag of canvas that, in spite of the stiffness of the material, was bulging with the weight of the contents. John Woolwin exclaimed to himself and then hastily unknotted the sinew that closed the mouth of the bag. It was a trying task, for the sinew was hard and dried, but the strong fingers of Woolwin worked it off eventually, and, spreading the mouth of the bag, he called to Alice to raise the lamp high, while he peered into the interior. What Alice could see was only a smear of dull yellow, but presently her father uttered a low cry of amazement, thrust in his thumb and forefinger, and brought it out with a pinch of stuff he sprinkled into his palm—a glistening shower of yellow particles.

"Great guns!" exclaimed the trapper. "D'you see, Alice? It's gold dust . . . three pounds of it . . . four pounds of it, I guess. Gold dust!"

"The man of Slumber Mountain!" cried the girl. "That's it. The man of Slumber Mountain."

Her father could hardly hear her. For the moment all that mattered was not who had brought the precious stuff, but how much of it was in the bag. First he hurried to the kitchen and returned with the scales. Then into the scales pan slumped the yellow heap, and the hand of the scales jerked across.

"There's enough," said Woolwin. "There ain't as much as I thought, but there's more than the six hundred that I owe to Morris. There's a good sight more'n six hundred in that pile."

Then, after he had poured the dust back into the bag, he recurred to the remark of his daughter: "Aye, Alice, it *must* be him! But what's brought him down here with all of this? What made him risk his life with Zachary to get it to us? I don't understand him . . . I don't make him out. I take pretty near two thousand away from him, and then he turns around and gives me this."

They sat together in the chilly night and wondered over it. But all of their wondering brought them no nearer to a solution of the mystery. The suggestion of John Woolwin seemed possible, no matter how strange it was. The man of Slumber Mountain, he said, must be an outlaw who had taken refuge among the peaks of that inaccessible summit, just as the outlaw, Silver King, had taken refuge there. In fear of his life he had concealed himself, perhaps dwelling in a cave, but never daring to show his face. When the food was taken up the mountain to him by the girl, he had been filled with gratitude, and he had desired to come down for a last time to leave some token of his thanks among them. This little bag of gold, perhaps washed out on the side of the mountain, was his present, or his payment, if one chose to look on it in that light. And John Woolwin was rather inclined to view it in this manner.

"To a gent like him," said the trapper, "condemned to death and a goner, if he shows his face among folks, money ain't nothing at all. What d'you suppose that he cares about the money I've taken from him? He might have a million, but little good it would do him. No, sir, what he wants is grub, and he'll pay high to get a hold of it. I'll bet that load of stuff that you brought him was the finest sight that he ever laid eyes on. I'll bet that he thought he was a millionaire when he got it."

His daughter had different opinions, but she did not voice them. She knew from old experience that there was a certain point at which her mind and the mind of her father branched off and began traveling toward unrelated goals. When there was anything to be gained, she would combat his viewpoint, but when it was simply a matter of empty opinion, she became silent, as she did on this night, and went up to her room again.

But in what a different mood she reached it. She had spent the evening closing the door upon her past and preparing bitterly for the unknown future. She had keyed herself up to the loss of her home. She had prepared to bury, one and all, the things that linked her with her childhood. But now at a stroke all of this danger was removed, and she was restored to all that she had ever possessed, through the generosity of him who slew Zachary and left them the money. She had looked forward to a sleepless night of misery. Now in five minutes the wreckage of her girlhood was cleared from the bedspread, and she was asleep and smiling in her dreams. It was one of those profound sleeps in which an instant may seem the length of an entire night.

With the feeling that it must be dawn, she awakened suddenly, so bright was the light that poured into the room. She turned her head. It was only the light of the moon that streamed through the windows and gilded a broad square upon the floor and pushed away the walls and filled the distant corners with unfamiliar shadows. Yet it was not this strangeness that made her heart beat so wildly. Her whole body was trembling with excitement, as though she had faced a revolver, and yet her excitement was a happy one. An odd delight, such as she had never known, filled her. Her very lips were tingling. Then it was that she noticed the window had been changed. It had been open at both top and bottom when she fell asleep. Now it was closed at the top and opened to the full width from the bottom. Someone had entered the room while she slept and had altered the window. That someone could not be her father. His rather unwieldy weight would have made a terrific creaking on the flimsy boards of the floor of the room. It could not have been he, but someone, as deft of foot as a very spirit, had glided noiselessly across the room.

By this time she was out of bed, still trembling and still strangely unafraid. She fairly tingled with expectation, and yet it was not the thrill of terror. Indeed, she was new to herself. She could not have told her best friend how she felt. She leaned out the window. All the village of Shawnee was asleep in the moonshine, a silver town with that light on the roofs and turning the windows across the street into solid sheets of burnished metal. Shawnee, also, it seemed to her, was changed by the hour to such a place as she had never seen before. She did not recognize the familiar façade of the well-known blacksmith shop. The open sliding door revealed a mysterious cave of darkness.

What had happened? It was as though someone had whispered wonderful words at her ear during her sleep, a message that she was to pass on to another. Or was it a message she was to keep for herself? No matter what it was, she could not remember a single syllable of the words, but all the message had been wiped away in a few instants of sleep. No, not all the message, for there remained to her the sense of what had been said—the tingling, thrilling sense of happiness that had been near her and was to come again.

But who had entered that room? Or had some intruder climbed up—it was a simple task—to the top of the roof of the verandah and from the window peered in upon her? Had he then pushed up the lower sash? Had he seen her hands, lying pale on top of the bed covers? Had he slipped in through the opened window and leaned above her face? And had he whispered to her, asleep, that which he dared not speak to her waking? All at once, she pressed her hand to her lips, her strangely tingling lips, and her eyes flashed up of their accord and fixed upon the distant peaks of Slumber Mountain, a fairy summit rising through the haze of the moon.

Chapter Eight

"Father and Son"

"Business," said Ebenezer Morris, wagging his head wisely from side to side and assuming his air of greatest sagacity, in spite of the age of the maxim he was repeating, "business, Woolwin, is business. That's an old saw, but it's one that you seem unable to learn and remember. But I'm here on mighty disagreeable grounds today, my friend. I've given you time off, again and again. I've throwed in an extra week or an extra month for you to find the coin to pay your interest. But this year I've been cornered, so's I can't let you have any extra time, Woolwin. They've got me up against the wall. I need that six hundred dollars more'n I ever needed anything in my life. And . . . but you run along out of the room, Alice, and let me finish up this talk to your father. This ain't no place for a girl of your age, not when men are talking business."

The girl, instead of answering or obeying, merely smiled down upon him. She was standing near the window, holding the curtain with one hand, and her face had been turned toward the sunshine. But now she looked back into the shadow of the room and at the miser. Her father spoke for her.

"She brings me luck, Ebenezer," he said calmly. "That's why I like to have her here now. Every time I do anything when she's around, I get the best of it."

"I hope it works out that way today," said the man of money. "I sure do hope so." The hypocrite actually rolled his eyes up to the ceiling, as though invoking a divine witness to the goodness of his intentions and the kindness of his heart. "I don't want poor Alice to have to stay home from the big dance tonight because her eyes are red with crying. I sure don't want to see that."

"I can see," said Woolwin with perfect gravity and eyeing the money-lender with great fixity. "I can see that you've got a good heart, Morris, even if you do have to keep an eye on your dollars."

This bit of praise fairly opened the floodgates. Morris expanded his gestures and his vocabulary. "It's for your own good, Woolwin," he said. "I'm really doing it just for your own good. Time that you closed up your work as a rancher if you're going to be a trapper, because no man can do two things well. No man can do two things." He clapped his hands together to give point to his remark. "But when I was leaving, poor Charlie near got down on his knees to me. 'Dad,' said he to me, 'wait till tomorrow. Wait till after the dance. You ain't got no right to rob all of us of the pleasure of seeing Alice Woolwin at the dance and at her prettiest.' That's what he says to me. When I shook my head, he says . . . 'Then let me pay that interest out of my own money that I've saved up these last few years. I've got. . . .' But there I stopped him. I wouldn't listen to him. And here I am again. He's got the sort of a heart that makes a man throw away his good honest-earned money, that boy of mine has."

"I'm glad to hear that," said the trapper, "because he'll have a lot to throw away when you're dead, Morris."

"Tush! Folks talk big about my little savings. They don't amount to much . . . just what a thrifty man can lay up. Now, Woolwin, getting down to business. How long will it take you to move?"

"Move? Why should I move?"

The other cleared his throat. "Maybe you think I been talking for fun," he said. "Maybe you think I talk for the sake of hearing myself? But that ain't it, Woolwin. What I mean is that the time has come for a finish. You got to pay, or get out."

"Pay?" echoed Woolwin mildly.

"What sort of a bluff are you trying to work?" shouted Morris in a sudden and suspicious fury. "Are you going to beg off by saying that you didn't know that the day had come? I want that six hundred, or this house and the. . . ."

"Oh," said Woolwin, "is that what you're driving at? The six hundred? Is that what you're making all this fuss about? Here you are. Here's six hundred in gold, Morris."

Then he pushed a neatly tied little bag across the

table, first opening the top so that the moneylender could have a view of the contents. As for Ebenezer Morris, he had half risen from his chair in the violence of his emotions, and now he slumped down as though struck by a club. He crashed into the chair and seized upon the bag with shuddering fingers. He could only stare at the gleaming contents and then at the smiling, contemptuous face of Woolwin, so that at last, with something between a groan and a moan, he rose in haste and fled from the house. From the window Alice Woolwin saw the extortionist shamble hastily down the street, his body bowed and his attitude that of one who hastens through the cold, piercing rain.

Straight to his home went the miserable Ebenezer. As he closed the door softly behind him, he discovered a tall, handsome youth, sprawling at ease upon the couch on the far side of the room, sound asleep. He was a fine, wide-shouldered youth, dressed rather too gorgeously in the fashion of a spendthrift cowpuncher. The eye of the money-lender softened as it rested upon this form. Then he began to tiptoe across the apartment.

But the young fellow had been merely shamming sleep. Now he raised himself cautiously upon one elbow and marked, with a smile at once amused and contemptuous, the cautious and silent progress of his father. Suddenly he shouted. The father started and nearly fell, so great was the shock, while Charlie Morris went off into a peal of laughter, pointing a finger of ridicule at his sire. At length he sobered himself and recalled Ebenezer, who was on the verge of leaving the room in the midst of this outburst of mirth.

"Hey, governor. Come back a minute."

The money-lender turned reluctantly back. "Well?' he questioned.

"It worked, did it?" asked Charlie. "You threatened to drive 'em to the wall, and then you told 'em that you'd let 'em come clear if Alice was to take kindly to the idea of marrying me?"

"Why do you want her?" countered Ebenezer Morris desperately. "Ain't there other girls as pretty as her and as . . . ?"

"Forget the looks," shouted Charlie. "Don't you see what she is? She's the real thing. She's a diamond. There ain't nothing else like her around these parts. She's got class. Understand? She's got class. Looks? Well, she's good enough to look at, but, what's more, she's all gold under the surface. Why do I want her? Because I ain't a blind bat like you for asking that question! Ask any other young gent why he wants her? Why, most of 'em figure that she's so far above 'em that they don't even lift their eyes to her. Takes a gent with some nerve to even do that. But go on, now, and tell me how they took it?"

Perspiration stood out on the forehead of Ebenezer. He could not speak. There was a sudden roar of rage from the son who leaped at the older man, as though he would crush the shrinking body in his strong, young hands.

"Did you see that deal fall through on you? Did you let that sure thing fall through? Did you let the girl *cry* you out of it?"

Ebenezer fairly wrung his hands in his grief and in his shame. "Charlie, I thought I had 'em cornered. But when I had backed 'em into the wall, and I was just about to tell 'em that you could find a way out of it for them . . . just at that minute he pushes this across the table at me." He dropped the little canvas sack into the hand of Charlie.

"What is it?" demanded the latter.

"Gold!"

"Gold?"

He dashed the heavy parcel to the floor. The worn old canvas ripped. A flash of gold dust spurted like yellow water upon the floor. Charlie Morris in a blind rage ground his heel upon the packet, and the gold spurted again on all sides, while the father raised a strange wail, stretching out his hands to the wasting gold and fixing his eyes upon the savage face of his son.

"You mean old scoundrel . . . you miserly old skinflint!" shouted Charlie. "You took the gold sooner'n make happiness for me. You don't put no value on me. You'd rather have your rotten coin . . . and be damned to you for it. I wish all the gold in the world was boiling in hell, and you in the midst of the stew!"

"Charlie," gasped out the trembling miser. "On my word of honor, I . . . !"

"Forget what you meant! What you did is the thing that counts. Now she knows that I wanted to buy her. . . ."

"I didn't tell them that."

At this news the face of the other lost some of its purple. He stepped back and sank upon the couch from which he had just risen. As he set about straightening the bandanna that had become disarranged, his father thumped down upon his knees and began to brush up the precious dust.

"She ain't learned that, then? She don't know that I put in a bid for her?" he asked. "Well, then there's a chance still . . . there's a chance still. Gimme that!" He snatched the little bag of gold from his father's hand.

"I want some more than this . . . I want this much again."

Ebenezer started to protest, but then he changed his mind. Charlie had just returned from a long trip into the Southland, and he dreaded lest harsh treatment should banish the precious youth again. So he shambled off to his room and came back with exactly what Charlie had demanded—six hundred dollars in greenbacks.

"Charlie," he could not avoid saying, "I dunno what you want it for, but here it is. It strips almost all the money I have in the house away from. . . ."

"That's a lie," said the tall youth easily. "That's a lie and a loud 'un. You ain't seen the day in the past thirty years when you ain't had twenty times as much as. . . ."

A shrill, choking cry from his father stopped him. The eyes of the old man were on fire with terror.

"You fool!" he shrilled. "D'you want to bring murder on us both? And I tell you this . . . little as there is left, there's enough to murder the two of us."

Charlie Morris, a little sobered by this outbreak, only cast a disdainful glance at his father and then turned away, dropping both bundles of money into his pockets.

He went straight to the house of John Woolwin. He saw the father in the distance, saddling a horse. A sweetly singing voice guided him to Alice Woolwin in the garden. She stood up and nodded to him with a smile that, when she made out who he was, faded quickly.

The fading of that smile tore the very heart of Charlie Morris. By a careful campaign conducted over a stretch of many years, he had worked closer and closer into the affections of Alice Woolwin until he had been able to promise himself that she cared for him and cared deeply. The wildness that boiled in his nature he had exercised at a great distance from the home town, so that no whisper of his doing should ever reach the girl. He had even been able to use the vice of his father to offset his own handsome generosity. Now he went straight up the path, dragging off his hat as he came, conscious that his long, yellow hair, blowing in the sunshine and the wind, made not a bad effect.

"Alice," he said, stopping close to her and looking sadly down into her face, "my father has just told me what's happened, and it sure makes me sick inside. Money? Why, you must think that I've got the money craze worked into my soul because I'm his son. Is that what you think, Alice?"

She shook her head, but still the smile that came so readily to her lips was not there. "I'm not judging you, Charlie," she said. "I'm not even judging your father. Why, the best people in the world sometimes do bad things. I suppose . . . I suppose that just accidents start them down a trail, and then they have to keep on going to the end of it." She sighed and raised her eyes.

It seemed to Charlie, with a leaping heart, that that glance was meant for him, and that all of its pity was poured out in commiseration of the destiny toward which his father had started him. But, as a matter of fact, she was looking far past him and at the shaggy skies of Slumber Mountain with every crevice clear in the morning light.

"But I'm not started down that trail," said Charlie Morris. "I've come over here to bring back the money he took from your father. Here it is, and here's the same amount more."

He forced it into her hands. "Take it, Alice. Why, money is nothing to me. It . . . it simply makes me sick to think of taking it from you."

"You know I can't accept this from you, Charlie," she said a little angrily.

"You have to," he insisted. "It's the only way I can make up for what he's done. It's for the sake of your father, Alice. You know he's not much of a saver. This might come in handy. You can put it away and never let your father know that you have it until a pinch comes. And. . . ."

Here she stopped him by forcing the money back upon him. "Of course, I can't accept it," she said. "But this has given me a chance to see what you're made of, Charlie. I knew you were a lot of fine things before, but I never knew you had such a heart."

Tears of rejoicing sprang from the eyes of Charlie Morris. He could have wept in his gladness over his own good soul. He turned away before the spell should be broken and went moodily down the path, as though still crushed by what she had learned of his father. But she ran after him and caught his arm.

"No matter what your father may have done or said," she declared, "that doesn't mean anything about you, Charlie."

"Prove it!" said Charlie suddenly. "Come with me to the dance tonight."

And she answered on the spur of the moment: "I will."

Chapter Nine

"Jack Vane"

A soft answer turneth away wrath, but a quick answer often raises Cain, particularly if the answer falls from the lips of a pretty girl. In five minutes after Charlie Morris had left, with a guilty qualm of conscience, Alice remembered that she had already promised to go to that unlucky dance with Jude Cobbett. So she hastily ran down the street and communicated the bad news to Charlie Morris.

He received it with a smile, but with grinding teeth. Five minutes later he was on his way to see Jude Cobbett. Three minutes after that encounter Jude Cobbett, a bleeding pulp, where the hard fists of Charlie had slashed and pounded him, sat down and wrote a note to Alice.

Dear Alice:

I'm mighty sorry, but I got throwed by a bronco this afternoon and am all messed up, so's I can't very well go to the dance. Hoping you have a good time at the same.

Yours Truly,
Jude

The note was all that Alice learned of the affair, but the rest of the Cobbett family learned further details, and the result was that they turned out in force to attend the dance. Three gaunt and hard-faced girls, five gaunt and hard-fisted, quick-shooting men, they donned their best attire and went to the schoolhouse and prepared to see "what's what" in Shawnee. Above all, they wished to come in contact with young Charlie Morris. No matter how fast he might be with a gun—and his reputation was growing—no matter how deft he might be with his fists—and his skill had been demonstrated on stalwart Jude that very day—the Cobbetts had a profound faith that somewhere in their ranks could be found a man to account for him in any sort of a fight he elected to fight.

A murmur of what was to happen went abroad and dampened the ardor of the most innocent dancers who flocked to the schoolhouse. Alice, a late arrival on the arm of Charlie, sensed at a glance that there was trouble ahead of them. But when she asked Charlie, he said he could not imagine what was in the air, or why the entire Cobbett family glowered upon them so darkly. As a matter of fact, he understood at once what was coming, and he was by no means sorry for it.

Cowardice was not one of the faults in the make-up of the big man. He would have been delighted to show his prowess under the eye of the lady of his heart. Fists or guns, he cared not which. He was ready for all comers. In the meantime, he felt that his gorgeous outfit far outshone that of any man in the room, and, taken in connection with his height, his good looks, and his joyous manner, he felt, and rightly, that he was the center of attraction at the schoolhouse this evening.

Alice herself was so soon lost in the pleasure of scurrying feet and lilting music that she forgot to note an occasional scowl. It was the first dance in a month, and her feet were tingling with eagerness for the rhythm. Moreover, Charlie was a fine dancer. Not only could he be picked from the crowd by his brilliant attire, but he was also instantly noticeable by the grace with which he guided his partner through the mazes of the crowded dance floor.

The Cobbetts themselves forgot their animosity for a short time and entered the dancing, formidable couples that drifted slowly here and there in the center of the floor, where there was the greatest amount of space. Soon all, at least on the surface, was a scene of rejoicing, presided over from the teacher's platform by the violinist, expert in drawing piercing strains from his instrument, and a trombonist of vast lung power, and a player upon the drums. Violin, trombone, and drums might not seem utterly soul-satisfying to some, but to the men and girls of Shawnee it was quite good enough. There was the violin for the fancy work, the trombone to make one stir one's stumps, and the drums to keep one in time.

The girls worked very hard, for the dances were long, the intermissions short, and the men in the ratio of two to one. Brown-faced fellows had ridden in as far as fifty miles to loosen up their dancing muscles in Shawnee. Acquaintances who had not met for a year and a day were as convivial as though they had parted only the day before. The men and the women of the range, perhaps to make up for the long silences that stretched through their lives, were now cramming as much noise and movement into a few hours as possible and storing up memories that would keep their hearts warm for many a drab year to come. In the midst of it all there could not but come to Alice Woolwin the knowledge that she was the queen of the party, and that her partner was the king of all the men present.

She was dancing with another now, and chatting with him with all the amiability that had gained her the popularity no amount of good looks could have won. She saw Charlie Morris go by, trailing all eyes after him, as he spun the second prettiest girl through the mazes of a rapid waltz. Certainly there was nothing about him reminiscent of the dark, lean face and the rat-eyes of his father, and, though sometimes she thought with a shudder of how the miser had attempted to corner her father that very morning, she could not really associate him with the upstanding youth who now was the observed of all observers at the dance.

The music by this time was working in her like wine. It seemed to Alice that something that had come to her that other night when she wakened with the sense that a man had been in the room— that strange and delightful sense had grown and grown, a feeling of chilly terror and of uncertainty along with it—until, at last, it was beginning to invade her mind and color her perceptions with a rosy hue of romance. The singing of the violin was merely twisting in her consciousness a shining thread of happiness that led she knew not whither.

The dance ended, and she returned to her place in the row of chairs that ran clear around the big room, broken only at the doorways. Charlie Morris seated his last partner, saw her safely enmeshed in conversation with half a dozen admirers, and then hurried toward Alice across the floor, stepping lightly among the sauntering crowd of couples. It seemed to the girl that he was given precedence, and that men drew back before him to let him pass. A flush of pride rose hotly in her at the sight of her approaching cavalier. But on the way he was encountered by one fully as tall as he himself. It was Joseph Cobbett, his brown face stirred by a stiff grin, murmuring words that brought Charlie quickly about to face him. There they confronted each other for a few instants, and then they went on, each with the expression of a thunder cloud.

Charlie Morris shrugged away his sternness when he came to her, but she could see that under the surface he was hard as flint and prepared for trouble, while Cobbett went back toward the door to wait, with his long arms folded across his breast.

Charlie excused himself. He had to see a man—
business—she hardly heard the muttered excuse,
hardly saw the forced smile, and then he was gone
through the crowd. She saw him pass Cobbett and
enter the big anteroom beyond the opened double
doors—the anteroom, where the pupils hung up
their hats and their slickers in rainy weather, and
where the men were now hurrying out to get air.
As he went past Cobbett, the latter wheeled in, and
they walked on, side by side.

Then suddenly she knew what it was. They had
made a rendezvous to meet outside and fight. With
a thrill of horror she started up, but before she
could cry out she saw that which made her know
that she was entirely too late to interfere. For suddenly on every side the other men scattered back
from Morris and Cobbett. These two confronted
each other with a silent rage that she could guess
even at the distance, and then their right hands
jumped back at the same instant for the concealed
guns. Neither should have been carrying a weapon
in such an assembly as this, but both were armed.

She saw that, and she had set her teeth to harden
herself against the explosion that was to follow—
when another figure was injected into the picture.
It came like the flash that jets from the muzzle of
a revolver. It darted in between the two combatants
with a speed more than equal to that with which
all of the other men were recoiling. She could see
only the white glint of the face, only the white flash
of a speeding fist, and then that fist lodged under
the chin of Charlie Morris.

Her hero went down with his revolver, crashing

to the floor. Down went tall Charlie Morris and, spinning as he lay, fell on his face on the floor and lay there without a quiver. Then the stranger whirled upon Cobbett, who stood amazed, with the naked revolver in his hand.

She could hear him speak now, a ringing voice that went echoing into the room: "Gun fighting at a *dance?* You hound!"

There was a snarl from big Cobbett, but the stranger seemed to swell. He was not very much more than the average height, and he was less than the average breadth, except for his shoulders. But now his lithe body actually was distended by his anger as he confronted Cobbett.

"If you want to cool down," he said, "get outside the schoolhouse and stay there. If you want to fight, wait for me there, and I'll tend to you when I come out later on."

To the unutterable amazement of the girl, big Cobbett, despite all the long list of battles in which he had contended, did not answer with more than an inaudible growl. The stranger, in the meantime, turned his back upon Cobbett and upon the motionless figure that lay on the floor of the anteroom and walked into the dance area, whistling.

It was only when they heard his whistling that the crowd realized that the musicians had struck up the next dance. Still no one stirred to take to the floor until the stranger came straight up to Alice Woolwin, and then she found him a rather pale-faced fellow, by no means better looking than the average, and with nothing extraordinary about him except the brightness of his black eyes and the length and slenderness of his active hands. That such hands as these should have possessed the power to knock Charlie Morris senseless, she could not comprehend.

"Miss Woolwin," he was saying, "Charlie Morris has been telling me that he has this next dance with you, and that he's been delayed by a business argument, and has asked me to come in and see if you care to dance. Will you dance with me?"

It was only the last part of his speech that had any meaning for her. It came with a subtle change of the voice that caressed her ear, that passed into her soul with a peculiar and subtle charm. Without knowing what she did, she stood up, and instantly she was in his arms and being guided away into the dance. That she was doing an unforgivable thing—dancing with the man who had just knocked down her escort of the evening—did not occur to her. Neither did it come to her attention that, though the violinist was playing the "Blue Danube" with all his honest might and even a touch of skill, there was only a scattering of couples on the floor. As a matter of fact, the important events in the world were boiled down to the peculiar and cat-like grace with which the stranger was dancing, and the even more peculiar softness of the voice that was murmuring at her ear.

"I've been waiting out yonder in the anteroom for an hour. I hoped that he'd get out, and that then I could come in and talk to you. But when he came, and there was an excellent chance that the other fellow would take care of him, I had to follow a fool impulse and throw my opportunity away. He's only stunned, and, when he comes to, he'll get to his feet and start every man after a gun by calling out my name. But, except for Charlie Morris, I think there's no one else who knows me . . . not a soul."

"Who knows you, and who are you?"

"Guess. Can't you guess who I am?"

Suddenly she caught her breath.

"Stop thinking then and go on dancing," he said softly, but almost fiercely. "No matter what else you know, you know that this floor is smooth, this music is good, and this minute is mine. Less than a minute, perhaps, for then he'll be on his feet and shouting my name and cursing me, and then that's the end of my party."

"You are . . . ?"

"Nothing . . . no one . . . don't ask me," he pleaded. "I have no name. I'm only a man who's seen you and loves you . . . a man who has only sixty seconds to tell you that and then never see you again. For they'll chase me, if they don't get me here. Stop trembling, there's nothing to be afraid of, and be happy. Smile for me. If all that I'm risking is worth anything in your eyes, then smile for me, my dear."

"Oh," she whispered, "you are a madman, but a glorious madman, too. They'll do you no harm. I'll keep them from you. I'll. . . ."

"Ah, now you're smiling. And that's what I've come to see. Now, ten seconds of silence and the music. . . ."

It seemed to her that something poured through her from the tips of her fingers. The music, it appeared, she had never heard before, but now it fell

303

with incredible softness and beauty upon her ears. All other things were changed. The old violinist was changed into a great artist, the blatant trombone had become an organ note of mellow beauty, and the drummer was beating out a soft, quick pulse like the rhythm of her own life in her veins. She forgot all that and saw the pale, intense face so close to hers, filled with a veritable agony of happiness and of apprehension, all in one.

"I knew it would be like this," he said. "I knew it would be worth everything if I could touch you. Seeing you was a wonderful thing, but touching you is divine. You feel it, too, don't you? Just an echo of what's in me . . . something that changes the music . . . that. . . ."

"Ah, I don't know what it is . . . I. . . ."

She stopped, tore herself from his arms, and sprang in front of him. For there was Charlie Morris, his legs braced wide, a crimson stream running down his contorted face and a revolver in his hand, standing in the door of the anteroom, balancing his gun and looking for the man he wanted to kill.

"Where's Vane? Where's Jack Vane?"

The call brought a yell of surprise, rage, and fear from the men along the walls of the room. She saw on every hand the gleam of quickly drawn weapons.

"Start for the window right behind us," she said to Jack Vane. "And . . . God help you!"

There she stood with outstretched arms, running backward as though she would cover to the last his retreat with her body. But Jack Vane refused to take advantage of that shelter. Instead, he broke away to the side, raced across the floor, with a fusillade of bullets beginning to tear it from under his feet, and then he leaped through a window, almost like a swimmer, diving into deep water.

He owed his life to the crowded condition of the room. They dared not shoot until the people in the direction toward which he was running had scattered from his path, and it was only when he was at the window that they could begin to shoot to kill.

He was gone. Alice joined the rush for the window, but she, like all the rest, could see nothing. Half of the men started on the run for their horses to give chase, but then, far away, she heard a long thin whistle. She knew it was Jack Vane, calling his horse to him, and she also knew that Jack Vane would escape.

Chapter Ten

"The Whole Truth"

That surety left her before she had covered half of
the distance toward her house. When she reached
the house, she ran in to her father with a storm of
questions on her lips.

"Who's Jack Vane?" he repeated in answer to her
first outburst. "Why, he's the man who's thought to
have held up the P. B. & O. guards in the mail car
last year, blew the safe all by himself, and got clean
away with ten thousand. They chased him with a
posse, and . . . well, I know you don't like these stories, Alice, but the posse came off second best,
that's all I can tell you. But now tell *me*? What in
the world are you doing at home at this hour, and
why do you want to know about Jack Vane? If you
want to know, ask Morris. Don't you remember
that Charlie Morris was working as a railroad
guard at that time?"

She dropped into a chair, and her father with a cry of alarm knelt beside her.

"Are you sick, Alice?" he asked eagerly.

"Oh, Dad," she answered, "Jack Vane is the man of Slumber Mountain!"

John Woolwin started up. "Then no wonder he keeps low, but heaven help him. I know, Alice, this hits you hard. He saved me. It hits me hard, too. But he should have thought of what was coming to him before he robbed that train. And. . . ."

She sprang from the chair and faced him in a sudden rage. "How do you know what drove him?" she demanded. "How do you know what made him do it?" And then she ran from the room and raced up the stairs.

She'll come down again when her temper wears off, thought her father and settled down to his newspaper again. But she did not reappear, and, when he went to bed an hour later, there was still a light showing at her door.

After a time she put out the lamp and sat in the darkness, full of the riot of her thoughts. *What utter madness had brought him down to dare death in order that he might dance for one minute with me? But what a man in a million he was to have taken that chance! And where was the chase winding now?* She called to her mind all of the savage fighters and expert trailers in Shawnee. They were hard men in a hard country. They knew the ground like the palms of their hands, and they were expert with their weapons. If ever they had a fair sight of Jack Vane, there would be an end of the refugee that instant. Moreover, they had fast horses. The very horses darted into her memory, one by one. *How could Jack Vane withstand their long challenge?*

A thread of sad beauty wandered into her thoughts, and then she wakened with a start to the fact that it was the air of the "Blue Danube" being whistled underneath her window. She sprang from the bed and stood panting in the full shaft of the moonshine that poured through the window. She looked out, and there unmistakably he sat upon his horse, his horse whose sweating limbs were turned to a liquid silver in the moonlight. Yes, there he was in full view, while up and down the street there were still lights burning, and hither and yon the voices of men were drifting through the placid night air. He saw her outline in the window and waved to her. At the gesture a sudden weakness went through her to her feet. She ran down the stairs and passed hastily out at the front door. She whipped around the corner of the house, and then she stood before him, with her hands clenched and her whisper fierce.

"You wild man . . . you wild man! Don't you know that they're hunting for you up and down, and that . . . ?"

"I suppose they are."

"And that they'll see you here? Oh, how did you give them the slip?"

"Ask Julia . . . God bless her! This horse's four feet and her big honest heart are what saved me . . . and not the first time, either. But the rest of that doesn't matter. What really counts is this one thing . . . that you knew I'd come."

"I knew you'd come? No, no, don't dismount! If

they should take you at such a disadvantage. . . ."

But in spite of her he was on his feet and confronting her.

"Knew you'd come?" she said, reverting to his remark. "I never dreamed you'd do anything so mad."

"Ah, but you did. For you were in that room with the light turned out, and yet you had all your clothes on. If you weren't waiting for me to come back, what *were* you waiting for?" His voice changed. "I'd forgotten one important thing, and that's why I'm here. Can you guess what I forgot to do, Alice?"

"I? Guess? Keep away, because. . . ."

But her arms had lost their strength, and they were numb against him. They crumbled at his touch, and she was in his hold. She could not even fight away the hand that tilted her chin. Then, with sheer weakness, her head fell back. His lips were on her lips. Afterward she was swaying in his arms, half laughing, half weeping, in the steep shadow that fell from the eaves of the house. And what he said she had not the slightest idea, but his voice— ah, that she knew and could remember forever.

"Then I was right," she said. "It was you who came into the room . . . ?"

"And kissed you, Alice? Yes, when I saw you up yonder on Slumber Mountain, I swore to myself that you were the loveliest creature on God's wonderful earth. But I also swore that I would not be a fool. I would not come down and put my head into the lion's mouth. Well, the more I swore, the more I had to come. So I came, as you know. I lingered around the town until I learned a few facts. So I left some money. I've washed out a tidy lot on Slumber Mountain, and was sorry about the dog. But afterward I had to see your face again, and the only way was to climb up to the window of your room and wait for the moon. I did that, and the moon was a horrible long time coming. Then it went, inch by inch, across the floor and climbed up the side of your bed and reached the spread and then went over your hand. How could I help it? I slipped through the window. I leaned by the bed and saw your dear face in the shadow. And could I help kissing you, Alice? But afterward, when I was gone, I couldn't forget. I had kissed you sleeping. I had to kiss you waking, with your eyes open and looking into my eyes, with your arms around me, as they are now. Do you see? If I had to die for it, why death was only a little thing . . . and now . . . do you understand?"

She could only nod. She was too full for speech.

"And afterward you'll wait for me, Alice?"

"Wait for you? There *is* no one else. But what is it all coming to? Where will you take me some day?"

"Into a happy home, God willing. Listen to me, dear. What they have told you, I suppose, about the train robbery is only half of the truth. It's true I tried to rob that train, and I'm plumb sorry for ever having the notion come into my head. It's also true that there was money stolen, but not by me. After I broke into the safe, I was recognized by one of the guards, Charlie Morris. I got scared, and I took off. It must have been the guards . . . or maybe just one of them . . . that helped themselves to the coin and blamed me for it. That was simple. When they chased me with the posse, I shot four men. I admit that. Two of them got well right away. One of them was sick for a long time, and one of them finally had to have his arm cut off. Well, Alice, that's why I've been living like a hermit on Slumber Mountain. I've been waiting up there, working the little claim I've found, and saving the money until I could go down and buy myself a good name again by paying the man who lost his arm what he needs to live on, and by repaying the express company every cent that I was supposed to have taken from it. Now do you understand, Alice? Do you see why there's something to wait for?"

Alice didn't know if she understood or not. All she really knew that night was a bounding happiness that did not end even when the horseman and his horse disappeared among the shadows of the trees.

About the Author

Max Brand is the best-known pen name of Frederick Faust, creator of Dr. Kildare, Destry, and many other fictional characters popular with readers and viewers worldwide. Faust wrote for a variety of audiences in many genres. His enormous output, totaling approximately thirty million words or the equivalent of 530 ordinary books, covered nearly every field: crime, fantasy, historical romance, espionage, Westerns, science fiction, adventure, animal stories, love, war, fashionable society, big business and big medicine. Eighty motion pictures have been based on his work along with many radio and television programs. For good measure he also published four volumes of poetry. Perhaps no other author has reached more people in more different ways.

Born in Seattle in 1892, orphaned early, Faust grew up in the rural San Joaquin Valley of California. At Berkeley he became a student rebel and one-man literary movement, contributing prodigiously to all campus publications. Denied a degree because of unconventional conduct, he embarked on a series of adventures culminating in New York City where, after a period of near starvation, he received simultaneous recognition as a serious poet and successful popular-prose writer. Later, he traveled widely, making his home in New York, then in Florence, and finally in Los Angeles.

Once the United States entered the Second World War, Faust abandoned his lucrative writing career and his work as a screenwriter to serve as a war correspondent with the infantry in Italy, despite his fifty-one years and a bad heart. He was killed during a night attack on a hilltop village held by the German army. New books based on magazine serials or unpublished manuscripts or restored versions continue to appear so that, alive or dead, he has averaged a new book every four months for seventy-five years. In the United States alone nine publishers now issue his work. Beyond this, some work by him is newly reprinted every week of every year in one or another format somewhere in the world. His popularity continues to grow throughout the world.

ACKNOWLEDGMENTS

"The Outlaw Crew" by Max Brand first appeared in Street & Smith's Western Story Magazine (2/20/32). Copyright © 1932 by Street & Smith Publications, Inc. Copyright © renewed 1959 by Dorothy Faust. Copyright © 1997 for restored material by Jane Faust Easton and Adriana Faust Bianchi. Acknowledgment is made to Condé Nast Publications, Inc., for their cooperation.

"The Coward" first appeared under the title "Under His Shirt" by Max Brand in Street & Smith's Western Story Magazine (1/27/23). Copyright © 1923 by Street & Smith Publications, Inc. Copyright © renewed 1950 by Dorothy Faust. Copyright © 1997 by Jane Faust Easton and Adriana Faust Bianchi for restored material. Acknowledgment is made to Condé Nast Publications, Inc., for their cooperation.

"Slumber Mountain" by John Frederick first appeared in Street & Smith's Western Story Magazine (7/8/22). Copyright © 1922 by Street & Smith Publications, Inc. Copyright © renewed 1950 by Dorothy Faust. Copyright © 1997 by Jane Faust Easton and Adriana Faust Bianchi for restored material. Acknowledgment is made to Condé Nast Publications, Inc., for their cooperation.

T. V. OLSEN

Winner of the Golden Spur Award

THE STALKING MOON

Army scout Sam Vetch is finally ready to settle down and start a new life on that quiet New Mexico ranch he's been saving for all these years. He has no way of knowing that his cherished wife had once been the woman of Salvaje, the notorious Apache chieftain known as The Ghost—and that she has borne two sons by him. When Salvaje comes to claim what is his, the duel begins—a deadly contest between two men of strong will, cast-iron courage, and fatal honor—a duel that can only end in tragedy under the stalking moon.

_4180-4 $4.50 US/$5.50 CAN

HIGHPOCKETS

DOUGLAS SAVAGE

In the autumn of his days, Highpockets stumbles upon a half-frozen immigrant boy, nearly dead and terrified after being separated from his family's wagon train. For one long, brutal winter Highpockets tries to teach the boy all he needs to know to survive in a land as dangerous as it is beautiful. But will it be enough to see both man and boy through the deadly trial that is still to come?

___4400-5 $3.99 US/$4.99 CAN

Dorchester Publishing Co., Inc.
P.O. Box 6640
Wayne, PA 19087-8640

Please add $1.75 for shipping and handling for the first book and $.50 for each book thereafter. NY, NYC, and PA residents, please add appropriate sales tax. No cash, stamps, or C.O.D.s. All orders shipped within 6 weeks via postal service book rate. Canadian orders require $2.00 extra postage and must be paid in U.S. dollars through a U.S. banking facility.

Name_____
Address_____
City_____State_____Zip_____
I have enclosed $_____ in payment for the checked book(s).
Payment <u>must</u> accompany all orders. ☐ Please send a free catalog.
    CHECK OUT OUR WEBSITE! www.dorchesterpub.com

CHIRICAHUA

"Some of the best writing the American West can claim!"
—Brian Garfield, Bestselling Author of
Death Wish

Led by the dreaded Geronimo and Chatto, a band of Chiricahua Apache warriors sweep up out of Mexico in a red deathwind. Their vow—to destroy every white life in their bloody path across the Arizona Territory. But between the swirling forces of white and red hatred, history sends a lone Indian rider named Pa-nayo-tishn, The Coyote Saw Him, crying peace—and the fate of the Chiricahuas and all free Apaches is altered forever.

The Spur Award–winning Novel of the West

___4266-5 $4.50 US/$5.50

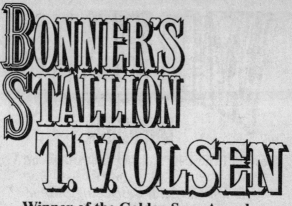

BONNER'S STALLION
T. V. OLSEN

Winner of the Golden Spur Award

Bonner's life is the kind that makes a man hard, makes him love the high country, and makes him fear nothing but being limited by another man's fenceposts. Suddenly it looks as if his life is going to get even harder. He has already lost his woman. Now he is about to lose his son and his mountain ranch to a rich and powerful enemy—a man who hates to see any living thing breathing free. That is when El Diablo Rojo, the feared and hated rogue stallion, comes back into Bonner's life. He and Bonner have one thing in common...they are survivors.

___4276-2 $4.50 US/$5.50 CAN

Dorchester Publishing Co., Inc.
P.O. Box 6640
Wayne, PA 19087-8640

Please add $1.75 for shipping and handling for the first book and $.50 for each book thereafter. NY, NYC, and PA residents, please add appropriate sales tax. No cash, stamps, or C.O.D.s. All orders shipped within 6 weeks via postal service book rate. Canadian orders require $2.00 extra postage and must be paid in U.S. dollars through a U.S. banking facility.

Name_____
Address_____
City_____State_____Zip_____
I have enclosed $_____ in payment for the checked book(s).
Payment <u>must</u> accompany all orders. ☐ Please send a free catalog.